THE GLASS COCKPIT

BY THE SAME AUTHOR

Novels

APES ON A TISSUE PAPER BRIDGE
THE DINGLE WAR
THE PILOT
CAT FIVE
CONTROL TOWER
THE DIVORCE

Nonfiction

In collaboration with John Stobart
STOBART: THE REDISCOVERY OF AMERICA'S
MARITIME HERITAGE

Motion Pictures

DAY OF THE PAINTER
(American Academy Award)
THE PILOT

THE GLASS COCKPIT

ROBERT P. DAVIS

ST. MARTIN'S PRESS NEW YORK

DESIGN BY DIANE STEVENSON / SNAP·HAUS GRAPHICS

Library of Congress Cataloging-in-Publication Data

Davis, Robert P.
The glass cockpit / Robert P. Davis.
p. cm.
"A Thomas Dunne book."
ISBN 0-312-05438-6
PS3554.A9377G5 1991
813'.54—dc20 90-48356
CIP

First Edition: May 1991
10 9 8 7 6 5 4 3 2 1

Dedicated to Patricia E. Tierney
for her help and patience.

Author's Note

UNFORTUNATELY TOO MUCH OF THIS NOVEL IS true.

There are serious shortfalls of proven equipment, in many control towers. The cockpits of civil airliners should carry collision avoidance equipment. This new equipment is supposedly on the way, and what happened in this novel on a March morning in Tulsa will, most likely, never happen in future years.

When I sent the first draft to the Air Traffic Manager of Tulsa, Oklahoma's International Airport for technical editing, some mistakes were noted and corrections made. But the FAA official did not say that the sequence of events portrayed in this novel were beyond reality; this accident could happen with the present state of equipment in many American control towers and aboard our airliners.

The Trent 270, the big jet that appears in this novel, might be the first airliner ever designed, on a conceptual level, for a work of fiction. Its creation was a most rewarding and enjoyable effort even though the plane will never be built.

Professional pilots and designers who read this book might claim that the aircraft that they fly, or know the details of on an engineering or operational level, would not respond as the Trent 270 does in this novel. That is understandable. Although the principles of mechanics and flight characteristics are generally identical for all fixed wing, powered aircraft, there are still vast differences in the operational and emergency procedures for each aircraft. The Trent 270 is one step beyond what is out there now or perhaps on the drawing boards. So the reader will have to go along with the hypothetical flight manual that our design team worked out for this new glass cockpit airliner.

The Trent 270 was designed within the limits of known and workable technology, meeting the requirements of Part 25 of the FAA Certification Rules and Group A of the British Civil Aviation Authority, or what is called the British Civil Airworthiness Requirements, the (BCARS).

New York, N.Y.
January 1991

Acknowledgments

I AM INDEBTED TO A NUMBER OF PEOPLE AND ORGANIZATIONS who have given me advice and guidance on Air Traffic procedures, and on many design aspects that went into the Trent 270 and the turbines for this new aircraft. H. Ric Hedges of Tulsa was particularly helpful, along with William A. Becton, Air Traffic Manager of the Tulsa, Oklahoma International Airport Control Tower. I owe much thanks to John C. Williams and Gordon Harrison, development and systems engineers, and to the late Arthur Koch of the Choate School who first taught me the finer points of large aircraft design.

I am also grateful to Ruth Cavin of St. Martin's Press for her wise editing, as well as my agent, Oscar Collier, who was my first editor. I want to thank Pat Tierney, who went over the final draft with me, and Diane Memmelaar, who spent many hours typing various versions of *The Glass Cockpit*. Lastly, from each person you fly with in a life time, something is learned; much of what appears in this book came from those with whom I have shared many cockpits over the years.

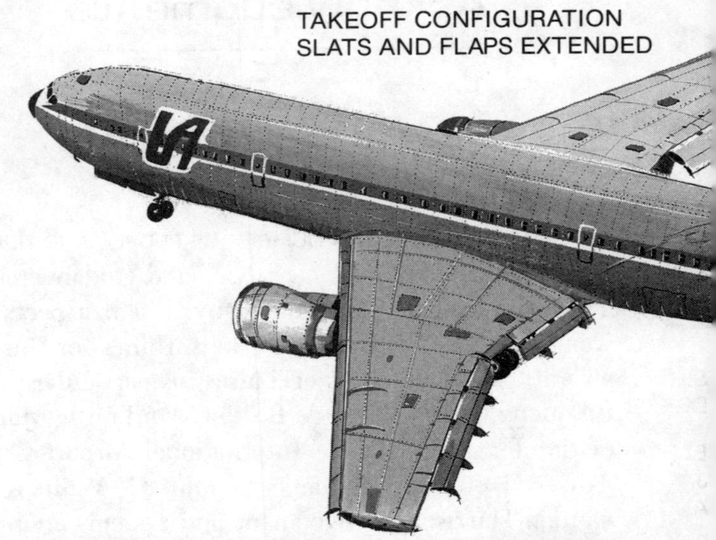

TRENT 270 DAMAGE CONDITION

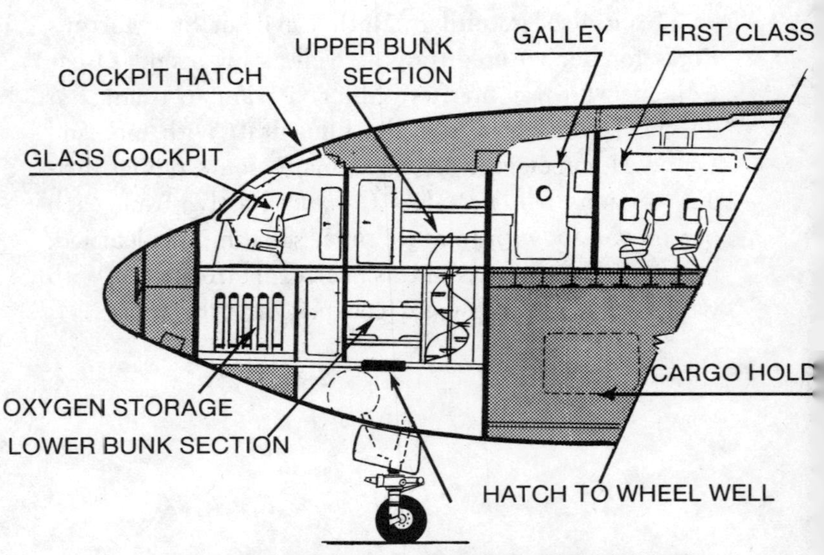

FORWARD INBOARD PROFILE

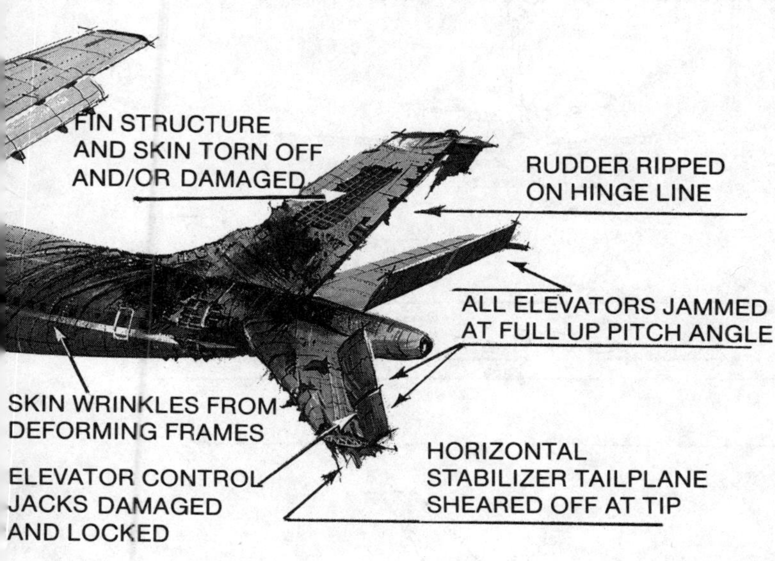

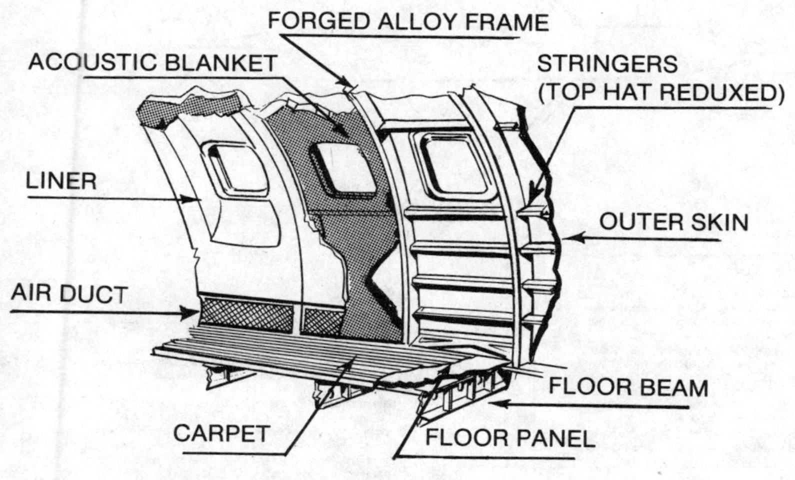

STRUCTURAL SECTION

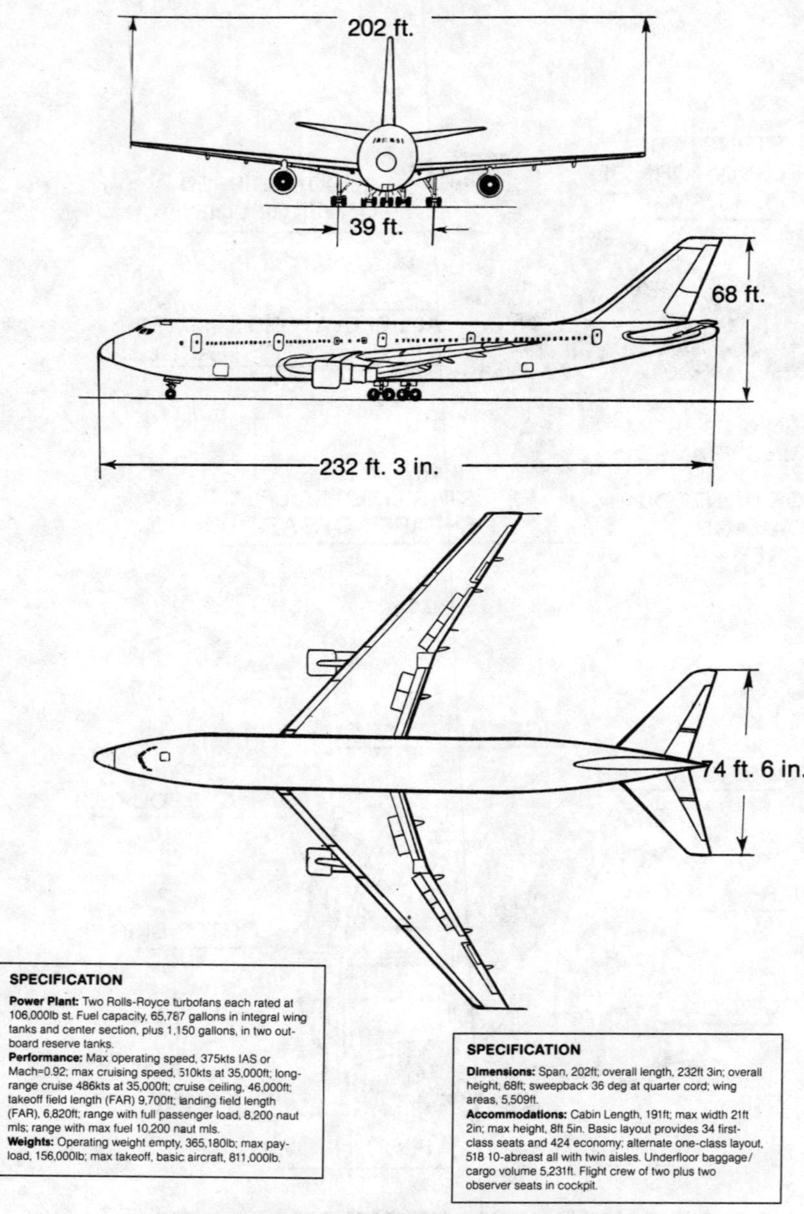

SPECIFICATION

Power Plant: Two Rolls-Royce turbofans each rated at 106,000lb st. Fuel capacity, 65,787 gallons in integral wing tanks and center section, plus 1,150 gallons, in two outboard reserve tanks.
Performance: Max operating speed, 375kts IAS or Mach=0.92; max cruising speed, 510kts at 35,000ft; long-range cruise 486kts at 35,000ft; cruise ceiling, 46,000ft; takeoff field length (FAR) 9,700ft; landing field length (FAR), 6,820ft; range with full passenger load, 8,200 naut mls; range with max fuel 10,200 naut mls.
Weights: Operating weight empty, 365,180lb; max payload, 156,000lb; max takeoff, basic aircraft, 811,000lb.

SPECIFICATION

Dimensions: Span, 202ft; overall length, 232ft 3in; overall height, 68ft; sweepback 36 deg at quarter cord; wing areas, 5,509ft.
Accommodations: Cabin Length, 191ft; max width 21ft 2in; max height, 8ft 5in. Basic layout provides 34 first-class seats and 424 economy; alternate one-class layout, 518 10-abreast all with twin aisles. Underfloor baggage/cargo volume 5,231ft. Flight crew of two plus two observer seats in cockpit.

TRENT 270 (THREE VIEW)

THE GLASS COCKPIT

4:52 A.M. Central Standard Time
TULSA, OKLAHOMA
FRIDAY, MARCH 10, 1989

•

IN A FEW SECONDS, THE ALARM would waken Captain Glen Doyle on a day he was scheduled for a check ride from Tulsa to Chicago. In fewer than six hours, millions of people in more than sixty countries would be watching him on TV, trapped in his glass cockpit. Many of them would be praying for him.

When the alarm went off, Doyle automatically pressed the snooze button, but silencing the clock only made more evident the screaming winds of a powerful blizzard. Just as automatically, he whispered, "It's all right. . . ," turning to reassure Louise, who was always terrified of storms. Feeling like a fool as he began to drift into sleep again, he wondered how long it would take to rid himself of these reflexes. Louise had been dead for five years.

When the alarm woke him again, the pilot heard the howl of the wind and the pelting of sleet against his window. He immediately called Intra-Continental Airlines operations. They couldn't be flying on a morning like this, he thought.

"This is Doyle. Are they departing flights?"

"Yeah, the east runway is plowed; they're taking in traffic."

"What's the terminal say?"

"Let me look here. Ah, it says we've got eight hundred overcast, half-mile visibility in blowing snow, temperature nailed at twenty-four degrees. Improvement by ten o'clock local. Fast-moving low pressure south of us."

"So we're going?"

"Right."

Everyone called him Lucky. A tall, rangy man with a handsome face that was deeply tanned, he looked as if he worked outside or played golf every day under a cruel sun. But he was an aviation romantic: Lucky Doyle's craggy looks came from flying open cockpit airplanes. He first flew these jobs spraying Florida crops. Years later his mount was an antique Waco biplane he had restored rib by rib with affection and skill in a feed barn north of Tulsa. When Lucky wasn't flying an airliner, this heretic against high tech was up cruising the cotton-ball clouds in his 1932 plane, a member of a lost flying world that he had re-created partly to solve his identity crisis.

A good storyteller, this purebred aviator was proud of his meager roots. He told it this way:

"Hell, I was born at the far end of an old Florida grass strip. We had this rusty trailer parked there in prickly grass. First thing I ever remember hearing were engines of the spray planes taking off at dawn, right over my homemade bed."

Around Belle Glade, a steamy farm community near Lake Okeechobee, people thought Glen Doyle was born to be a pilot. Lucky soloed at sixteen; he was deftly shooting crops at seventeen.

It was dangerous dirty work. The spray plane had to start far down on the open produce field where the flagman signaled the spot to begin the next pass. With white powder trailing off the lower wing, the spray pilot would approach the windbreaks, usually tall Australian Pines. At the final moment, so he could powder the last rows of vegetables, the "spray boy" yanked his stick back, firewalling his throttle for a snap climb over the trees.

If the engine coughed at that moment, the branches snagged the plane like a witch's bony fingers, and it usually was all over for the pilot and his equipment. One day when Lucky was hitting a lettuce section, the big radial engine of his biplane hiccupped during a climbout beside the stiff pines. With lightning-fast instincts, Lucky flipped a wing up as it brushed the tree tops. In one long swathe of crackling twigs, his airspeed peeled off as the lower right wing crumpled and opened. By this time the cunning young airman had his equipment into a nose-down slip away from the trees, heading back toward the lettuce heads. It was a semicontrolled crash: The gear and the wing were ripped off, and he plowed a ditch in the damp ebony soil for sixty feet. Lucky busted the bird into a spray of pieces. He also busted the odds, for very few spray pilots ever walked away from an engine balk at the windbreaks, but he climbed out with just a blue bump on his knee. And from that day on no one called him Glen. He was now Lucky Doyle, a legendary pilot around the sizzling rimlands of the "Glades."

At nineteen, the banks had lent the rail-thin natural pilot enough capital to buy a two-plane spray operation. With its profits, he put himself through a junior college, studying engineering and airframe mechanics. Lucky's dreams of flying adventures went far beyond the croplands of south Florida. He decided he would become a carrier-based jet pilot, nothing less, since they needed young men with his skills for the rapidly developing war in Vietnam. Then Lucky faced his first career setback: He could work the handle of a wrench as well as the control stick of a plane. The need for skilled airframe men was a higher Navy priority than the need for pilots. Lucky's dream of being a fighter pilot tumbled around him. He was a fast, dextrous crew chief: Still, fixing jets wasn't like landing a hot one between the snag cables of a busy carrier deck. After a four-year tour off "hell's peninsula," Lucky returned to the stink of chemicals in the juicy heart of Florida. But few remembered him down on the mucklands; good spray boys were roamers with short lives. His home, the rusty trailer, had been towed away; his mother had died, and his father was once more a guest of the Glades Correctional Institution for passing bad checks.

With cash he had banked from his Navy years, Lucky picked up his floatplane and multiengine tickets at a south Florida flight school. Then he headed for the last frontier of undiluted flying: Alaska. There he found a wife and a floatplane job all in the same month. The year was 1970.

During the winter, when the small planes were resting in hangars, their floats off for repair, Lucky started flying transports, hauling supplies over the Brooks Range to the arctic oil patches. The aviator was positioned perfectly when the North Slope pipeline was announced. He and an old Australian bush flyer, Frank A'hearn, bought a large, creaky, twin-engine Caribou, a cargo plane, and they started flying pipe sections up to the North Slope. This was pure seat-of-the-pants aviating. Whiteouts—low arctic clouds blending with snow-covered surfaces to form a vast whiteness—grumpy engines, edgy electronics, and a hundred other intractables were everyday events for these men. But during the North Slope days, Lucky and Frank were part of a rare love affair with their ancient transport. Their passion for the plane probably kept her in the air, for the wracking Caribou had 39,000 hours on its airframe. The big hull whined in strange places as if she had lungs and a hidden voice that wailed with the pains of age.

The lesson driven in by the North Slope flying was self-reliance: Survival meant much more than good air sense. A "sourdough" pilot had to be a mechanic, skilled with tig welding and sheet metal work, able to handle all his tools blindfolded, because that's the way it was in a sudden whiteout that reduced visibility to zero. When the pipeline was signed off, hundreds of Alaskan pilots were grounded. Lucky and Frank sold their worn-out equipment and headed south. Frank opened an aircraft conversion shop in Fort Smith, Arkansas, and Lucky started flying right seat for Intra-Continental Airlines, a medium-sized Tulsa-based carrier.

That's when his luck began to slide.

The sourdough aviator started to commit the unpardonable cockpit sin: He actually flew the jets himself, by hand. All the others, "jet drivers" as Lucky called them, simply slapped on the flight director, pushed buttons and let the gyros and computer chips take over. Out of spite and deserved pride, Lucky continued to fly with his fingers. The chief pilot, André Bouchard, admired the high-tech cockpits, however.

"Lucky," he said repeatedly, "we're all impressed that you hand-fly, but people don't do that too much anymore. The autopilot feels the slightest change in altitude . . . corrects it quicker than the human hand. And it's much more fuel efficient to let the microprocessors do the work. I'm sorry to say it, but the computer does some things better than you do."

Lucky rebelled. He abhorred the buttons and let everyone know it, becoming something of a paradox, as if he had been hauled out of the open cockpit age and mistakenly dropped into the super-high-tech generation. When he became captain, Lucky's war on the computerized cockpits was so well known around the western end of the airline industry that check pilots used to tell their men: "Don't pull a Lucky Doyle. 'Keep in the loop.' "

Loop was one of the new cockpit buzz words. To "keep in the loop" meant to set up the computer, or flight director, for the assigned course and altitude. Then the airline pilot's job, after creating the loop, was to monitor the progress of the integrated circuits by scanning the cathode-ray tubes that decorated the smart cockpits. Being "out of the loop" meant not keeping an eye on things, or letting the plane get ahead of the pilot.

Lucky was usually "out of the loop" because he seldom punched up the computer to create the loop in the first place. He was his own adamant man. That was how it was going to be as long as he flew for I.A.

But that wasn't going to be much longer. The airline was falling victim to a "friendly" merger with South Central, a St. Louis–based nonunion carrier. The day that Lucky was taking his check ride, the deal was supposed to be closed and the preliminary papers signed.

Early the evening before it had started to snow, and by nine o'clock it was a foot high on Lucky's farm north of Tulsa. He sat alone that Thursday night, realizing that the merger would eliminate his job along with approximately 1,500 others. Since he was going to be pink-slipped anyhow, Lucky decided to hand-fly the bird all the way up to Chicago's O'Hare with a stop at St. Louis, his usual route. It was part pride and part defiance, but Lucky wasn't going to give into the glass cockpit on his last check ride with I.A.

To most airline pilots the new cockpit was a beautiful handout. Information such as location, course, engine condition, ground speed, and time to the next waypoint could be called up on glass screens that displayed almost anything the pilot wanted to know and more. The colorful images reminded some pilots of the early arcade computer games. There was a magic to it. Airline pilots, it seemed to some airline executives, were taking home higher and higher salaries for doing less and less. Unlike Doyle, however, most pilots were not affronted by computerized flight decks. The hallowed place was becoming an executive suite, and those who sat there hour after hour were more like office managers than pilots. The theory of the glass cockpit was crew reduction. It was also designed to eliminate pilot error. Somehow, the correlation didn't quite work. Pilot errors continued.

This created an ideological division. There were still some Lucky Doyles left in the system, pilots who wanted to fly the plane instead of letting the autopilot do it. To an arctic aviator like Doyle, the glass cockpit was an invidious step backward. By dehumanizing the flight deck, Lucky felt that hundreds of bored pilots were being created. They were becoming lethal. To Lucky these dulled pilots were forgetting the basics of flight, such as putting the flaps down for takeoff or forgetting that proper airspeeds are essential to big jet operations.

"Hell, how can a bored pilot be sharp, ready for a full-blown emergency?" Lucky used to ask people around the I.A. operations in Tulsa.

He was thought to be a persistent holdout, likable but a little odd for not getting into the proper loop. To the younger pilots, Lucky was a leftover with a lot of tough hours scratched in his logs. Underneath, though, even cathode-ray addicts knew that there was some truth in every heresy. Some airline pilots were silently asking themselves: "Could I really handle an extreme in-flight crisis?" A few of them, even those seduced by microchip flying, asked themselves an even deeper question: "Might I unwittingly create a crisis?"

5:07 A.M. CST (TULSA)

●

THE WIND THAT CHALLENGED Lucky frightened Connie Esposito. The bash of sleet against the windows jolted her awake. For two years now, she and Lucky had been a unit in every sense of the word: in bed, in the cockpit—and in the kitchen, where they were a gourmet cooking team. They seemed perfect together. Yet when it came to flying airliners, they shared very little. But Lucky and Connie respected each other's methods, even though their attitudes toward the glass cockpit were widely divergent.

Connie was intoxicated by computers, health clubs, jogging, jumbo jets and women's rights. She was a striking young divorced woman of thirty-six who had been born perfectly into her age. Everyone liked Connie because she had a quick and frequent smile, and her skin seemed to glow from inside, reflecting her warm heart. Still, she confused everyone she met. Her hair was red and she had azure eyes, so blue that she looked more Irish than Italian. "Proof of the stubbornness of the genes you inherited from your Irish mother," her father would tease her.

As the daughter of a Boston-based, American Airlines pilot, Connie remembered with clear anguish the months directly before and after her father had to surrender his left seat at the age of sixty. Her mother said it killed the man. Captain Esposito was devastated, totally unprepared for the eviction from his cockpit. During that first spring he tried to work in his garden, but every time a jet flew overhead, inbound to Logan, he looked up and the pain edged deeper.

When the expilot died suddenly, the doctors weren't quite sure of the etiology, so they put down cardiac arrest. Connie knew different. This bright, sensitive young woman realized what had been happening to her father; the silent suffering of a grounded airman had slowly killed him. Those memories intensified her concern about Lucky's situation. Who was going to want a hands-on left seater whose world had been reshaped to such an extent that his brand of flying was seemingly unnecessary and unacceptable?

The night before, Connie had cried for Lucky, and when she awoke that morning to the chorus of the fast curling winds, she saw the knotted balls of Kleenex by her bedside table. Twelve of them. Being a practiced crier, she could time her tears by the Kleenex—her flowing emotions had lasted for nearly an hour.

She, too, called I.A. operations that morning and then phoned Lucky to see how he sounded. Maybe he would reject the flight to avoid going through the meaningless check ride when there was little to check at that point.

Connie tried to sound bright.

"Hi, Lucky. Some day for a check ride."

He sounded his usual confident self. "Didn't think

they would be departing . . . appears worse than it is, I guess."

"They must know something we don't," she said, trying to match his casual tone. "Are you going to slap it on the buttons for old Bouchard?"

"No, I decided to hand-fly it."

"Why not let him decide? Bouchard might be able to help find you another seat." There was a long pause. When Lucky came back, his voice was suddenly flat and paced. She could almost feel the man's desolation.

"I couldn't find a right seat on an air taxi. We both know that, Connie."

"Lucky, don't talk like that. There's a lot of room for a guy with your hours."

"Where?"

"I don't know exactly. We'll work on it together. You're valuable, Lucky, never stop thinking that. And be sure of one thing, I love you very much."

"And I love you with all I got, but my time is over."

"Let's just give Bouchard his ride and talk about it tonight. Are the roads open out there?"

"Yes, I heard the plows go by. I'll be there about the usual time."

"Good. Drive with a light foot."

Connie put the phone down and walked to the window of her Tulsa garden duplex. The blaze from the streetlight etched the edges of the whirling snowflakes. They seemed to be driven sidewise by the caprice of the wind, and the flakes spun down toward the ground like a million tiny tornadoes. Some of the white funnels landed and built the drifts higher; others didn't quite make it to the ground. The spinning flakes went upward again, and they would disappear into the low-scudding clouds.

When the mystery of the tiny snow swirls no longer

held her attention, Connie thought about Lucky. It wasn't merely the prospect of a great pilot's being edged out by a takeover; she knew it would affect their two-year relationship, which was heading toward marriage. There were twenty-nine women on the flight deck of I.A. All were copilots except one. The assistant head of the pilots' house union had overheard management talking about the termination profile after the takeover. Only two women would go, recent low timers. Connie, with three years up front, would remain and that would deepen Lucky's troubles. She would fly; he would stay home. It might even end their relationship, she thought with anguish. That puzzling disease called cockpit elimination wasn't in the medical books, but Connie knew it existed nevertheless. She just didn't want her Lucky to die of it. An image of her father slipped across her mind, and she remembered the conversation in his hospital room shortly before he died.

"I think Sal would have wanted you to become a pilot."

Sal was her brother, who had been shot down in the early days of Vietnam. Before enlisting, he had been a copilot with American, and his father was very proud of him. Then he was killed.

"I'll be a pilot," Connie promised her father offhandedly.

Connie soon forgot about her idle promise to take flying lessons. But after nine years with a major Boston insurance company, she felt lifeless; she had a tedious job and a demanding, prosaic husband. Connie remembered her words to her father, then, and she learned to fly, eventually moving all the way up to an Air Transport Pilot Rating.

As Connie stared at the snow, she thought of Lucky's battle—a terrible losing battle to outwit the flawless autopilot. Two fears had always nagged Connie: getting tied up with men who seemed to be going crazy, and perhaps even worse, with pilots who were not satisfied unless they were testing fate almost daily. Her first serious love affair, just after graduating from Syracuse University, was with a political activist who worked in the Boston public defender's office as a lawyer. At night he made speeches and organized rallies on behalf of animal rights in Boston medical experiments. He started to drink heavily and do wild things, like handing out Protect the Animals buttons in jury assembly rooms, until he was censured by the judiciary.

One day the Boston police called Connie to say that her lawyer friend had killed himself with a gun he'd signed out from the evidence department at the police station. Shortly after, she decided that she didn't need crazies in her life. As a defense, she picked out a dull, steady man and married him. That was not the answer either.

Her second fear was of becoming involved romantically with pilots on the edge. Her father used to say, "Commercial aviation attracts two types of people. The right guys. The rock-steady professionals who fly the airliners by the book, day after day, year after year. And then there's the fringe element. Spray boys, the airshow barnstormers, movie stunt pilots, the bush guys, and high-risk test pilots. Stay away from that breed. They attract women, but they're dangerous husbands. Many of them don't last long."

Lucky Doyle, Connie reasoned, might combine the worst traits in a man according to her father's definition and the dark experience she had had with the young lawyer who blew his head off.

At first Connie put up with Lucky's hand-flying. Why not? He pulled it off damned well. Then he told her he wasn't sure of the fuel gauges on the advanced type of jet they were flying, the Trent 270, a new British import.

Connie was shocked. So were the I.A. linemen the first time they saw Lucky putting a wooden dipstick into the tanks to measure the fuel quantity.

"Lucky, you look like a fool out there with that stick. Fuel quantity, pressure, and flow gauges are damn accurate and you know it."

"I don't know it. Up north we often found differences between the cockpit readouts and what was really in the tanks."

"But this jet is state of the art."

"I know, but I like to do things my way. Makes me feel better."

"I love you, Lucky. But I sure don't understand you."

"Few people do."

Connie, who usually flew with Lucky as his first officer, wondered if she should consult the flight surgeon the first time she saw the homemade dipstick. She thought that Lucky was losing it. Every I.A. employee who heard about the famous dipstick thought so, too, but Connie decided not to talk to the doctor about Lucky. She hoped that measuring fuel the old-fashioned way was just a passing phase of his curious personality: an odd blend of air safety on one end and dangerous aviation on the other.

Connie accepted Lucky's addiction to high-hazard flying; it seemed to be born in him. Now the risks were reduced to Sunday afternoon acrobatics in his rebuilt 1932 silk-and-wood plane.

She could understand some of Lucky's romance with forgotten flying. In earlier aviation days, she reckoned, part of the experience was not knowing everything;

now anything could be known by button tapping. Part of the impassioned mystery of flying had been ripped out by the high-tech boys. There was little adventure now. Few expectations. No discoveries. The computerized, cockpits not only pointed out the problems with colored blinks, they suggested and at times demanded the solutions. These ruling micro chips were programmed to almost eliminate pilot error while reducing the path of human judgment. Perhaps that was the authority factor that Lucky Doyle detested and feared. Connie knew that to Lucky the glass cockpit meant the abandonment of an old familiar device that had been in airplanes since the Wright brothers. The pilot's wheel, his yoke, was gone, replaced by a handle to each side of the pilot and the copilot. It was a small stick, like those in the video games, and on the stick were buttons to be pushed for this and that. And where the wheel had been for some ninety years there was a folddown plastic desk.

Deeply concerned about Lucky, how he was going to react to losing his job, Connie phoned Frank A'hearn in Fort Smith shortly after the dipstick appeared. He wasn't surprised to hear from her. There had been stories for months about the I.A. deal and the loss of pilot jobs up in Tulsa. Some called the merger, or takeover, a disguised ploy of union busting.

Lucky had never come to the conversion shop asking for a job. Some Lucky Doyle tales had drifted back to Frank's shop. Louie Bonner, an old, grizzled North Slope pilot who worked for Frank, had rushed into the office one morning.

"You heard what Lucky is doin' on those two-seventies? He don't trust the birds."

"They dropped a few but that doesn't mean it's a bad plane, just a controversial one."

"But Lucky thinks the fuel transmitters are way off."

"Can't be," Frank laughed. "What do you mean?"

"Well, Lucky's made this dipstick for himself, has it marked off in pounds and gallons, down to an eighth of an inch. He keeps goin' up on the wing and havin' the linemen pull the caps. Puts the stick down in the tanks."

"You're shittin' me, Louie."

"Naw, heard it four times. But I guess someone talked to Doyle. They said he broke up the dipstick."

"That was smart of Lucky. I wonder if he really distrusts that two-seventy. What do you think of a jet that heavy with just two holes? Hell, it's larger than a seven-forty-seven with four engines," Frank said.

Connie told Frank that she didn't like the way Lucky was acting. Sometimes he was as morbid as if his world were ending. Then his mood would soar; once he said he'd open a restaurant that served only crepes.

"Connie, his world ended a long time ago. Lucky's the only one who doesn't know it," Frank said.

"He's having his last check ride today in all this mess. I was thinking of good news for the guy."

"Like what?"

"Well, you deliver all sorts of cargo planes. Why can't Lucky ferry the equipment? He's checked out in DC sixes and sevens. You name it, he's flown it."

"We're not insured for ferry work. The seller flies the equipment in here, the buyer flies it out. We shoot a few test flights, but Louie Bonner does that. One thing I have to tell you, Connie. Lucky has made a bad name for himself. This hand-flying to outwit the autopilot, and making his own dipstick, for Chrissake! Can't you talk him out of that crap?"

"I tried."

"People think he's crackers."

"It's just Lucky's way of reacting," Connie said mechanically.

"I know that. I told him he wouldn't be a good penguin."

"What do you mean?"

"One night we were having a drink after we pulled into Tulsa. I told Lucky that I flew supplies down to the Antarctic one time. On the layover they showed us this penguin rookery. All the little birds were doing the same thing. I stood looking at those penguins waddling all in a line. They reminded me of airline pilots, black and white uniforms marching together. Every damned bird was a conformist. After I told Lucky about the crazy birds, I said to him, 'You'll never be a penguin-type airline pilot. That's not you, Lucky.' Well, he agreed. At first I thought he'd come down here and join me. He'd have been perfect. Good welder. Took engineering in college, knows aircraft structures. He'd be great at sales. You tell him my door is still open."

"I appreciate that you really care about Lucky. I love the guy."

"Lucky has to realize that his kind of sky jockeying is over. It wasn't easy for me to accept it, but I got used to being grounded. Can't stay up there forever."

"He's only forty-five, Frank."

"It's his attitude. Lucky never understood why they didn't make him a jet pilot in the Navy."

"That's over. Lucky told me all about that," Connie said.

"Yeah, but he still believes that article they wrote about us."

"What article?" Connie asked quickly. She thought she knew everything about Lucky and his past.

"The one this reporter from L.A. did for the *Sunday Examiner*."

"Never saw it."

"Ask Lucky about it. I'm sure he saved it."

"What was the article about?"

"This reporter spent three days with us flying around in the shitty part of winter. He sort of made human monuments out of us."

"To what?" she asked quickly. "Insanity?"

"Nothing like that. The guy compared our kind of flying to an art form. He said we were pioneer poets with wings. It was just baloney. We were up there for big bucks. Lucky knew that, but he liked to believe he was practicing some kind of art or poetry. He wasn't. I can tell you."

"So Lucky read it wrong. He dreams. Some of that's okay."

"Yeah, but the guy has to know where he is. Lucky's a victim of electronic supremacy, if you want to call it that. He's also taking a few hits because of airline deregulation. Fewer carriers. Union busting. Lucky just has to come to terms with who he is . . . where he is. As soon as he figures that out, he'll be solving his problem."

"That's true. But to me, having just two big mouths on that monster looks wrong. An aircraft designer told me one time, 'what looks right is usually right,' " Louie said.

"Maybe. But I wonder if size can kill a turbine? It sure as hell knocked off the dinosaur. Could it be the same with turbine design?"

"There's got to be an upper limit. But has the Trent reached it?" Louie asked skeptically.

"Don't worry, poor engine designs always show up."

"That's what I'm worried about." Frank sighed. "If one more of those Trents go in, that jet has had it!"

They both thought of Lucky Doyle flying the huge two-engine Trent. They didn't like it.

5:40 A.M. CST (TULSA)

●

———————THE SOUTH CENTRAL CORPORate jet was just minutes northeast of Tulsa. Only two passengers were aboard: Augie Hartman, the young South Central president, and Pete Rosen, an even younger reporter for the *Tulsa Leader*. Part of South Central's takeover bid was that Intra-Continental's Tulsa corporate headquarters would remain there. That section of the deal was unbendable, according to Ron Alcott, the seventy-year-old pilot-founder of Intra-Continental. He had started the carrier in Tulsa with one DC–3 in 1938, and the airline "belonged" to Tulsa. It was a city tradition almost as strong as the connection to oil drilling and the rise of the natural gas industries.

Augie Hartman, however, was a devious man who was planning to remove the board one by one. When he had unequivocal control, he would vote for relocation of the airline's headquarters to St. Louis.

Pete Rosen, the twenty-five-year-old Tulsa reporter, suspected Augie of unfair manipulation in the I.A. deal. He had gone to his editor asking for an assignment to cover the new man in town, the South Central dealmaker.

"Is there an angle on this?" the editor, Mike Wills, asked.

"In a way," Pete replied. "Actually, there're two angles. One is Hartman himself. He's not an airline man; he's a thirty-one-year-old accountant who turned three regional carriers around. That's why they brought him in. He's the antithesis of old Ron Alcott. Ron knows and loves aviation. Hartman is ignorant of planes, not interested in either them or air safety. He's all numbers, a real bottom-line guy. Then there's something else. Two months after Augie took his seat with South Central, their load factor went up and I.A.'s dropped off, way off."

"What did Hartman change?" the editor asked.

"I feel the financial public relations firm that Hartman hired, a tough Chicago bunch, was behind it."

"What are you getting at, Pete?"

"I think Augie set out to undermine passenger confidence in I.A. by bringing up the safety factor over and over again."

"You think they're planting stories?"

"That would be Hartman's style. I have some leads, but nothing's in yet."

"That's heavy," Mike said, sensing a strong story, "but it wouldn't stall the merger. They're closing next Friday."

"I realize that, but I think our readers should get a handle on Hartman and his real plans for I.A. So I'd like to go up to St. Louis and interview the man. I have another tip on this," Pete added.

"From where?"

"Can't tell you."

"What the hell do you mean? I'm the editor. Where did it come from?"

"South Central. I know someone on the *Post Dispatch.* The merger agreement says that Hartman will uphold the I.A. house union contracts. But South Central is a nonunion carrier. Pay scales are twenty percent below those of the machinists' and pilots' union. That's twenty percent under I.A.'s house union, too. So Hartman is going to bust the I.A. union by asking the guys to take cuts. They won't do that. Then he'll fire them when their contracts are up and hire nonunion people. No one's job is safe."

"Will he pull the bankruptcy trick, as Lorenzo did with Eastern and Continental?"

"No. He doesn't have to get that drastic. Hartman's dealing with a house union. The method will be different, but the result will be the same."

"A sad end for Ron Alcott and I.A. My father used to fly down to Dallas with them. Took me along when I was a kid. The airline industry's a mess. An old carrier like I.A. being forced under by a single little bastard. Okay. You have the assignment."

What Pete hadn't told Mike was that he had stashed a mole in the Chicago public relations office. The corporate spy had reported the connection between Augie and the stories about I.A.'s "safety problems." If the editor gave him the feature story, Rosen was planning to offer the I.A. piece as hard news for the front page. It would be Pete Rosen's break at the *Tulsa Leader*, perhaps his way into investigative reporting.

Rosen and his mole had discovered Hartman's stealthy plan: It was rooted in the Trent 270.

Five years earlier, after years of airframe and turbine development design, Trent Aircraft Ltd. of Bristol, England, Saab and Rolls-Royce had just about bet their economic futures on the radical new design. It was the largest two-engine jet in the world, slightly larger than a 747, the Trent 270 could carry more than five hundred passengers in some configurations.

Just as Frank and Louie had discussed, the wisdom of breaking the 100,000-pound thrust mark with a giant, high bypass ratio powerplant evoked the most heated debate in the world's aircraft industry. No subject had created more anguish.

Were the bold new engines killers, technical marvels, examples of turbine design audacity and economic brilliance? Or would they enter history as the power plants that crippled airlines and brought three highly respected names in aviation industry to their knees?

There was no one answer. The editor of *Aviation Week & Space Technology*, the most respected trade journal of commercial and military aviation, said at an industry meeting, "I can report without a doubt that our book has never experienced such a cascade of mail and pro and con stories as we have seen on the Trent two-seventy. But the controversy goes even deeper. There is no middle ground of opinion regarding this airliner. Just as many respected authorities in our field condemn the new British-Swedish entry as being an example of wreckless design as those equally qualified experts who say that the Trent two-seventy, while unprecedently forward in turbine technology, represents a sound solution for today's higher fuel costs."

When the Trent entered service, fuel prices were relatively low. Experts said that hanging two engines on an airframe that by common sense needed at least three and maybe four turbines was foolhardy. "A total disregard for passenger safety," the aviation editor of *The Guardian* said. But the Trent 270 had met the airworthiness requirements of the British Civil Aviation Authority.

All the aviation insiders knew that airworthiness is a subjective term. It measures, in an almost abstract way, risk against achieved reliability. Still, there was one area of certification under British and U.S. standards that was not up for controversy: Controllability on takeoff with one engine out.

"How could one turbine lift an aircraft weighing about eight hundred thousand pounds that would still be controllable?" many asked. Pilots and designers know that when an engine mounted on a wing goes out on takeoff, the aircraft suffers asymmetrical thrust. Very simply the plane turns into the dead engine with frightening speed if the pilot doesn't jam in full opposite rudder to halt the impending loss of control.

With a turbine opening of almost twelve feet hanging off each wing, those critical of the 270 from the start said, "No bloody pilot will be able to control that roll into the dead engine."

Those dedicated cynics had not taken into account the brilliance of the Trent design team. Realizing that the huge frontal drag element was hanging out there to snag the aircraft with a dead engine on takeoff, they took charge of the contingent problem.

The first step was to design extremely large control surfaces and a high fin to control the aircraft at low speeds with an engine out. Then the glass cockpit designers arrived at a computer solution that would not only identify the inoperative engine, but put the microchips in command of directional control, kicking in full opposite rudder with speed faster than the keenest pilot could use his left or right foot.

The 270 adversaries were dumbfounded.

Not only was the new aircraft fully controllable in a one-engine takeoff, the huge plane demonstrated responsive actions in yaw, pitch, and roll with and without the emergency computer operating. The FAA certification of the Trent 270 brought even more positive results.

"The damn thing even climbs with one fan cold and dead. Amazing!" said an ancient aircraft designer who had worked with both Donald Douglass and Bill Boeing.

Despite its built-in safety backups, the Trent 270 experienced three crashes within two years of certification. But not one accident was associated with the turbines; even if the 270 had been designed with four turbines, like the 747, the same tragedies would have resulted.

The worst accident occurred in Hong Kong, where a Trent 270 struck several apartment houses in marginal weather conditions when the captain should have executed a missed approach instead of continuing his landing. The pernicious rumors said that the glass cockpit systems aboard the advanced new aircraft were faulty. Two other crashes, one in Singapore and another at Dublin, ran the Trent 270 death toll to more than one hundred sixty. The Hong Kong accident was definitely pilot error. The others were associated with the jet's hydraulic system, which evoked landing gear failures. An emergency Air Directive grounded all 270s and the design fault was corrected.

The initial Eastern Hemisphere reception of the new two-engine giant had been positive, with two hundred deliveries. In the Western Hemisphere, the sales were limp, except for I.A. They ordered twelve units, and Aeromexico took four 270s for their European service.

Ron Alcott placed the mammoth Trent 270 into an unusual service. The aircraft, with its new flap design and mission adaptive wing, could take off from the ten-thousand-foot Tulsa runway. Direct international service from the "Oil City" to London and Paris was inaugurated with enthusiastic passenger response. When the price of jet fuel rose dramatically, most airlines hiked their fares by ten percent or more. Not I.A. Ron and his marketing group pulled what they thought was the coup of the industry. They lowered their short-haul fares by placing the Trent 270 on domestic routes, some under five hundred miles.

The theory was sound. If the fuel-efficient 270 could board 390 or more revenue fares, the airline would profit over the competition by high density loading from passengers taking advantage of lower priced tickets. It worked for a while. Then the I.A. regulars turned away. They didn't think that the new British jet was safe.

Even though not one I.A. passenger ever suffered an injury, there were four incidents associated with the 270 that eroded confidence in the new airliner. Three I.A. Trents made unscheduled landings associated with electrical and turbine oil pressure problems. The flight crews felt that these actions were merely precautionary landings; that they had not been forced down by acute inflight emergencies. The public saw these landings as a serious portent of future trouble, even disaster.

With passenger confidence in the 270 on the line, Augie Hartman made his strategic move. He hired a marginal Chicago PR firm to go to work, hammering away at the Trent safety record. All they had to do was raise the question of the aircraft's safety with editors in the cities served by I.A. along with South Central.

"Is the two-seventy safe?" was the question they promoted. The passengers decided. After an avalanche of these planted pieces, the effects began to be felt. The load factor for the I.A. 270 flights slipped dramatically. The aircraft appeared to be doomed. The Hartman plan worked, and the banks were not willing to restructure I.A.'s heavy debt schedule. Ron Alcott had bought the wrong aircraft; a semicongenial takeover was the only alternative.

Pete Rosen was given the assignment he had asked

for, but he could not have imagined where it would take him.

About six o'clock on the morning of the blizzard Doug Halsey, a wealthy forty-nine-year-old developer, was jarred from his sleep by the cracking branches of the ice-loaded trees. As his head cleared, Doug's ears began to pick up the moans of the slashing wind intermixed with occasional volleys of sleet pinging off the slate roof of his expensive Tulsa home. The night before, Doug had called the Flight Service Station at the Tulsa International Airport. He had been told that the weather would be improving by ten o'clock the next morning, so he had not taken a drink that evening. He was flying his own plane up to Omaha, and he carefully observed the FAA rule: eight hours from bottle to throttle.

Doug phoned the Flight Service Station once more. He didn't ask for a complete briefing, but he was informed of the deep low-pressure system affecting Tulsa with attendant IFR conditions, meaning that the weather was marginal, to say the least, and only pilots with current instrument ratings and a plane certified to fly into known icing conditions were permitted to take off.

"We have flight precautions for moderate rime icing in clouds. The freezing level is six thousand feet. Possibility of moderate turbulence below eight thousand feet."

To someone with solid instrument flight experience, the weather at Tulsa and the briefing would have signaled a no-go situation especially for a pilot flying alone.

When Doug put the phone down, his wife rolled over in bed. "How can you fly in this storm?" she asked.

"The plane is certified to fly into known icing conditions," he reassured her.

"Don't you think you ought wait until the storm passes?"

"No. I have an important meeting up in Omaha. If the airliners are taking off, so can I."

"But Doug, you don't have an airliner."

"In a sense I do. My plane is equipped with just about everything that the big boys have on their panels. I didn't spare any expense when it came to safety. Don't worry, the storm sounds worse than it is."

Doug Halsey was the epitome of the emerging, rich American. As a very successful developer and architect, he wanted his rewards, the medallions of wealth. On the coasts the status prop was a yacht; in the Midwest, though, the move was to fast, private aircraft. Owning a jet was not seen as ostentation but as a serious business tool that provided freedom from airline counters and the delight of going anywhere at any time. To Doug it meant complete self-determination: a triumph over delayed airline schedules, canceled flights, and lost baggage.

The purchase of his Rockwell turboprop was a symbolic rite of passage. The aircraft broker at nearby Richard Lloyd Jones Field knew Doug's type: the man who wanted the freedom of flying but had not yet spent one minute in a cockpit. The broker had a proven method of dealing with the new rich who were after limitless self-expression.

"I don't mind selling you a turboprop or a pure jet, but first I'd like to sell you safety. You can't just be another pilot in today's crowded skies. You have to be up there as one of the best."

Doug liked the word *best*. He thought of himself as someone who tried for that level in his family life and in his career. Doug was shown a gleaming turboprop. Inside were the scent of real leather, a small buffet, a head, six passenger seats and a baffling cockpit. The console had rows of round windows with white numbers inside.

"Of course, we want to upgrade the instruments —state of the art—you never want to take chances," the broker repeated.

Doug agreed. On the afternoon he signed the $275,000 check for his new Rockwell turboprop, Doug took his first flight lesson—not from a kid trying to build time but from a white-haired, ex–airline captain who was hired by the broker for those special students with deep pockets. In four weeks Doug had obtained all his necessary FAA licenses, even one that was not required: the instrument ticket.

Just after Christmas he flew on business trips to Topeka, Chicago, Midland and Dallas. All the flights were under Visual Flight Rules, fair weather, so it was not necessary to file an instrument flight plan.

On one particular flight from Little Rock, Tulsa fell below Visual Flight Rules, and Doug filed an instrument flight plan while en route. The controller sensed that he was a "squirrel," a low-time private pilot. When Doug was handed off to the approach controller at Tulsa, the word *squirrel* was used by the air traffic control center. They could tell the squirrels by the way they spoke on the radio: slowly, and repeatedly with terms used incorrectly.

Doug was not in the least apprehensive the first time he flew in the clouds. The turboprop was in perfect control, being flown by the autopilot. The Tulsa Approach Controller, knowing he had a "squirrel", spoke slowly, giving Doug a number of headings so he could establish his aircraft on the Instrument Landing System to Runway 17 Right. Doug tuned his navigation equipment to the runway localizer frequency, 111.1, pushed the button marked APP on the autopilot, meaning that the electronic signals from the runway landing system

gineer, pilot and businessman who headed up the five-generation airframe company located, as it had been for seventy-two years, on the outskirts of Bristol.

Intra-Continental, a medium-sized carrier by United States standards, remained just barely segregated from the airline swallow-ups that followed deregulation in the United States. Both Pryce-Smith and Ron Alcott were pilots of the old school, although not a school as ancient as the one Lucky Doyle was onto. Still, both the U.S. and British corporate heads were men of grit who would not give up or give in. There was a high price tag to individuality, however.

Ron Alcott was the only American to buy the Trent 270, and Ian was the only man who could have rolled this controversial, outsized aircraft out of his fabrication hangars. In doing so, both men were trapped by deep fiscal problems.

Ron could not service Intra-Continental's debt load. The 270s carried high price tags, and Ian wasn't selling nearly enough of these giant two-engine airliners to overcome the high development costs.

This was reckoning day for both companies. If I.A. could not restructure their payment schedules, then the carrier would fall prey to Augie Hartman. They would know the answer sometime during the next two hours when the loan officers of the various banks met to decide if their only way out was to allow the South Central merger. For Ian, the situation was graver. If the ad hoc committee that had been assembled to aid the distressed airframe manufacturer could not come up with a solution, two events would be faced by Trent Aviation: the cancellation of their 270 program and the amalgamation of Trent into the national giant, British Aerospace. The handsome forty-nine-year-old leader of Trent Aviation was taking the 270 crisis as a personal defeat. It was the same for Ron Alcott. Both men would end their long and notable aviation careers on a sharp note of shame if Augie Hartman prevailed.

Because both companies were suffering together, Ron Alcott had sent his affable chairman, Lou Walters, to Bristol to be by Ian's side if the Trent rescue operation failed. Lou, nearly seventy, had been a pilot in World War II with the Eighth Air Force. With Alex Anderson, the vice president of maintenance, Walters was one of I.A.'s grand old guard, part of the founding group.

Why was the publicity against the aircraft so sharp? Everyone was asking.

Ian decided to find out. He hired the aviation consulting firm, Kendal Associates of London, to explore the matter. And on this day their chairman, Sir Hugh Hamilton, an ex–Spitfire pilot, was to arrive at Trent headquarters to render his report. He had told the Trent executives that shocking facts had been uncovered. Ian and Lou Walters started lunch in the executive dining room at Trent's Bristol plant before the Kendal executive arrived.

"Tell me, Ian, if you had to design the Trent two-seventy all over again, would you change a thing?" Lou asked.

It was a direct and brittle question in the light of what had happened to the aircraft in the press and in the accident columns.

"If I had to redesign that two-seventy starting tomorrow, it would be the exact same design. Not a bolt would be relocated."

The bald Lou Walters, a man who looked as tough at seventy as he had at thirty, smiled. He had known that would be the answer.

"I knew you would say that. It makes this damned situation all the more tragic."

"I can't believe what's happened to both of us. How is Ron taking it?" Ian asked.

"As bad as I am. Over ten thousand jobs will be lost in Tulsa. It's the defeat of Alcott's life."

Their commiserating over what had happened was interrupted as a tall man, Sir Hugh Hamilton, edged toward the table. After quick introductions, he got down to business.

"All this will be presented to both Intra-Continental and Trent Aviation in a two-hundred-page report tomorrow. But I thought it was my duty to tell you gentlemen the highlights."

"Good of you," Ian said. "I couldn't sleep last night wondering about what you people discovered."

"Our report appears in two sections," Sir Hugh replied. "The Trent two-seventy we find, after a complete analysis of all systems and design elements, is a very fine aircraft—advanced, stable, engineered and fabricated well, economically sound and about as safe a big jet as could be built at this stage in aviation technology. The accidents and incidents surrounding the two-seventy have been blown far out of proportion, but I will get to that in the second part of the report. The Hong Kong accident appears to have been caused entirely by the captain's lack of respect for the numbers on his landing plate.

"The other two accidents as you know related to hydraulic problems. These have been remedied. No further problems have arisen.

"Now to the second part of our report. We've discovered some frightful conduct on the part of Mr. Hartman and others at South Central. Basically, in one sentence gentlemen, Hartman, and to some extent others who will have to be deposed, engaged a rather underhanded Chicago PR firm to plant negative safety articles on the Trent two-seventy."

Ian and Lou crossed sharp glances and leaned forward. They could not believe what they were hearing.

"How does one do that with responsible aviation editors?" Ian asked.

"Very carefully and subtly. First this Hartman chap hired a group of marginal aviation writers in five states. They visited editors they knew, not revealing, of course, that they were being paid to present one-sided articles on the Trent design and safety questions. These writers had always been independent. That's what the editors assumed. And they bought these danger stories saying that the aircraft was too big for only two turbines. We all know what happens once you put a false seed in someone's mind. It grows to be a fact. The idea of the unsafe Trent took shape. It was picked up by the wire services. And the sad part here is that Trent Aviation and your company, Mr. Walters, could not counter a campaign that you didn't know about."

"That bastard Hartman!" Lou blasted.

"From our side, too," Ian said. "But to mount a PR counterattack would take time . . . a lawsuit, even more time. And that's what we don't have. The lenders are closing in on both of us."

"I know that," the consultant said. "It's probably too late. But if we put out a story on our findings, it might buy time."

Ian agreed with a dip of his head. They might gain some satisfaction, but that wouldn't repair the damage.

Jack Haverly, the Air Traffic Manager of the Tulsa tower, was having a hard time keeping on the road. He wondered, as Connie and Lucky had, how they could be moving air traffic out in weather like this.

Jack thought of the Tulsa control tower as home. His wife had left him many years ago, and his three children were now grown and scattered about the country. The sixty-four people who worked under Jack were, in a way, his family. He knew their birthdays, their problems, their home lives. Jack thought of himself as a lovable porcupine. That's what an Air Traffic Manager had to be: soft on the inside and damned prickly outside.

As he inched along behind a semi just outside of Tulsa, Jack picked up his car phone and clicked in the tower number.

"Juan? Jack. I'm poking my way in. Where are you now?"

"On top. In the cab."

"What's the runway visual range?"

"Let me look at the readout on the RVR." The deputy chief moved over to his runway visual range readout and noted the figures.

"About a thousand feet, Jack."

"You sure that damned thing is working?"

"Why?"

"I'm driving in. I can hardly see the truck right in front of me."

"I know. A lot of the operations people called. They couldn't believe we were moving traffic, but I can see the lights and the outline of the American Airlines hangar. That's about three hundred yards across from the tower. I'd say the RVR projector's reading okay."

"Why is the airport above minimums and everyone else around Tulsa is socked in?"

"Damned if I know."

"How's the runway work going?" Jack asked.

"The east side is not bad . . . pilots say traction's okay. In twenty minutes I'm going to close it to traffic for about thirty minutes and let the plows take another run."

"How about the west side?"

"That's closed. We're handling corporate traffic on three-five right. I'll get the plows over to the other side after the next sweep."

"Anything else I should know?"

"Just that five guys said they couldn't get their cars going for the morning shift. They're digging them out of deep snow. Also we're picking up a lot of wing icing at the gates. Line crews are working like hell on the deicing."

"Are we on a gate hold?"

"No, but it's coming in about twenty minutes, Center says. As soon as I lock traffic in here, I'll start the plows."

"Can you see the west runway?"

"No."

"Wish we had that ground radar."

"You know it. But we're keeping the ground traffic far enough apart, holding flights at the intersections until we get confirmation of the crossovers. Everything's going real slow, but it's okay for now."

Jack clicked off the phone and continued to squint at the huge truck in front of him with a Christmas tree of red lights strung around the rear doors. He wondered why anyone would want to drive in this stuff. And again he asked himself, "How could the airport be open?" As long as he'd been at the Tulsa tower, he never remembered a snowstorm quite like this one.

The operations room on the first level of the Tulsa airport was choked with I.A. pilots clustered around the long corkboard that held floppy sheets of weather data. Connie and Lucky said hello to a few friends. In a sense it was a series of goodbys.

The airline personnel had been split between those who were surviving the merger and those who were receiving termination letters. Most executives were being fitted with golden or even platinum parachutes, but men like Lucky and hundreds of others, from gate agents to reservation people, were getting slim severance checks with a simulated personal letter from Ron Alcott.

With a fistful of dispatch papers, Connie and Lucky boarded the Trent 270 at the gate on the east concourse, which I.A. had all to itself. They said hello and had a few words with the flight attendants. Connie put on her old raincoat, which she kept in one of the two hanging lockers in the cockpit. Then she slushed around outside the jet for the visual preflight inspection. She ordered the wings deiced and entered the cockpit once more. Lucky, who had been filing the flight plan, put on his old fedora again and the coat that looked as if it belonged at the Salvation Army store. He left to do his own walkaround. This was not required for the captain, but Lucky liked to see things for himself.

Connie was filing her nails when the cockpit door burst open and a pink-faced, panting man with rolls of sweat coming off his smooth forehead entered, blowing out breaths of steam.

"Captain Bouchard! Have you been jogging in all this?"

"Oh, yes, just taking a short run. Have to change," he said in his singsong way.

He was a small, almost frail-looking man, not the sort of person one would expect to find in an early jet fighter twisting around the skies over Korea.

"I'll be downstairs getting ready. Where is Lucky?"

"Out on his walkaround."

"Good." The chief pilot disappeared from the glass cockpit.

Ten minutes later, showered and dressed in his custom uniform, André entered the cockpit again. "Frightful day, isn't it?" he said to Connie.

"Unusual storm to say the least. I never saw one like it. Captain Bouchard, I wanted to talk to you about something while Lucky's out doing his walkaround."

"Of course. Anything, Miss Esposito."

"Could you possibly put in a good word for Lucky? He's come to the realization that computer flying is here to stay."

"That's hard for me to believe. He was the last of the hand-fliers. A good pilot but charmingly obsolete. I'm not too sure I can recommend him. But I like Lucky very much. If I didn't, I wouldn't let you two handle this jet. That's how much faith I have in both of you. Real pros. Now Lucky has strange ideas, wouldn't you say? He's not a systems man. I'm not sure there's a place left for old-style pilots. They're gone now, unneeded."

"There has to be a place for him."

I'll keep an eye out for Lucky. Now, I have news for you!"

"I'm not on the transition list?"

André extended his thin lips into a smile.

"You *are* on the transition list. You will be flying with South Central as a captain. I have recommended you for a left seat on the Seven Thirty-Seven equipment, South Central's first female skipper."

Connie was stunned. It took a minute or two for this to sink in. Lucky was on the beach, and she would be flying left seat for the new merged carrier. What would that do to Lucky and their relationship? She thanked the chief pilot dazedly. An airline captain. Her father would have been so proud.

"Captain Bouchard," she said, "would you do me a favor? Would you not mention this to Lucky until we get to Chicago today?"

"If you wish it. Now one last point," he went on. "This morning we have a dozen Girl Scouts from all over the state who have come to Tulsa as science merit badge winners. They're going with us this morning as far as St. Louis, where they change to another flight for Savannah. That's where the Girl Scouts originated, my wife said. As a special favor to me and Ron Alcott, I would like you to explain to the Scouts, as many as we can squeeze in here, how the modern cockpit works. I would have chosen Lucky, but I know his quirks."

"Yes, I'll—I'll be glad to. I'll give the girls the cockpit tour."

Ten minutes later the uniformed girls were boarded, and Connie was explaining the wonders of the glass cockpit and all its electronic capabilities. She hoped all the claims she was making for it were true, but she wasn't sure. And all the time she babbled on about electronic displays, she thought of Lucky without a job and aviation plucked out of his life.

When Jack Haverly finally approached Tulsa International through the crawling and stalled traffic, the blowing grayness and the size of the flipping snowflakes seemed to moderate, as if the airport were stationed in some neutral zone. He heard the roar of a jet overhead coming down the alley. There was only the high shrill sound; nothing to see. The ceiling was still low and skirting. Jack turned off onto the conduit road, which had just been plowed, and entered the field at the far end where the control tower could be reached without crossing a runway or taxiway.

He was surprised at the emptiness of the parking lot. Usually, at a peak traffic hour such as this, there would be three rows of cars. Once inside, Juan Gomez told Jack that there were three sick calls and that five controllers for the shift had phoned to say they were delayed but on their way in.

Jack decided not to work in his office until more of the crew arrived. He went down the hall to the radar room, a long dark cavern lighted by the pea-green glow floating off the banks of radar scopes. It was in this room that the flights were handed off from Air Traffic Control Center as they came within the jurisdiction of the Tulsa tower. The area was called the ARSA, or Airport Radar Service Area.

"So where are we, Juan?" Jack asked his deputy.

"Well, when we got the first gate hold, I had the plows work the long runway on the east. That's in good condition now . . . traction's not bad. Not too much blowing snow. Then I sent the plows over to the west runway. They're scraping that now."

"Anything else I should know about?"

"We're moving the flights from the gates very slowly. We've got three airport cars out there helping us spot the ground traffic. Each pilot just follows the tire tracks of the jet in front of him. I keep a car in between each bird until we swing them onto the active."

"That's the way to do it . . . but I still wish we had ground radar so we could see the entire field. Okay, we don't. Now who's on the snow committee and where are they?"

"Two of the pilots called in and said they would be late."

"They were supposed to be here all night," Jack retorted with an edge to his voice.

"Two of them were. They went home at seven."

"Why didn't they wait for replacements?"

"Don't know. The fellow on duty now is a TWA skipper. He's over at the General Aviation Building having breakfast while the plows work the west side. He's got a handheld radio with him."

"I'll talk to him later and find out where the other guys are."

"I asked him. He doesn't know," Juan said.

"I thought the snow committee was better organized than that."

"It is. But a lot of these boys drive in a long way, and they don't get paid for walking around the runways all night."

After he was certain that the radar room was manned sufficiently, Jack took the elevator seventy-four feet up to the cab. Although the sleet was hitting the tinted glass windows, the controllers seemed at ease, even though they couldn't see the entire field—only part of the long east runway.

Across the field, smothered in the gauze-like shroud of snow, the General Aviation Building looked like a soft-edged pastel drawing. On the first floor were the FAA offices, the Flight Service Station, a restaurant, and some aviation insurance brokerage offices. Upstairs, various offices were rented to corporate flight departments.

Before Doug Halsey arrived, he had called the fixed base operator handling his plane and asked that his turboprop be tugged out and prepared for flight. Doug was not used to heavy snow operations. It was better to leave the aircraft inside the hangar to obviate ice buildups on the wings. It was against the fire rules to refuel a plane in a hangar, but they could have pumped the kerosene aboard at the last minute, outside, as close to Doug's departure time as possible. Doug went to the Flight Service Station for a final weather briefing. He was warned once more about the icing level now at 5,000 feet. He shrugged and again said smugly that he was certified to enter areas of known icing.

"About thirty minutes after takeoff you should break out in clear skies. Tops are at eight thousand now," the briefer said. Doug took a few notes, casually looked at the radar summary posted on the board and left for the restaurant.

He was confident that morning as he drank his muddy airport coffee, and he hummed to himself while he filled out his flight plan. And all the time, as the west runway was being plowed, his plane was sitting out in front waiting for him, and the wings were icing up inch by inch.

In Bristol, once Hartman had been singled out for malfeasance, a certain curse seemed to have been exorcised. In Tulsa, the weather had eased up a bit, and although the controllers could not see the entire field or who was at which intersection, the traffic was moving in and out slowly. Five additional controllers had arrived; the tower was now adequately manned. In the cockpit of I.A. 19, FAA designation N 9690 WC—Whiskey Charley, as the flight was to be identified—Lucky Doyle's frayed nerves had settled down. But he would still hand-fly the bird. In some cases, in gusty winds, it was the way to go.

9:16 A.M. CST (TULSA)

DOUG HALSEY WAS ENJOYING his second cup of coffee in the airport restaurant. He, too, felt secure and happy. He was a financial success and now he was an instant pilot with a plane that was absolutely safe because there were backups for the backups.

Unlike Lucky Doyle, Doug thanked God for the fly-by-wire cockpit. Those little things to push and program eased his mind; his turboprop just about flew itself if the right buttons were touched and the correct program entered. Doug was good at that. In fact, right now he couldn't understand why there was a group of corporate pilots clustered down the hall looking at the update on the radar summary. He thought they were probably overcautious, or even timid about coming out to tackle weather like this.

Doug left the restaurant, looked out of the window, and saw two plows returning to the east side of the airport. Believing that the west runway was plowed and ready for use, he filed his flight plan and breezed through the pretakeoff list. Doug naturally thought that the plowed west runway was open for business.

The Tulsa International Airport is actually two airports in a sense, with the control tower between them. On the east side was the longest runway, the one used by commercial airliners. On Doug's side, the western end, was a shorter strip that the smaller planes and corporate jets used. Doug had always requested the Romeo Two Intersection takeoffs. It was a taxiway that intersected with the west runway about half way down the strip. He had been told by his instructor to use the entire length of the available runway in case of an engine out on takeoff, but Doug, like other pilots, usually requested an intersection takeoff. Always lightly loaded, he found that he was airborne well before the end of the runway. This cut a few minutes off his flight time, and a few minutes saved here and there added up to hours for more productivity.

And like everything else that had happened to him so far in his brief career in aviation, the abbreviated takeoff worked out splendidly. Never a close call. It had all been as advertised by the man who sold him the aircraft and the retired captain who taught him to fly the complicated machine.

"It's a piece of cake as long as you think it out and follow the checklists," the instructor had repeated often.

Doug believed he was proficient when it came to routines: After all, architecture, he reasoned, was actually procedure and checklists. It was something like flying, he decided, a blend of restrictions, basics, decision making, and, yes, creativity.

Doug was so confident of his abilities and the high-tech capabilities of his aircraft that he put on a cassette tape of the speech on architecture that he had missed. He called the tower, which he could not see in the storm.

Without ground radar, the controllers were just as blind as he was. Doug asked for his usual intersection takeoff.

The ground controller said, "Alpha Two, intersection departure approved."

Doug's mind was on the recording of the speech; he heard only the words, ". . . Two, intersection approved."

He reported back to the ground control, "Intersection departure approved."

But the two men were talking about different intersections. Romeo Two was on Doug's side, the runway closed to traffic, although the architect didn't realize that. It had been plowed but still not signed off by the snow committee for flight operations.

The ground controller had cleared Doug to the opposite side of the field, to the longer east runway where the Alpha Two intersection was located. Doug simply taxied to his usual position at Romeo Two on the west runway and held short, as he was instructed. The controller told him that he wanted to depart a large jet before him. Doug did not understand why a large jet was using the short runway, but being occupied with the words flowing over the cassette, he didn't question the ground controller. Neither did the ground controller confirm Doug's exact position.

Just at that moment the Trent was rounding into position, holding short on the long east runway, 35 Right. The British jet had crept forward, following the blurred outline and strobe lights of an American 727. There was a high level of confidence in each cockpit.

9:30 A.M. CST (Over TULSA COUNTY)

"FIVE FOUR VICTOR, YOU'RE cleared for takeoff."

"Cleared for takeoff," Doug said. "Five Four Victor is rolling."

Doug pushed up his turbine levers and started his takeoff run. He scanned his engine instruments: Everything was in the green, and long before the end of the blurred runway he pulled back on his yoke and the plane took off without incident. He retracted his gear and was told by the local controller to contact departure control. Doug popped in the new frequency on the digital reading radio and announced, "Five Four Victor is with you."

Just before Doug's words were spoken, the departure controller had looked down the radar line for a fraction of a second. He glanced back at the display and noticed Doug's target, but he did not study the position long enough. His eyes had to adjust from the darkness of the room to the floating glow off the radar display.

"November Five Four Victor, radar contact," he said. "Turn right heading zero four zero."

"Right to zero four zero," Doug repeated slowly.

Whiskey Charlie was cleared for takeoff and Lucky eased up the levers of his two turbines. The Trent, pushed by 240,000 pounds of thrust, dashed down the east runway into a fuzzy blur of sleet and tumbling snowflakes. Connie started to read out the various speeds.

At V–2, the go or no-go speed, she said, "We're looking good, Lucky . . . you have Velocity Two."

He eased back on the sidestick and the jet rotated, lifting the big round nose into the spray of snow as the jet created its own wide path in the weather-filled air.

"Positive rate of climb," Connie said.

"Gear up," Lucky responded.

The enormous Trent, so big that it seemed to rule the skies, was on its way to St. Louis. The takeoff had been perfect, and everyone in the cockpit exchanged smiling looks.

By this time Doug Halsey was well into his right turn. Suddenly the conflict alert rang beside the Departure Scope in the tower. The controller froze. He had never heard the alarm before, only a simulation at the FAA Oklahoma City training facility.

"I.A. nineteen, turn right to zero five zero, right now!" he shouted. "We have traffic out of place! Collision course! Five, Four, Victor, turn left immediately to two, five, zero. Two five zero!"

Doug was on autopilot. He turned the directional bug to the new course instead of flipping the wheel to the left to overpower the autopilot. His turboprop made a slow coordinated turn. But Lucky slammed over his sidestick instantly, so hard that the jet banked deeply to the right.

Doug should have been hand-flying. That was his deadly blunder.

9:33 A.M. CST
(Over TULSA COUNTY)

•

———————AT EXACTLY TEN SECONDS after nine thirty-three that morning, Doug Halsey looked through the heated windshield of his turboprop and saw an odd shape. It was the last sight of his life.

At a speed of one hundred twenty miles an hour, the turboprop plunged into the guts of Whiskey Charlie on the lower side of the tail section. In microseconds, the Trent's far aft ribs were partly crushed, as if they had been crafted from balsa wood. Had Doug's plane been five times heavier, the weight of commuter equipment, the crash would have severed the 270's entire tail. Both aircraft would have tumbled out of the ice-laden clouds just north of the airport. But the blow from the smaller plane didn't cause a total structural failure of the big British jet. As Doug's nose ripped into the airliner, his canted wing sliced part of Whiskey Charlie's horizontal stabilizer off as if it were made of butter.

When the munched nose of the turboprop had pushed up and over what was left of the 270's tail, the smaller plane's left propeller, turning at 1,800 revolutions a minute, caught Whiskey Charlie's rudder section. The small plane jerked around; the prop dug deep into the Trent's structure, grinding, serrating, wedging, and chewing up whatever was inside with the fast action of a food processor reducing a solid onion to minced parts.

The great jet shuddered violently. This pulsation coughed out what was left of Doug's plane, a grinding noise rose above the chortle of the wind, and a gray powdery mass of aircraft pieces were spewed up. Black engine oil and kerosene were flung about as the turboprop's tanks ruptured and the engines were peeled open, and wreckage was whipped into one liquid mass full of curled metal chunks.

The whole appalling sequence took just three seconds from the time the small plane's nose made the initial contact with the 270 until the splattering and grinding had run its boomeranging course.

Suddenly, the gray sky erupted into a geyser of blazing jet fuel as the flames shot up and widened. The inferno seemed suspended in the air, as if it were part of the wild sky. At one side of the blazing ball, Whiskey Charlie was like a great whale plowing through a fogbound sea. The jet's tail section was roasted, its alloy skin glowed white-hot for a second. By all counts there should have been a second explosion when the fuel and hydraulic liquid stored in Whiskey Charlie's tail cone had almost reached the flash point. But not quite. The frigid, churning air cooled down the tail cone's rippled skin. The 270 escaped without a fiery trail, or far worse, a detonation that would have splattered the tail section into a million bits of scattered alloy.

The molten fragments of Doug Halsey's self-flying, foolproof plane dropped away. The largest piece was the left engine: Every other section had been pulverized by the impact. Doug was burned black so quickly that he felt no pain. Death came so rapidly that there was no time for even a sliver of a thought.

The concussion waves flowed like orchestrated shudders through the various cabins of Lucky's jet. Passengers in the rear screamed.

The sound of the impact was bomb-like. Ripples came in surges through the wrenched airframe as if giant fingers were massaging the plane. These tormenting sounds and fluctuations faded somewhat toward the front of the long 270. They were absorbed by the very length of the jet: 232 feet from tip to tail.

Still, the three in the cockpit knew what had happened long before the others aboard the jet. The second the turboprop hacked its way into the tail section, the control sidestick popped out of Lucky's fingers. Then the tiny column seemed to ease forward. It remained in a neutral position even though the 270 was still pitched in its initial climbout attitude, its nose about twelve degrees high, its altitude going through two thousand feet.

The crew had heard the controller's heated instructions: the course corrections, the warning of an aircraft out of place, so when the sidestick did its dance, all three in the cockpit knew what had happened. It was a full-blown collision in the tail, the most vulnerable place that any aircraft could be hit.

Connie looked first at André, who was leaning forward from his observer's position with his arms folded on the rear of Lucky's high-backed pilot's seat. His head shot straight up. His mouth opened to an oval and he panicked. What terrified Connie even more, if that was possible in those hellish seconds illuminated by the red instrument lights, was Lucky's fixed gaze. He did not react. His facial muscles, the ones she thought she knew so well, seemed carved from stone.

With the same expressionless face, Lucky tried the various controls. He pushed the sidestick one way, then another, but there was no change in the pitch attitude. Without the slightest show of desperation or dismay, Lucky tested his roll axis, banking gently left and right. That worked.

Then Connie saw him push the left rudder pedal. That should have swung the jet in that direction, but because they were still in the dense clouds, the course change could only be detected by the Heading Situation Indicator, or the HSI, one of the most important instruments on the panel of any airliner. The course reading remained constant.

The rudder was gone.

This did not mean that the 270 could no longer turn. Since the wing controls, the ailerons, were totally intact, the jet could be turned slowly by banking, but the rate of turn invoked by rudder pressure was absent.

Connie recognized the critical problem at once. She knew that Lucky understood it too, even though nothing about his face or actions appeared to underscore the crisis.

"How the fuck are you going to get the nose down and cut this climb?" she asked herself under her breath, wanting to scream at Lucky to shock him into the deathly reality.

They were in their takeoff configuration: flaps and leading-edge slats were set to reduce the stall speed of the jet. If Lucky retracted his flaps, it would cause a stall, that awesome moment when an airplane stops flying and starts falling.

Then there were the trim tabs, miniature control surfaces on the trailing edge of the two inner elevators, that were used to trim the up-and-down pitch of the plane. Connie saw Lucky's left pinky finger gingerly reach for the trim button on the left side of his sidestick. She outwardly scoffed at that. If the elevators were gone, how could the trim tabs attached to those control surfaces still function?

But they did. To her astonishment, the nose came down about two or three degrees. Just as that happened the airspeed picked up to about one hundred sixty knots. Lucky did the next best thing: He tickled off some thrust so that the turbines would not overheat from the extreme pressure ratios used for the full-thrust takeoff. The scream of the blades lessened. The ice balls could be heard more clearly bouncing off the jet's skin, and the airspeed dipped back to around one hundred forty knots. Lucky continued to ease back his two thrust levers until the sidestick started to shake, which meant that the stall was coming up fast. To prevent that, Lucky edged his thrust levers forward until the vibrative, buffet warnings subsided. Then he leaned back in his seat and yawned.

"Yawn all day, fellow," Connie said to herself. She wanted him to share her terror. But he didn't.

Finally Lucky said calmly, "Connie, darling, go to number two hydraulic system, please."

She hit the switchover button. Lucky once again tried the sidestick and rudder pedals. Nothing.

"Number three, please," he said just as softly.

The same thing.

"Go back to number one, now."

From afternoons of pulling Cuban Eights and Snap Rolls in Lucky's old Waco, Connie had learned the nature of the truly calm airman. Lucky was a guy who knew himself and his plane. Upside down, in a loop, or flying level, he would hum above the wind song a melody of old airplanes with two wings and lots of wires and struts holding things together.

Often she would look into her rear mirror in the

first of the two holes that were cockpits. Sitting outside while flying, Lucky told her, was the only way to taste the full brew. The oval mirror had a vital purpose: It was canted in such a way that Lucky could keep an eye on her face. When they were pulling loops, or back slides, he wanted to make sure she wasn't blacking out. All this was supposed to be challenging fun, not some cerebral collapse even for a second. Connie would also look into the mirror and watch Lucky's interesting face. Whenever he rounded out in a perfect, round loop, his square jaw would extend a bit, as if to say, "How do you like that, you big-ass clouds? Nice one, huh?"

She knew he was controlled and confident. But during those moments right after the collision, Lucky seemed particularly placid and detached as if it had been just a rough slice of air and a little flexing of the control surfaces.

He broke his calm with a verbal explosion. It was so loud that it dulled the clang of the ice balls and the siren of the wind.

"If you're still there, Tulsa approach, why aren't you speaking? Or have you lost your voice along with your ability to keep traffic apart?"

"No, sir," Jack Haverly said. (He had replaced the approach controller.) Jack had not contacted I.A. 19, for his display revealed that little had changed. The distinct target of the giant jet was unmoved by the collision. The radar showed that the plane was still on course, still in its initial climbout as if nothing were wrong.

"You were hit by a turboprop. How seriously are you damaged, sir?"

"Oh, just a few minor problems. I say minor because we're heading up toward outer space. Going into orbit forever, just going to keep circling the globe, around and around."

"Say again, sir."

"We have three hundred and nineteen aboard. We've lost all pitch control. The elevators must be jammed in the up angle. All we can do is climb with almost full thrust. How's that for a little spice to liven things up?"

"What are your intentions, sir?" Jack said, not knowing how to respond to Lucky's caustic tone.

"I'm going to land back in Tulsa. I'm planning a special dinner tonight," Lucky continued in the same sarcastic voice.

"I understand, sir," Jack said, trying to figure out how Lucky was planning to land when he could only climb.

"Just hang on this frequency," Lucky ordered. "Might be needing your assistance."

He clicked off and picked up the phone for his first PA of the flight. Before he could open his mouth, the cockpit buzzer rang. It was Linda, the head flight attendant.

"Lucky, has a bomb gone off? Some passengers are going crazy back here. They're starting to get up."

"That wasn't a bomb, we were hit by a private plane. Keep everyone seated. I'm just going to PA this."

"Ladies and gentlemen, this is Captain Doyle. That noise you heard sounded like a bomb. It wasn't. We took a glancing blow from a private plane. We experienced some damage to the tail section. With me in the cockpit, besides Miss Esposito, a very capable copilot, is Captain André Bouchard, the chief pilot for the airline. We know we can solve this problem, and I plan to be home in Tulsa for dinner tonight, as I just told the control tower. We request that you remain calm and stay seated, obeying the directions of the flight attendants. As soon as we know our course of action, I will be speaking with you again and coming back to the cabin to answer your questions. We are sorry about this failure of the air traffic controllers, but the damage problem will be solved."

As he closed the switch on the PA, Connie turned to him with a mixture of disdain and panic. "Why the hell did you promise them something like that?"

"How are you so sure you'll be home tonight?" André asked weakly.

"Lucky, I don't know what you have in mind, but let me shake you up a bit," she said tightly. "We're heading for the Coffin Corner! There's an altitude where the air is too thin for a jet to remain flying. So it falls. Remember?"

"I know that," he replied calmly.

"We'll go over the top and spin down. We can't unstall this bird. The elevators are jammed! And look at that fuel burnoff! The turbine temperature gauges creeping up! We'll either run out of fuel, blow the engines off the pods, or go over the top. There's not a damned thing you can do about it!"

"I plan to make it. I told you that."

"How?" She was almost yelling. "How?"

"Listen, both of you. I'm scared, okay? But I've been in jams before. Many of them. The first thing I learned was not to panic and to keep the attitude positive."

"I agree," Connie said. "But just between us, how do we solve this?"

"I don't know yet. But there *has* to be a solution. I may be a little crazy, as some people say, but I'm not dumb. If anyone can figure this out, I can. Believe me. I'll handle this. I know crisis management like very few others do." He reached over and kissed her tenderly. "Stay with me in spirit. All of us will be in Tulsa tonight and without a scratch."

Connie looked at Lucky as if he were a dreamer, a

man who was mad; so far over the line that he actually thought he would be the recipient of a miracle. That's what it would take, Connie thought. Maybe a bag of miracles. She had been right in the first place. The man was unfit to fly. His dipstick was a telling clue. And now it was too late, she thought.

She chided herself for not talking to the I.A. Flight Surgeon when she had had a chance.

9:38 A.M. CST
(Over TULSA COUNTY)

●

——————IT HAD BEEN JUST OVER FIVE minutes since the collision.

Although most control towers look the same, tall and skinny with a glass hat on top, each one has a certain personality of its own in the surrealistic world of separating aircraft. The Tulsa tower had experienced some near-misses, but they had never run two planes together nor, as another euphemism described it, had it ever caused a "shot gun wedding."

The tone of the Tulsa tower was actually set by Jack Haverly. He was softspoken and never frenzied, unusual characteristics for an Air Traffic Manager. Jack informed the Kansas City Air Route Control Center of the situation to their facility Area Manager.

"We have a General Aviation turboprop off the scope, and I.A. flight Nineteen, a Trent Two-Seventy, has heavy tail damage. Persons aboard, three hundred and nineteen."

Kansas City ARCC advised all inbound flights to Tulsa to divert. The second requirement of the Tulsa crisis management program was to inform the Airport Authority that there had been a midair collision and that all flights would be gate-held until further notice. The third and last call was to the Tulsa Airport security office, informing them that a plane was off the scope in a certain area and that I.A. 19 had been hit. The airport security then contacted the hospital emergency and trauma teams to head for the airport along with additional fire fighting equipment. It was the Airport Authority's job to notify the I.A. corporate office of the midair collision, but when they called at about 9:40 that morning, no one answered the phone at the corporate communications office because of late arrivals caused by the storm. The receptionist took the Airport Authority's number and said she would leave word to call back immediately.

The twenty-one men and women in the tower remained mute and stunned. Each wondered how the hell it could have happened. There was only one runway open, traffic was light and well separated because of the weather. Yet Doug Halsey's plane, the General Aviation aircraft, the "attacker" as it was called, was at least two miles out of place.

Nobody said it, but although no one in that tower knew precisely what had caused the tragic mix-up, they all knew what could have easily prevented the needless collision. It was all the more ironic and maddening because the federal government had had the funds for ground radar for years, but the government had packed these monies away in an Aviation Trust Fund that was held as a credit to offset the binge of reckless Washington spending. And now the fiscal cosmetics were about to backfire in a ball of flames. The controllers began to wonder how that would be explained just like the Detroit ground accident when a plane became lost in runway fog. The Detroit Tower was also without ground radar.

Some of the controllers were pilots, some not, but each person in that tower shared Connie's anguish. The jet was going over the top. Saving it was only wild dreaming.

"Whiskey Charlie, any new developments?" Jack said into his mike.

"Nothing . . . I'm trying to figure something out," Lucky said.

"We're standing by. Airport's closed. You have the whole sky."

Then, turning away from his mike, Jack snapped, "Call the garage."

The cab supervisor picked up the phone and was told that the plowing of the west runway had been finished twenty minutes before, and that the runway was open.

"What do you mean it's open?" Jack asked slowly.

"Well, we called the snow committee pilot, a TWA man. Couldn't get him at first. Then we did, so he's out there someplace."

Jack slammed down the phone and picked up another mike, which connected him with the ground frequency used by cars on the taxiways. Then the TWA pilot came through.

"Got a crazy thing over here on the Three-Five Left. There're tire tracks coming off the Romeo intersection. I followed them down the runway and they disappeared. So we've got a bogus departure off the west runway, but it was closed. Someone fouled up."

"And you didn't see anything?" Jack asked.

"I was having breakfast."

"You were having breakfast! I hope the eggs were good because we just had a midair collision. That crazy guy who made the tracks in the snow plowed into a Trent Two-Seventy."

"Holy God!"

"Stay right where you are. We're coming over with the videotape camera."

"Better hurry. The snow will cover those tracks real fast."

Jack told Juan and two others to grab the video camera and rush over to west side. It would be the best evidence they had that it was not entirely a control tower error. Doug had departed from the wrong runway. Jack turned to the ground controller and asked, "How come he was over there when the runway was closed?"

"The pilot confirmed his position, Jack."

"What did he say?"

"It's on the tape, but he confirmed his intersection position."

"There are a lot of intersections on this field. Come on!"

"Play the tape back."

"Don't worry. We will."

9:42 A.M. CST (Over TULSA COUNTY)

LINDA GLEN ENTERED THE cockpit.

"Lucky, I've flown too long not to know we're messed up plenty. It's all over, isn't it?"

"Sure it is," Connie said. "Any asshole would know."

"Shut the hell up, both of you! It's not over! I'm just beginning to sort this out. Go back and look sweet and smile," Lucky said crisply.

As Linda left the glass cockpit, Alex Anderson, the I.A. maintenance chief, shuffled in. Anderson was an old-time pilot who was flying as a passenger on Whiskey Charlie. He was out of the Lucky school, detached and so cool that he didn't even offer the slightest hint of the impending disaster.

"Looked out the aft windows, Lucky. We seem to have horizontal tail damage. Can't see too much. Any ideas?"

"I think I can solve this with some radical tactics."

"What can I do?"

"Just go back there and keep an eye on the far aft liners. Give me the word if they start to deform. That'll be our first clue that we're coming apart."

"This jet is built like a tank. We might not have to face structural failure. But I'll keep an eye on it and find out how many I.A. maintenance people are on board. I know most of them by sight."

Then Alex smiled at Connie.

"It ain't over yet by a long shot, lady," he said.

Another clue began to hang in the tight air of the flight deck. Of all the senses, that of smell is the least explored or understood. Still, high timers, especially seat-of-the-pants pilots like Lucky Doyle, could enter a cockpit blindfolded and by its scent they could say, "This is a DC–Three, a DC–Six, or a Two-Seventy." The smell of the old planes was that of trapped human odors mixed with the distinctive fragrance of ancient cracked-leather seats worn down by thousands of rumps over the years. To Lucky this smelled like a real cockpit, the grubby true airplane smell like that the early aviators sniffed. The air was pungent with the never-ending reek of hot oil and exhaust plumes. The burning oil was as pleasant and sweet as the finest perfume.

When the 270 came along, it had an electronic smell to the cockpit, a high-tech odor, strange little smells leaking from the jungles of microchips. It was sickening to Lucky and a few others like him. Most modern pilots thought the electronic smell meant safety, backups that could never go wrong. But Lucky told Connie one time that the 270 cockpit smelled wrong, unhealthy. But now the computer cockpit fragrance was overrun by the scent of sweating panic. Lucky thought the place smelled deathly, like one of those rooms in a nursing home with beds occupied by people about to die. Lucky punched the mike button.

"Departure control—I.A. Nineteen."

"I.A. Nineteen, Tulsa Departure Control. My name is Jack Haverly. I'll be right here all the while."

"I'm Lucky Doyle. Take this down. Damage remains the same. No pitch control. Aircraft stable. Our best climb rate on the edge of a stall is about one hundred thirty feet a minute, sometimes less. We are now at three thousand seven hundred feet. Our speed is one hundred and forty-five knots. Do you confirm?"

"We confirm that, sir. Can you make a gentle turn left or right?"

"Affirmative. I tried that. It works but just barely. Does I.A. corporate know about the collision?"

"We left word with corporate, but no one was in yet."

"Now Jack, you're going to be very important here," Lucky said. "Can you get the engineering section or the president of Trent Aircraft in England on the phone for me? Then I want you to call a man named Frank A'hearn in Fort Smith, Arkansas. That's four five six . . . six eight nine zero, area code five zero one. And I'd like to speak to Ron Alcott at I.A. to tell him what's happened. Then I want to be able to speak to the three parties on the same frequency. Is that possible with a phone patch?"

"It's possible. We'll get to the phone company immediately. There's a contingency plan for that. But Lucky, what are your intentions?"

"I told you . . . we're landing back in Tulsa. Everything will be okay."

"Great."

"How long will this take?" Lucky asked.

"Give me ten minutes."

"Remember, every second counts. We're burning fuel off at a high rate . . . we can't suck them dry before we figure out a solution here."

"At your present rate of consumption, how much flight time is left, Lucky?"

"My copilot, Connie Esposito, is just working that out now."

Connie punched her cockpit computer feeding in figures: passengers and crew aboard; position and weight in the two cargo holds; fuel on board and other details. She checked her fuel pressure and flow rate, which in turn could be translated by the computer into minutes and seconds of fuel remaining. To make sure there was no misunderstanding, Connie slipped Lucky a note with the final figures.

"Jack," Lucky said into his mike, "I'm reading nine fifty-five and ten seconds Central Standard Time. At this rate of burnoff, we'll be fuel exhausted at twelve-twenty local time. I repeat. At about twelve-twenty, we'll be dry. That gives us two hours and twenty-five minutes to punch out a solution. As soon as you contact those people, even before the telephone patch, tell them how many are aboard, our altitude, and that there are two hours and twenty-five minutes to execute our actions. Make sure you drive that point home so these guys can start some fast-lane thinking."

9:58 A.M. CST (TULSA)

PETE ROSEN WAS SITTING AT his desk in the *Tulsa Leader* building when the call came in from his news source at the police department, about fifteen minutes after the accident.

"Pete, want a big one? It'll be worth five steak dinners with a good wine."

"All right, what do you have?"

"An I.A. flight with over three hundred aboard just had a midair collision with a private plane. The private guy's down in a million pieces just north of Owasso, only one aboard."

"How many killed in the airliner?" Pete asked hastily.

"No one, yet."

"What do you mean, yet?"

"The tower just called our office. The tail of the jet is screwed up somehow. The plane's just going up. That's all it can do, just climb. Some fellow at the tower said that the flight was headed for outer space."

"Outer space. I'm sure that can't happen."

"It was a phrase somebody used. Maybe it was sort of figurative."

"He must've said it was *like* entering outer space. What are they going to do about it?"

"They're trying to bring the flight back, but the trouble is they can't come down. They can only go up."

"Thanks, I'll call you back."

Pete Rosen then phoned the control tower, which confirmed that I.A. Flight 19, bound first for St. Louis, then Chicago, had experienced a midair collision with a private plane. There were no other details. Pete phoned his source at I.A., Martha Dobbs, assistant head of the airline's human resources department.

"Are you kidding?" she said in a half-whisper.

"No, it just came through the police department. The tower confirmed it. You mean no one over there knows?"

"I'll try to find out."

"They say there's over three hundred up there, and the plane can only climb—like it's entering outer space. I don't think that's possible, but someone used that term."

The Whiskey Charlie story had a bizarre syntax all its own. It was eventually traced to Pete Rosen, for in the history of calamity reporting, few stories ever drew so much attention. No one aboard the airliner had sustained the slightest injury, yet the story as written by Rosen was not only a fast-breaking piece, it was a double bellringer on the wire services throughout the world. It exploded across front pages and interrupted radio and TV programming.

Pete wanted to add a bit of flavor to his reporting, to grab his first front-page byline. He recalled something one of the professors had said when he attended journalism school, "Give your story a little spice, but make sure it's peppered with truth, and the spice may be taken as a possibility."

Pete, knowing nothing about aviation, wasn't sure that the I.A. jet could enter space. Probably not, but he was told that someone in the tower said so. Pete thought it was the pepper his professor had referred to, so he wrote the story as a bulletin, saying in part, "According to reliable sources at the Tulsa International Airport Control Tower, Flight 19 can only climb, as if heading for outer space." The tag line was typed by Pete as an attention seeker only. He thought the "as if" was enough of a disclaimer and that the phrase would be edited out.

When he finished the bulletin, he walked over to the national editor, but because the *Leader* was printed late in the evening as a morning paper, the editor wasn't due in until later that day. Pete should have gone down two floors to the editor of the *Times*, the afternoon paper, for copy approval. He decided, instead, to hit the wire service first as a bulletin, and then speak to the *Times* editor about an afternoon story with more details.

The impact of the "outer space" reference had an effect that Pete never imagined. He thought that any reasonable person would know that an airliner is never in danger of entering outer space, that anyone it would obviously check it out or delete the phrase. But the wire service in New York dispatched the story to more than 2,000 subscribers in eighty-nine countries without a double check or a deletion.

It was afternoon in England. On Fleet Street the *London Dispatch* wire editor ran to his senior to show her the bulletin. They set up the headline using Pete's outer space angle. Before running it, they intended to check with Trent Aviation in Bristol if there had been a collision.

AMERICAN AIRLINER WITH 319 ABOARD INVOLVED IN MIDAIR COLLISION OVER OKLAHOMA. HUGE ENGLISH JET CAN ONLY CLIMB, COULD POSSIBLY ENTER OUTER SPACE.

And that was the start of the Whiskey Charlie media odyssey, the event that almost brought the entire world to a standstill.

The first word of the tragedy to reach the I.A. office was routed to Ron Alcott from Jack Haverly. The airline president was called from the conference room where the committee was chiseling away at the fine points of the merger. Ron picked up the phone in his own office down the hall. Haverly explained the situation. Ron remained calm except for the reference to outer space.

"Who said that?"

"The pilot, Captain Doyle. He said the flight was headed toward outer space. The jet can only climb. He meant it as a joke, of course."

"Well, don't repeat that or say anything to the press. Have everyone contact our corporate relations people here. Give me a call when you have everyone on the line."

Ron Alcott was stunned. At first he thought it might have had something to do with the merger, a retaliatory act by some of the unions. But that was too extreme, Ron thought. He wrote down the control tower number and then phoned Bristol to speak to Ian Pryce-Smith and Lou Walters as Jack Haverly was placing the call to Frank A'hearn in Fort Smith.

"Miss Barnes, have Cap Kimble get right up here. And tell those in the conference room that something important has come up."

In less than a minute, Ian was on the phone, with

Lou Walters listening on the other extension. Both men thought that the call concerned the merger. They were not prepared for what Ron was about to say.

"Bad news. Our Flight Nineteen, the Trent, just had a midair collision north of Tulsa. Took place in a snowstorm."

"How many went down with the flight?" Ian asked slowly, not wanting to hear the answer.

"No one, yet. Thank God. They're working out a radio and phone patch to the flight now. Apparently the tail is badly damaged. All they can do is climb. Around twelve fifteen or maybe a few minutes later, they'll be out of fuel."

Lou Walters cried out, "What a hell of a thing! My God!"

"Can't believe it yet . . . just can't," Ron replied.

"Pilot to pilot. Do they have a chance?" Lou asked slowly.

"Don't know. A thousand things are going through my mind. I'll have to put a chase plane up. When they bust out of the cloud tops, we'll survey the damage."

Ian cut in.

"That's right, Ron. We can't make a prediction until we have a fast look at what's going on back there."

After a long pause, Ron continued. "This fellow in the tower, guy named Jack Haverly, said they were hit by a private twin-engine turboprop. Our pilot is a man I know, Lucky Doyle. He wants to speak to an aircraft repair shop in Fort Smith. Doyle used to fly up in the Arctic with the fellow who owns it . . . Australian, named Frank A'hearn. It'll be a few minutes before we can organize a radio-phone link to the cockpit."

As Ian continued to speak with Ron, Lou dropped his phone and moved past Ian's antique desk to the window. The man was severely shaken. He had an impulse to cry out, something to express what he felt, and from the window he stared at the bare branches of an ancient oak tree. The thought of the collision shook Lou down to his roots. He had joined Ron Alcott just after World War II. He remembered the early years of launching the carrier with particular fondness. Their spirits had never dimmed. The industry was a gentlemen's club annexed to something called honor. As the airlines worked for their load factors, a sense of duty and obligation went along with it. Lou was honored to serve the flying public; the standards were high; the service was something special, as if the passenger were an honored guest. It was a proud business: Lou Walters was certain of that. The airline chairman wasn't sure when the erosion had begun: before deregulation or after? He only knew, as they all did, that a sad time came with it.

It seemed to Lou as though his beloved industry had picked up a bad bunch of hitchhikers. The cherished honor was gone. The haunting brilliance of aviation was forfeited. It was now a gaudy game of takeovers and sharply designed bankruptcies, and how could an arrogant little bastard like Augie Hartman take such a stab at an old and respected airline? Worse: How could so much tradition cave in to such an alien? Lou pondered that. The chairman had seen many other standards slowly slip, as if a valued world was vanishing before his eyes. Planes were falling apart in the skies; Lou was certain that those appalling incidents—the rot at the core surfacing—could have been prevented. All it would have taken was time, money, and good care in the hangars. The mechanic's total devotion to his plane had ebbed in many cases, like a long true love affair that collapses, yielding to expediency. But the mechanics were under new and hostile pressures.

And the passengers.

They had lost their honored guest status, Lou thought. Now they were treated as so many products, assembly-line figures necessary but unwelcome by the new airline elite. Lou Walters could not adjust to these alterations any more than Lucky Doyle could accept the glass cockpit.

Ron Alcott also dreaded the changes in the industry he had helped to establish. It was a brand-new game with no holds barred. Ron was grateful that he had seen the best days of civil aviation: the rise of passenger confidence; the quenching of the public's fears of flying; the coming of the jet age and finally supersonic flight. Now he was glad to be leaving the field of fire. Still, he desperately didn't want to go out this way, as the man associated with possibly the worst crash in the history of American aviation.

Ron felt stranded, helpless. He thought of Lucky Doyle, the man who had control of the Trent. Was he up to this? Was anyone?

In one sense Alcott admired the Arctic aviator who flew an ancient Waco for fun. He was a basic pilot, but he was *not* a team player. Alcott remembered with mixed feelings why André had wanted to drop Lucky from the transition list.

"An airline captain these days has to fit into an organizational notch," Bouchard had said. "He's no longer up there alone, doing his own thing. The good left seater must relate to the system and his aircraft. I judge pilots in one way. A single question has to be asked: When everything falls apart, how is this guy going to handle things? Will he come around and work with the book, or will he try to make his own way? That's my doubt about Lucky Doyle."

Ron believed that he had an obligation to tell Lou and Ian something about the man in charge of that 270 cockpit, as unsettling as the comments might be. He tried to decide how to put it, how to adjust his words, knead them into a palatable flow of speech. In the end, he started simply telling what he knew.

"The captain is a fellow named Doyle, Lucky Doyle they call him. He used to fly up in the Arctic . . . authentic seat-of-the-pants guy . . . one of those hand-flyers."

"Do you have faith in him or not?" Ian interrupted.

"I guess so, but with Lucky is our chief pilot, André Bouchard, a top guy. The copilot is a woman, very bright they say. Yes, I have faith in that cockpit crew. As a group, I mean."

A high-time pilot himself, Ian felt concerned about the word *group*. They could assist the pilot in command, but Ian knew that there had to be one head in that cockpit with absolute authority: a captain they could trust. Was a seat-of-the-pants guy the right fit? Ron could detect the doubt on the edge of Ian's voice. He knew Ron well. They had worked together introducing the 270 to the American market, blending the outsized jet into the I.A. route system.

"Ron, here's how I feel. The damned thing looks perfectly rotten, a lost cause. At lunch today Lou asked me if I would change anything in the 270 if I had to do it all over again. I said no. It's a fine, tough aircraft. We didn't shortcut a thing, not one bolt, not a single fitting. Everything's as it should be. We built that plane as if our lives depended on it. That's turning out to be literally true. The equipment just might be able to take this. I don't know what can be done, if anything; I don't know if this—ah—*unorthodox* pilot can just make things worse."

"No one can predict that, Ian. How many times has this ever happened? Large jets don't pull out of a collision. They go in. There's no learning curve. No experience. I don't know what the hell this Doyle is going to do. Maybe he doesn't know. We'll just have to wait. But there's one consolation. If Doyle doesn't come around, André Bouchard can take over. There's a good man."

The thought rattled Ian even more. "I don't want a battle in that cockpit. It's desperate enough—just about hopeless—as things stand now."

"We'll just have to see."

"Strange that this occurred on the day of the closing, isn't it?" Ian commented.

"I thought of that," Ron replied.

"Any ideas?"

"No, I think this was a control system error . . . nothing else."

"We'll have our engineers alerted and speak to you again as soon as we're in contact with the flight."

Ron put the phone down and was staring at the wall blankly when Cap, the tall, rangy public relations head entered the office without knocking.

"I just heard, Ron. I'm sorry. I can't believe it."

"You work all your life to build a great airline, and the very day all your efforts go to a man like Hartman, you'd think that would be enough. But hell no. Then you're told that one of your jets is hanging on the edge of a stall with over three hundred aboard. Today's aviation—it *isn't* aviation."

10:10 A.M. CST (TULSA)

•

4:10 P.M. GMT (BRISTOL)

THEY WAITED IN SILENCE. For a time a row of clouds blocked out the fast-fading light. Suddenly the low sun was glancing in through the tall windows in Ian Pryce-Smith's richly paneled office, casting a network of shadows on the curling patterns of the Persian rug. Ian, a stolid man, pushed his banister-back chair away. He stuffed his hands in the pockets of his Savile Row pinstriped suit, pressed slowly to his feet, and ambled along the light patterns crisscrossing the multicolored carpet. When he arrived at the smaller desk where Lou Walters was sitting, Ian flashed a wide smile.

"It's far from over, old boy."

"Hope you're right, Ian. I have nine thousand hours in my log, and I've never heard of an airliner surviving a midair collision in the tail section. Fuselage . . . maybe . . . a wingtip, yes. But the tail, hell no! Ron was on target with that one."

Just then the call came in from Jack Haverly at the Tulsa tower. Lou handed the phone to Ian.

"Yes, this is Ian Pryce-Smith. I understand we'll be patched into the cockpit of the I.A. flight?"

"That's right. We have Mr. Alcott on the line, and we're working on the Fort Smith call."

"All right. Would you give me the Fort Smith number? We want to chat with Mr. A'hearn privately."

While Ian continued to talk to the Tulsa tower, Lou placed the transatlantic call to Frank's conversion shop.

"We'll probably be transferring this call to our engineering section in the next building," Ian told Haverly. "Hold on while I set that up." He called Henry Gibbons, the chief engineer, who was only two offices away.

"Henry," Ian said, "we have an emergency. One of the I.A. Trents was just in a midair collision. Could you step in here straight away? The flight's still airborne, somehow. About two hours of fuel aboard."

"I'll be right there, Ian."

Back with the tower, Ian said, "Mr. Haverly—"

"Jack."

"All right. And my name's Ian. With me is the I.A. chairman, Lou Walters. Henry Gibbons, our chief engineer, will be on the line in a minute. In the meantime, we'll be speaking to Fort Smith. Perhaps you could fill me in on what happened?"

"We have a heavy snowstorm here. This fellow in a turboprop somehow took off from the wrong runway. If we had ground radar, we would have seen that he was out of position. We didn't turn him fast enough and they collided."

At that point a stooped round-faced man with pure white hair spurted into the office. Ian pointed to the phone on the coffee table in front of the large couch.

"Henry Gibbons, our chief engineer, has just joined us," Ian told Haverly. "What was the tone of this Doyle fellow?"

"He was angry at first. Don't blame him," Jack said. "Then he told me about the damage. They're still in their climb. I'm looking at the target on my scope now."

"Was he panicked? Could you tell?"

"No. Lucky said he was going to return to Tulsa as if he were sure of it. Then he asked for the three-way phone patch."

By the way the two Bristol men looked at each other, trying to veil their fright, Lou Walters could tell they were not optimistic. Lou wished he were at Ron Alcott's side through this, and he imagined the total agony of the man he had worked with for so many years. Lou also knew that it had been years since André Bouchard had been on the line as a left seater, and the chairman was not encouraged by Ron's description of Lucky Doyle. And like many old timers, Lou did not completely accept women in the cockpit.

But Ron's hasty comments about Lucky Doyle were bland compared to what was coming next from Frank A'hearn, who was now on the line from his office in Fort Smith.

"My breath has been sucked away by this," Frank said. "I'm out of words. I know Lucky and Connie, the copilot, very well. I flew with Doyle up in the Arctic."

"This sounds like a pretty grim mess to us," Ian said. "But we're going to give it one hell of a try—if we only can figure out what to do. Doyle told the control tower he plans to return—at least he's thinking positively. I suppose he needs your help. Frank, what about the man?"

"Sir Ian, I flew with him. Frankly, I don't see any way out of this, but if anyone in the world can save that plane, Lucky Doyle can. I've been with him in in-flight emergencies. He keeps his head and he uses his imagination."

"Ron referred to him as a seat-of-the-pants man."

"He is that. But this is the time you need someone with a brain of his own instead of an electronic chip. There's no computer program for this kind of disaster."

Pryce-Smith hesitated. "I'm afraid that I'd have more faith in a pilot who let his computer help him out of a jam."

"I can see that, and in most circumstances, you're probably right. But I stand by what I said. Lucky's a self-styled 1930s kind of airman, a hands-on flyer, anti-computer. And I must tell you this: Lucky doesn't always trust the gauges; after all, his life and the lives of his crew and passengers depend on the information they give him."

"What do you mean?" Gibbons, the chief engineer, demanded.

"Lucky used to go up on the wing of the two-seventy after a topoff and measure the fuel in the tanks with a homemade dipstick. I taught him that up in Alaska. Our fuel transmitters were always off on the Caribou we owned together up there."

"Then we have a disturbed man in that Two-Seventy cockpit," Henry Gibbons said angrily. "Everyone knows that the fuel transmitters are accurate right down to the liter. They're state of the art. You know that." Gibbons had supervised the design of the fuel quantity gauges.

"Yes, sir, I do know that. But don't write Lucky off because of a measuring stick. When the going gets rough, Doyle's right there. And God knows, it's rough now."

Jack Haverly said that the phone patch was through.

Lou crossed to Ian. He whispered, "I haven't been in a cockpit for years. For God's sake, have Doyle explain things simply when he's on the line."

Ian nodded. After establishing first names, he took

the lead. "Lucky, Lou Walters, the I.A. chairman, is with us today. He's not current, so no high-tech explanations, please."

"I'll try," Lucky said. "Basically, we're like a lumbering goose climbing higher and higher after taking a full load of buckshot. I've got flaps in and leading edge slats down. The guy who smacked us chewed up our tail. The elevators are pitched up. That forces the tail down, the nose up, as you know. All I can do is climb. I need power, high pressure ratios, to overcome my drag. Like the injured goose, as soon as he stops flapping as hard as he can, he falls out of the air and crashes.

"My airspeed is one thirty-eight. Fuel remaining is just about two hours at this setting, but that could change as we climb. So at twelve-twenty, our time, we'll be over the top and spin in. But I doubt if we'll reach "Coffin Corner" today. My oil temp's heating up. So we're in danger of blowing the turbines off the pods."

"May I ask a question, Lucky?" Henry interrupted.

"Please do."

"You didn't mention trim control."

"Sorry about that. I have some trim left. It's far forward. That brought my snoot down some, maybe three degrees."

"Surely," Henry said, "that's coming off an independent system. Well, now, Lucky, that's a full pocket of bloody trouble, isn't it?"

"I'd say it's all the way down to my socks."

"The control tower chap mentioned that you plan to return to Tulsa."

"Yes, sir. That's my plan."

Ian slowly turned his head around to catch Lou Walters' eyes. The doubt they shared had its counterpart in Frank A'hearn's look as he crossed glances with his test pilot, Louie Bonner, who was sitting at an army surplus steel desk, another phone pushed to his ear. Henry had noted the damage assessment on a long yellow pad. He scanned it, working a slight smile onto his lips as he spoke.

"We want you to know that we have a virtual brain trust here, brilliant engineers and a supercomputer capable of four million operations a second. We know every inch of that Two-Seventy airframe. Tell us how you plan to bring her home."

By this time others were beginning to eavesdrop. Pete Rosen had dashed for his car as soon as his bulletin was filed. Grabbing his all-frequency radio, he was listening in as Lucky started his survival scheme.

"Now, I have to tell you gentlemen a little story. It's about coin collectors," Lucky said, his voice curiously stable.

"Ah, Lucky, Ian here. I'm just glancing at a ship's clock I have on the wall. If I'm right, we're about two hours to fuel exhaustion."

"I'll confirm that," Lucky replied mechanically.

"I'm one for a good yarn, old boy. But I think we just better get to the point and hear about the coin collectors later."

"Lucky, cut the shit. You're hanging by your ass up there," Frank A'hearn said in his deep Aussie voice. "Forget coin collectors, huh? No stories."

"Give me a chance, Frank. The coin collectors represent the solution. Happened aboard a United flight, or was it an American flight?"

"Lucky, please," Ian snapped.

"Fellows, stay with me. I'm in my own loop. So this flight has ninety rare coin collectors going to a convention in L.A. They sit in the back of the plane because that's where they think it's the safest. So on takeoff the skipper rotates and his nose pops way the hell up. He trims off, but the bird doesn't handle right. He lands and realizes that something's the matter. What? he asks. Can anyone guess?"

"You tell us, Lucky," Ian said again, lifting his eyes to the ship's clock.

"It's simple. You see, all the collectors packed about thirty pounds of coins in their takeon luggage. So they had over a ton of unknown weight back aft. Very simply, the coin collectors upset the center of gravity, the loading envelope. So that's my hint, the principle of the coin collectors."

There were empty stares in Bristol and Fort Smith. Ian slapped his hand over the phone and whispered with a husky voice, "He's bloody brain dead!"

"Lucky," Frank said, "That's very informative. Now let's get to your own untidy little problem."

"Sure, Frank. The only solution here is to upset our center of gravity."

"How?" Frank asked placatingly.

"You and I know that air-to-air transfers are possible. Frank, we'll need an air-to-air transfer. Tools, power packs, cables, all that gear we used up north."

"What are you going to do, Lucky?"

"Well, it's sort of like balancing one of those scales where you put weights on those dishes. What I'm going to do is upset the scales. I'll cut out weight in my left aft end. Chop up the galleys . . . take up the seats . . . transfer everything along with the passengers up to the front to press my nose down. I can't see any other solution."

"Let me ask you, Lucky," Frank said. "How do we send you the supplies? You can't open a door in flight."

"Hell, no. I plan to punch out one of the emergency escape hatches . . . I guess one of those over the wing."

There were bewildered looks on the Bristol end. A smile bloomed on Frank's face. It was a Doyle original, the old Aussie thought. Vintage Doyle.

Ian tapped his bony fingers on his inlaid Sheraton desk. Henry Gibbons sighed.

A former RAF pilot with four thousand flying hours, Ian sensed the field expediency in the Doyle scheme. Connie Esposito had the advantage of seeing Lucky's face come alive as he threaded them through the coin collectors yarn.

"Gentlemen, this is typical Doyle thinking," Frank said.

"Very nice, Lucky." Ian added, "I'd like to pick up the pace here. I'm reading one hour and fifty-six minutes of fuel left, and I would say your compressors are beginning to overheat."

"That's true," Lucky answered.

"We have the tools and men here," Frank said. "What about help on your end? It's a massive job, Lucky."

"I knew you'd ask that, Frank. I took it into consideration. I fly this route with Connie five times a week. The passenger composition is about the same day to day the flight attendants tell me. I.A. mechanics deadheading up to O'Hare. In fact, we have the best man, VP of Maintenance, Alex Anderson, on board. Then there's usually a load of ex-oilfield riggers. Young guys with heavy tool experience. The others are businessmen. I'd say I could find at least thirty good hands. Tough, experienced guys."

"I have a problem list here. So we'll eliminate the work crew problem. Stand by."

Frank asked Louie Bonner to start digging out a DC–6 they were preparing for delivery to Scotland and to gather up a load of portable tools.

"I'm back now, Lucky. As soon as you pop an escape

hatch, you'll have violent out flowing air. You might take a group of people out the hatch."

"Thought of that, too, Frank. I'm going to depressurize just before we pick up the monkey fist."

"What's a monkey fist?" Ian asked.

"It's a big knotted rope-end," Frank said. "Lucky wants me to drop this so his men can pull down a series of cargo nets with arctic suits and power tools."

Ian pushed to his feet. He was as shaken as his chief engineer.

"Lucky," Ian started trying to breathe easier and pace his words evenly and confidently. "What can we do to help? We have unlimited technical and computing capability, as we said."

"Good. First of all, see if the computer has a better solution, or perhaps your engineers might have something. Regardless, I'd request that you confirm my numbers, the weights that must be relocated and jettisoned."

"You'll have it straightaway."

Henry put down his phone. He moved over to Ian and whispered in Lou's ear.

"He's daft. Have Lucky go aft and assess the damage by the last galley. I don't want him hearing our conversation."

Ian bobbed his head in agreement.

"Lucky, Gibbons has a keen suggestion. Have you been aft to size up the damage in the tail end?"

"Not yet."

"May I suggest that you get on to that. Then come back with us. Look at your tailplane, for instance."

"Sure. Sure. What do you think, Frank, old buddy?"

"It's innovative, Lucky."

Connie leaned over and kissed Lucky's smiling face. She glanced at the collection of electronic displays. The cockpit microprocessors were as useless as a box of potato chips at this point.

"Ms. Esposito," Ron Alcott said.

"It's Connie."

"Has Lucky gone aft?"

"Yes, sir."

"Put André on the horn now."

She signaled Bouchard into Lucky's seat.

"Yes, Ron."

"What are we dealing with, André? You were going to fire Doyle because he's an adamant loner."

"Correct."

"This is the craziest thing I've ever heard in my fifty-one years in aviation."

"I agree."

"Damn it, André. We're dealing with a banana head."

"Quite," Ian cut in.

Frank decided to listen for a while. He sensed the real shape of the swelling tragedy. They were not speaking the same language.

It was as if the Tower of Babel were falling down, and no one could save it because the grammar and vocabulary were so polarized. Lucky feasted on perverse air problems! Only arctic and mountain pilots appreciated tastes like that. Frank felt that English engineers were probably brilliant in their own way, but was it Lucky's way? Probably not.

"André, what would you do?" Ron asked.

"Don't know. Is this flying or engineering?"

"That's a good question," Frank finally chirped in. "The best one yet."

"Stand by," Ian said as Henry whispered, "Put the chief pilot in charge."

"André, is Doyle capable of working with us? Is he all there?" Ian asked slowly.

"He seems very placid."

"For God's sake, André. You're the chief pilot. Is Doyle's head working?" Ron yelled. "Does he know the shit he's in?"

Connie's beautiful face reddened. She pushed her transmit button.

"Now look," she told them, "I know Lucky Doyle and his strengths. He thinks damned well. To you guys he seems like a medium-priced Indiana Jones, a plumber who didn't finish the course. To hell with all of you! He had the idea. Now help him. Don't tear the linings out of his head, or we'll all go in. I've always felt that he knew things about flying that no one else could grasp. Secrets."

"She's right," Frank said. "Give him a chance. Lucky said it. If you have something better, let's have it. And he might have secrets and tricks up his sleeves. I have twenty-two thousand hours in nine logs, but I can't think of a fucking thing better, or anything as clever as Doyle's idea. But while you criticize this man, gentlemen, just keep an eye on the clock. In the meantime, I'm loading up my DC–Six. I'm going out to help him."

Henry rose up on his toes and bellowed out, "This Aussie's right. But it can't work!"

"Why, Henry?" Ian asked.

"There's not enough time to effect an air-to-air transfer and to start cutting out the guts of a huge bird. Secondly, moving people around is foolhardy. They aren't strong, trained young soldiers. Passengers come in all varieties. Young, old, strong, weak, sick, well. They're not a bunch of sandbags that can be moved around like silent ballast. They have emotions. Fear leading to panic is going to get the upper hand here. On a scientific level, Doyle is right. Yes, by the relocation of weight, an aircraft's loading envelope, the design centers, can be altered to make the nose heavy. But here we are facing a critical fuel problem."

"Then what's your answer?" Ian asked.

"I don't have it yet. But I will. Engineers will solve this problem. Not an imaginative pilot. In fact, gentlemen, I'm sorry to say, there's no such thing as a creative airline pilot. It's a deadly contradiction. A sound cockpit man goes by the book. If the book has to be rewritten we'll do it on our end. Remember, we wrote the flight manual the first time. We're the ones to rewrite the emergency procedures the second time around. I applaud Doyle for his ideas and tenacity. But what we need is technology, not sheer guts!"

"I hope you're right, Henry," Ian said. "Go to it with everything you have."

"Don't worry."

As Henry left the office, each man was confused as well as petrified.

10:19 A.M. CST (Over TULSA COUNTY)

•

WHISKEY CHARLIE'S DIGITAL ALtimeter read 6,900 feet. Engine compressor heat and oil temperatures were just nearing the caution zones on the glass monitoring panels.

Connie and André stared at the displays. Then, as if a bounty had been awarded to them, the blackness of the clouds lightened: The red glare of the cockpit lights paled. The transition accelerated as the sky became a light blue haze. Suddenly, Whiskey Charlie broke out of the clouds. Below was the undulating dark blanket of the weakening blizzard. Above, there was a vastness of violet blue. Deceptive. Threatening. André and Connie knew that these were enemy skies full of icy air and thinning density levels. She clicked her transmit button.

"We're out of the cloud cover."

"Do you see a Beech Baron off to your left?" Jack Haverly asked.

Connie found the speck in the sky.

"Connie, I'm Bill Hamilton. We might have met in I.A. Operations. I've been with the carrier for twenty years as a left seater. Ron Alcott asked me to get up here and take a look at the damage back there."

"I know Hamilton. Good man." André said.

"How are you, Bill?" Lucky said pressing his transmit button.

"How are *you* doing? That's the question."

"Not bad. I guess. But I'm going to get this baby down safely."

"I was thinking of options. You don't have very many if the damage profile is what you suspect."

"The Brits didn't sound optimistic."

"Didn't think so either."

"Have any ideas, Bill?"

"Not at this point. But whatever has to be done, it'll be a first. I've never heard of a heavy airliner surviving a tail collision. You're damn lucky just to be flying."

"I know. That's why I'll try anything to keep it that way. My name isn't Lucky Doyle for nothing."

And that's what it was going to take, Bill Hamilton thought as his small plane neared the hideous sight of the struggling airliner. Luck, guts, and skill. Plenty of each.

4:50 P.M. GMT (BRISTOL)

•

THE THREE EXECUTIVE BUILDINGS of the Trent works sat on the hummock of a grassy hill. They were three floors high, with narrow windows carved deeply into chipped rose brick, vestiges of the original woolen mill. When Ian's grandfather first became intoxicated with wood and silk blended together to take men into the air, it was the vast sheep meadows surrounding the mill that made him buy the place. The grass had slowly given away to cement aprons, and fabrication hangars stretched on for as long as the eye could see.

Of the three ex–woolen mills, the last one, known as the "brain building," was Henry Gibbons's other company home. He had two offices, one near Ian and the other executives and another on the third floor of the last building. This was the design control center. The heart of the Trent thinking machine.

On the first floor of the brain building were the offices of the hands-on fabrication engineers and detail design men. These were the groups that wrote the flight and repair manuals. Others took the concept and development drawings from the senior design engineers upstairs and turned a new program into reality, or what was called fab drawings, the op sheets. From these masses of drawings, sometimes six hundred for a single-landing gear design, the tooling was created to punch out the parts for forgings and extrusions and then final assembly.

In this design and fabrication process, there was a caste system as old as the British aviation industry. At the Trent Works, the design engineers on the second floor did the thinking, the inventing, the innovating. Those on the first floor were the doers who turned ideas into working drawings, which would then be fabricated into things that one could touch and put together with fasteners or welds: ribs, spares, stringers, struts and over twenty thousand other parts that went into an airliner.

Those on the upper floors of the Trent brain building thought that the lads downstairs were merely mechanical practitioners. They were there to carry forward the work of the idea men. The competitive spirit was mutual. The engineers downstairs felt that they were the realists; their job was to save the developing design from the flights of fancy, the impractical dreams of the theorists.

The men—and a few women—on the first floor usually wore work aprons, since they kept in constant touch with the fab floors, the hangars where the aircraft were built. These engineers and draftsmen were called the "muckies." They worked with tools; held parts in their hands and they knew a tee joint weld from a flange joint weld. These people got grit under their nails and they were proud of it, for they knew the materials and structures of big aircraft. They were proud of their pragmatics, their skills at turning "flighty ideas," as they used to call some of the upstairs efforts, into workable shapes that could be produced with that delicate blend of reliability and service life.

These were the Trent people with flying certificates in their pockets, the ones who could lay in a perfect weld rather than just talk about it. But in the pecking order, the brain boys felt that they were authors, the originators of the new design; all the others were aides, functionaries, floor men with tools in their hands.

Suddenly, as news of the Tulsa accident spread about the buildings, those on the first floor rallied. They were the ones to save the crippled airliner, not the computer and high tech princes upstairs. The day had come for the practical people to show their stuff. They could get Lucky's 270 down safely, not the others. Henry Gibbons didn't see it that way.

The key to everything, in Henry's opinion, was on the second floor: two hundred engineers, each with a specialty, crowded that area. At the far end, toward the fabrication hangars, was the computer section. It had no windows, and one had to enter the sacred place via two doors; the last access was opened only by slipping a plastic card into a release slot. Inside was the design-by-wire brain, the altar, the ultra supercomputer that cost more than $11 million pounds with all the options. It came in only one color. It was this mastermind that had concocted the Trent version of the glass cockpit, with Henry's help. Ian was puzzled by the idea of one computer designing another. At the other end of this floor were the development design rooms where a new aircraft was born. In the middle were private offices, including Gibbons's, plus a conference room.

Henry had suffered a slight heart attack the year before. He was told to lose weight and exercise. There were five elevators in the brain building, but the chief engineer had chosen to use the stairs each day; it provided all the panting a man needed. He usually walked up briskly, one step after another, but on this Friday Gibbons bounded up two steps at a time. He reached the last landing out of breath and with a line of beaded sweat on his flushed face.

There was an old pensioner up there, Mr. Waffles, armed with a feather duster. His job was to empty the computer printout bins and to make certain that there was a freshly starched white coat for each engineer ready on the hooks by eight o'clock every morning. Henry believed that a knee-length white coat indicated science and skill, professionalism.

Mr. Waffles helped Henry into his whites, distinguished from the others by two pockets across his broad chest instead of one.

"It's dreadful, sir. Just heard."

"I know, Mr. Waffles. It seems so bloody unfair. Nothing has gone right with that aircraft."

"I've been praying, sir. Called home and me wife is going to the church. She believes in candles, sir. Puts a couple of pence in the box each week and lights one off."

"Call her again, Mr. Waffles. Tell her to light the whole place up and send me the bill. We'll need a world of candles going."

The elderly man smiled at the chubby chief engineer as Henry rushed into the conference room where his senior design team had assembled to hear the details. Each man knew that if the jet circling lazily over Tulsa didn't land safely somehow, there would be no more white coats on the hooks. Maybe the building would be plowed under for a housing development: That was how serious things were at the Bristol facility.

The engineers had been encouraged when word seeped back that their 270, according to the research firm, was a sound and honest piece of advanced design. Henry had told the group that Ian was getting on the phone to potential customers to explain Augie Hartman's smear work.

There would be jobs in the future, Henry had reported to his men; now he was about to tell them that they faced not only sparse economic futures but deeply damaged reputations. The engineers had been silent waiting for Henry; they stood as he walked in. Each man had a pad, pencil, and a pocket calculator. The atmosphere was one of fear, as if they all were about to be marched out and shot. Naturally, they thought of those in danger of their lives aboard Whiskey Charlie; however, when they tried to think what to do about them, to a man (or woman), each designer felt entirely lost.

As the chief engineer finished his painful report of the Doyle plan, the "white coats," as Mr. Waffles called them, were even more dismayed; it was the final blow for the 270. Most of them were jarred speechless, and Henry could read their thoughts. Of course, his senior engineers agreed with him that the pilot was bats.

"Does anyone have a comment?" Henry asked.

An elderly senior design man raised his wrinkled hand.

"In-flight altering of gravity centers has never been attempted, sir. There could be flight control and handling problems. Will the structure take the forward loads? No one has ever explored it that I know of, Mr. Gibbons."

"I've never heard of it," someone else chimed in.

"There's a lot of nevers in this," Henry said. "Gentlemen, perhaps we should approach it this way. Consider yourselves in that cockpit. Now you're the man in control. What would you do, given these grisly facts?"

Finally, at the far end of the table, a bony man with high cheekbones and tight olive skin snapped the ensuing hush. His name was Dr. Kagune, and he was the human factors engineer from West Bengal, India.

"Sir, I am not a man who solves hideous problems.

My job is to prevent them, as we all do in this room when we set out a new design. I have not the slightest idea of what I would do if I were sitting in that Two-Seventy cockpit.

"My field is people engineering. This Doyle. You have given us a negative profile of him. The entire question, in my mind, is this man's leadership abilities. Obviously, he is helpless, or almost so. What kind of man is he? How strong? You have told us that he handled equipment in terrible places like the Arctic. I once knew a pilot who flew near my home, up north in Nepal. Very poor conditions, thin air, wind shears, ice and cold. The roof of the world. Being interested in human reactions, why people survive and how, I asked this pilot about his work. What were the keys to existing in that enemy territory? He said that each day he wrote a new combat survival manual. Each morning he met a slightly different battle with the elements. 'One learns,' he said to me, 'the great value of improvisation.' Much like the quick thinking of a theater group, who, given a subject, will work out a plot line, a story that comes out and flows forward by words made up instantaneously. In a way, this Doyle fellow is put on the same stage by what has happened. My point, sir, is this. I believe that a man who flies the Nepal routes must be a different breed by the demands of the task.

"Some might judge such a man to be unstable because of the way his mind rockets off this way and that way in odd, unpredictable directions. It seems to me that we have such a person in the two-seventy cockpit today. I see him as a plus, an improviser. The question is an old one. Will his mind and body continue to function at top levels throughout the grueling experience? We will see. We also must adjust our attitudes toward the man. How we handle Captain Doyle, it seems to me, is just as important as our solution."

The Oxonian tones of the Indian doctor trailed off into barely heard whispers as if they were dicta from the ancient world of his birth. He waited for his words to sink in. Then, as if his lungs had been refueled, he put a tag on his message.

". . . just as important as our solution—if any."

Henry was moved by Dr. Kagune's assessment.

One man at the table, the senior systems engineer, spoke up. "I think I know why the elevators are trapped in the far-up position."

"Tell us," Henry said.

"I was noting a few of the probable impact forces against the tail of the aircraft. I believe they were so great that all the screw jacks were knocked out of position."

"I see," Henry said. "That would seem logical. What would you do about it, given those circumstances?"

The question backed the man into a corner.

"Up there, nothing, sir. Down here, yes, I could solve it. The point is this. This is no way to perform an operation in the air. Whatever work is done must come from the inside, as this pilot has proposed. Even then he is limited. He cannot reach into the tail section from the cabin areas."

The phone rang in short blasts.

"Ian here. Henry, we have the damage reports on the line now. The chase plane is there. Chap named Hamilton. He's an I.A. captain. Have the department heads monitor, please."

The chief engineer pointed to the eleven phones on the highly waxed oval conference table.

"Here it is, gentlemen," the pilot began. "Are we all reading?"

"Yes, yes," Ian cut in briskly, speaking from the main building. "What do you see?"

"I'm flying close in by the side of the Trent. Almost

the entire rudder is off, with heavy bruising and missing skin panels on the vertical fin."

"Any deformation?" Henry asked.

"Negative."

"How did the rudder separate? Was it sheared off?"

"There's a small part of the top rudder section still atached. The vest was sheared off, a massive hinge failure."

Each engineer noted that on his pad.

"Now I'm below the left horizontal tail. It's sheared off about four feet in from the end. Both elevators are jammed in the extreme up position."

"Are they vibrating in the least?" Henry asked.

"No, but there's hydraulic oil leaking out from somewhere. And the lower fuselage just forward of the horizontal tail is quite smashed up with skin wrinkles. They're shooting up and over the aft galley load door. Hell, it looks like a crinkled chewing gum wrapper."

"How many wrinkles?" Henry asked swiftly.

"I'll go around and count them on the other side. It's a damned mess back there."

As the chase pilot continued his depressing damage report, each detail seemed to confirm a death warrant for Whiskey Charlie.

When Bill Hamilton finished and clicked off, Henry said into the phone, "Ian, the equipment is damaged far beyond Doyle's grasp. We've got elongating skin wrinkles. That tells us that we have a progressive frame failure. It seems that we lost longitudinal strength. And I might ask, what's holding the tail onto the rest of the hull?"

"The pressure bulkhead?" Ian questioned.

"Quite correct and this is what Doyle wishes to cut through as I understand it. He wants to empty that tail weight."

"Run the imaging on the computer. Let's take a look at the damage progression," Ian ordered.

Henry leaned against the door jamb of the conference room with his short, round arms folded. He nodded to each man as he left for the computer section to run the structural program.

The tall Indian doctor looked down at Henry. "I am sorry, Mr. Gibbons, that I was so direct. But I believe the solution must be treated on a human as well as scientific level."

"I appreciate your input. On this floor, perhaps we leave the human being too far behind. That might be our shortcoming, indeed."

"I did not want to imply heartlessness, sir. The problem is diverse. We must take our considerations on many levels. The pilot, his crew, the passengers, each must be worked into the overall scheme. If any of those fails seriously, it will matter little how brilliant are our engineering solutions."

Henry looked into the unblinking eyes of the Indian. They seemed to be burrowing into him. Gibbons felt a chill. "Yes . . . yes. I know what you are saying."

"But I do have great human compassion, sir."

The Indian then turned and moved like a white bird in slow motion toward the door to the stairs, which led to the top floor, the human factors department.

Henry admitted to himself that he was somehow timid about the human factors group. He felt that they worked in some other orbit with information no one else in the "brain building" understood. When the door to the stairs swung open, Henry shifted his glance to the hall. Mr. Waffles was waxing the original paneled door to the men's room. The doors and the pitted oak floors were the only vestiges left by some passionate renovation architect when he turned the building from a noisy, working mill into a muted high-tech think tank. At least there was a hint of the past left, Henry thought, as he started for the computer section.

10:27 A.M. CST
(Over TULSA COUNTY)

●

——————IN THE FIFTY-FOUR MINUTES that had passed since the accident, an almost Kafkaesque atmosphere began to pervade the plane. The passenger reaction aboard Whiskey Charlie was bizarre and hybrid, the terror level oddly mixed. Those in the after-coach section were still praying and digging their fingernails into the arms of their seats. The wild clamor of the storm still assaulted the ears; the refuse from a large ruptured waste collection tank under the four lavatories behind the rear galley assaulted the noses of passenger and crew alike.

The farther one sat toward the front of the jet; however, the less the collision punch had been felt and heard. This disparity of fear was entirely due to the mammoth size of the 270. Some passengers up front associated the thundering vibrations in the rear of the plane with the onslaught of the ice blizzard, as if the noise of the crash was actually caused by the storm.

There were other visual and sound clues that separated the appearance of Whiskey Charlie's accident from other air disasters. Most such disasters begin and end in a few horrifying seconds, or several minutes at the most. Lucky had spoken calmly to the passengers on the PA system, promising a safe return to Tulsa. Some passengers believed him; others weren't so sure.

At least there was no smoke or fire; no damage that could be seen, and the airliner had not noticeably changed its direction of flight. From the time the passengers had boarded, the cabin had been completely bathed in fluorescent light, and all that could be seen from the windows were the tumbling, raven clouds flecked with wind-driven snowflakes. The noise and blackness of the sky only added to the passengers' anxiety after the accident. But when the 270's blunt nose rose out of the cloud tops into clear skies, the bright light that streamed into the cabin had a tempering emotional effect.

Still, the effulgent glow did not lessen all fears. The four young flight attendants who had been sitting in the aft jump seats when the turboprop ate into Whiskey Charlie's hindquarters were still petrified. In that section of the aircraft the collision was very evident. The crash accelerations back there had been so aggravated that the newspapers and paperbacks attendants read in brief quiet moments were jolted off the shelf. And far worse, the galley doors had flopped open one by one, and sixty plastic trays in the warming ovens were belted out with such force that they pitted the rear bulkhead. Piles of breakfast trays spewed their contents, which showered down on the young women; now the entire area was a warm lake of watery scrambled eggs.

The attendants screamed. Passengers nearby reacted the same way.

"It's a bomb! It's a bomb! We're being blown up!" one old lady had cried over and over; the Pan Am tragedy over Scotland was in everyone's mind.

"My God! We've had it!" a businessman in one of the far rear seats had yelled. "What the hell happened?"

Far up front an executive was working with a hand calculator on a series of marketing figures. He didn't know that there had been a crash because his tiny computer hardly budged in the cup of his fingers.

The storm that pounced upon Tulsa with such force wore itself out as fast as it had developed over the Pacific Ocean. The back wind, the high force of air from the northwest filling in the low pressure, chased the remaining clouds away. Patches of nut-brown earth could be seen below. Finally the thin, silver-fox tail clouds elongated; they separated and sailed off to the east.

Just at that moment the flight returned to the airport area. Most of the passengers, despite the seat belt sign on, ran to the right-hand windows. The airport with its two long runways, dark lines framed against the stark white snow borders, stood out as clearly as the city beyond. The entire Tulsa skyline could be seen in ultimate clarity as only a relatively low morning sun can etch sharp edges. The panoramic view from the windows on the right side evoked two emotional highs: Because they could see Tulsa, most of the passengers felt safer, and the sight of the airport implied a landing. That was a grossly false conclusion. The soft-spoken captain seemed to know what he was doing. He had said he would bring them back to the airport and there it was, right below them, although much farther below than ever. But that didn't seem to matter.

Before the flight had burst out of the shroud of blowing snow, Lucky's arrival in the cabin was a reassuring appearance. His uniform fit his trim body neatly; his shirt was clean and crisp; his tie pulled up right in place between the long points of his starched, clean collar. If this was a man in serious trouble with a life-threatening situation facing him, he didn't reveal a hint of it. Instead, Lucky wore the precise blend of a confident smile and a serious look of authority. When he stepped out, all eyes in first class swung toward him. Lucky nodded and said,

"Good morning again. I'll be back to answer your questions shortly."

Lucky then retreated to the forward galley where, at his request, the cabin attendants had identified and gathered the I.A. employees: nine maintenance men and six flight attendants, all deadheading up to St. Louis and Chicago, including Alex Anderson, the head of I.A. maintenance. Lucky laid out his plan of removing the rear seats from their rails and how he wished to displace the internal center of gravity to bring the nose down. Lucky glanced aft at the sea of taut faces staring at him. He explained his plan more in detail to Alex who listened carefully and said,

"It's a long shot, Lucky, but that's about the only shot you have as I see it."

There was one total skeptic aboard, Linda Glen. She liked Lucky and realized that he wasn't the usual, company-drilled airline pilot who sometimes lied to passengers. But she had heard perplexing rumors about the man and the affair with his cockpit lover. When Lucky finished talking to Alex, Linda took him aside.

"Lucky, what's going on? Are we helpless?"

"Yes and no. The elevators are jammed in the far up position. No matter what I do with the control stick, nothing happens. So we have to forget the elevators and try another way. We'll have to push the nose down by relocating our internal weight."

"But how?"

"By moving passengers and cutting out some weight aft. Linda, look at me closely. Do I look petrified? Tell me."

Linda, a hardened veteran of aft-end flying, studied Lucky Doyle's rugged face looking for traces of despair. Should this guy be worried? Linda asked herself.

Lucky could see the lingering doubt on her face.

"Listen to me," he said in a hard whisper. "If this is to work, we need passenger cooperation. No panic. And that's put together by your crew smiling. So kick in your widest smile, Linda. Have them grinning just as hard if you want that dinner in Tulsa tonight."

He said that with such conviction that Linda Glen was convinced.

"Of course, of course. We'll do just what you say, but you'd better give that small pepper-upper to the attendants in the aft section. We have one big mess back there, and four young kids are terrified."

"Okay. I'll go back there. You start a new-look crusade up here."

Then Lucky was gone. As he worked his way aft, he kept saying to the passengers,"Won't be long now. Things are going to be fine."

One man stopped him, saying, "Captain Doyle, I have to be in Chicago for a presentation at three. Any chance of that?"

"Of course, there's always a chance. But we'll need your help."

The appalling shambles in the galley did not diminish Lucky's cocksure smile. The crew had earnestly tried to tidy things up, but they appeared bedraggled and scared. On their starched white blouses were blotches of scrambled eggs.

"Will we get home, Captain?" one of them asked, holding a sodden pillowcase she was using to wipe up the flood of food bits from the deck.

"Of course we're going to make it. I want you gals to look bright, smiles all the way. We've already picked up a good group of I.A. maintenance fellows in the center cabin, so you people go into the heads, straighten up, and begin looking like your sparkling selves."

"Are we just supposed to look like that, or are we really going to make it?" another young woman asked.

"I'm confident. The aircraft is still in control. The engines are working fine. So fix yourselves up, and let's get it done as true professionals."

"Captain," one of the young attendants said, "one of the head doors doesn't open. Another one doesn't open very well, and a third one is starting to stick."

Lucky moved over and tried the second door handle. He pushed, but it was jammed. He tried the other two doors. One was difficult to open, but the last of the four lavatories seemed unaffected. Lucky should have picked up a clue as to what was happening but he didn't.

Connie shared some of Lucky's feelings, his dislike of the six big glass displays in the electronic cockpit. The glass cockpit had arrived because the computer could store limitless amounts of data. This innovation supplied complete monitoring of cruise control, navigation, graphic pictures of adverse weather, engine condition on a call-up basis. That was the positive side of the glass cockpit, the way Connie saw it, the elimination of extraneous information. There was another side to this cockpit: the computer was programmed to present impending problems. Suddenly, Connie saw on the glass display a warning that was bad news, a critical, blinking message: "REDUCE PRESSURE RATIO . . . DANGER . . . OVERHEATED TURBINES . . . REDUCE THRUST IMMEDIATELY."

She just sat and watched the warning, knowing that if she wiggled the power levers back, even a quarter of an inch, the mammoth jet would start to shake and that the shaking would be followed by a stall and a spin.

She wondered, did the computers know that? Of course they didn't, nor did they know what to do in case the elevators were jammed in the far up position by a "marriage" with a wayward turboprop.

Despite all the wizardry of the glass cockpit, the answer to their dilemma never came up on those full-color displays. It took Lucky's rapid-fire mind, his hands-on experience to make it a possibility that they'd get out of this hell. She thanked God he was aboard.

Although there was guarded optimism aboard Whiskey Charlie, the rising panic of the ground team at Bristol was evident. New reports from the chase plane came in, plus additional data from Connie on the speed, the pitch angle, and the warning of the turbine heat values. These data were fed into the graphic computer program along with the vast databank that Trent Aviation already had punched into the supercomputer.

First they saw the 270 airframe in full-dimensional color appear on the forty-two-inch screen. Then Henry introduced the variables: the calculated collision loads, the extent of the skin wrinkles and other data. With lightning speed, the display revealed a progressive frame collapse. Whiskey Charlie was slowly coming apart in the air!

Ian had been the most dispassionate, and now his heart beat so rapidly that he thought it would burst out of his chest. Henry had his lower lip caught in his teeth, which were yellowed by years of pipe smoking. His eyes narrowed as he watched the results of the computer analysis. Second by second the display showed the collapse of Whiskey Charlie's structure. It was one thing, Lou Walters thought, to be told the terrible truth by integrated circuits forming green letters racing across a screen, but to see it happening with pictorial clarity was ghoulish.

Henry touched a button on the enormous keyboard. Another iconography began to redraw itself in ghostly detail. This graphic episode showed the effect of Lucky's weight relocation. The progressive structural failure accelerated.

"Watch the effect," Henry said, trying to overcome the tightness of his throat.

"Now we see the nose coming down with the displaced weight just as this Doyle fellow predicted. But here's what he didn't know and he couldn't predict. He doesn't have the structural forecast data. It's not in the man's head—as much as he may think that he has a true grasp of things. I don't have to explain the developing episode, gentlemen."

The detailed computer visual revealed a faster and faster vibration of Whiskey Charlie's after section. Then it began to separate. The detail was made more horrifying because the imprint looked into the guts of the aircraft's anatomy like the high-resolution pictures of a scan on a person being crushed to death rib by rib. The jet's frames began to deform from sheer strain.

The tail section fell away. The detail even displayed the seats being flung out of the shattered fuselage as the whole jet nosed over and dove for the ground. The picture was relentless, as if it had to show every horror in the most minute detail. Just as the wings were ground off at their roots by the forces of the fall, Lou yelled.

"Turn that God damn thing off, Ian!"

As Lou Walters swung himself away from Whiskey Charlie's computer death, the old Tulsan saw the gaunt faces of the engineers rigid with fright as they watched their finest achievement destroying itself.

"Is it all over?" Ian asked Henry, with a directness that almost implied the answer.

"I don't know. If that scenario is carried out by Doyle, you see what happens. Very simply, gentlemen we're looking at a mode of failure here that's called unit strain. The two most fundamental load and reaction systems are torsion and bending. . . ."

"Henry, don't get into all this engineering." Lou Walters said briskly. "Just tell me what's happening, what we're going to do about it."

"What's happening is this. Because of the crash, the load forces, those in the forward section of the structure, are exceeding the opposing forces' resistance. The bending moments are being stretched to the point of failure. All aircraft structural forms are designed to take certain predictable loads. Here the modulus of elasticity is too great for the characteristics of the design and materials."

"In other words nothing can be done?" Lou asked,

"No. You can't shore up a failing structure in the air when time is running out."

"Then what's the answer?" Ian asked.

"I can't tell you what to do yet, only what can't be done. But that's part of crisis management. The first law is don't do the wrong thing."

"Where does that leave us?" Lou asked.

"As I said Mister Walters, we don't know yet."

"When will you know?"

"As fast as possible. We have a brilliant team here and the most powerful computer in the world. If we can't come up with the answer, then there is no answer, at least with conventional thinking."

"Maybe this will take radical thinking. Did you ever consider that?" Ian asked.

"In the history of aviation, Sir Ian, I've never heard of a solution coming out of radical thinking. New thinking with a sound engineering basis, yes. Renegade thinking, no!"

Ian was even more alarmed. Lucky was a true nonconformist, a purebred renegade.

10:36 A.M. CST
(Over TULSA COUNTY)

●

— — — — — — —JUST SEVENTEEN MINUTES after Whiskey Charlie burst out of the cloud tops, the first live pictures of the struggling, nose-high jet were picked up through a long lens of KOTV, the CBS affiliate in Tulsa. They had instantly chartered a twin-engine Cessna to cover the media windfall. The startlingly vivid pictures of Whiskey Charlie were beamed down to a remote truck, then to the repeater unit at the station.

Realizing that a network feed would come from KOTV, the station manager organized satellite time directly to the network's uplink station near New York.

When the head of CBS network news looked at the horrifying pictures overlaid with the actual sounds from Jack's tower from England, and the 270 cockpit, he immediately phoned down to master control.

"Have the news bulletin ready for punch-up. There's an airliner out of control over Tulsa. We're picking up sensational coverage. Get Rather to the news set . . . and find an aviation expert, quick. I'm going to cut in on the game show."

"We're taping now, so stand by for the feed in two minutes."

When they punched up the picture, all the networks, plus CNN and the independents, saw the once-in-a-lifetime opportunity and offered to pay for a time-shared audio visual feed.

The picture had a rare dimension to it, one that was unprecedented in the history of live TV coverage of a disaster in the making. It was the actual air-to-ground audio that gave the visual such agonizing realism. The voices were not merely scraps of words, like those one would hear over a shortwave set. Very high frequency radio used in aviation is free of clutter. And there were thousands of VHF receivers that could be bought at any radio store. So the audio went out raw and clear. Stations throughout the world ran it unedited, expletives and all. Other TV facilities taped the sound and laid it over the pictures at random.

The French television used the audio unedited. They also found a large clock from their prop shop and marked off 7:20 Paris time, or 12:20 Central Standard Time with a large red band. That would be the hour and minute that the jet would burn off the last ounce of fuel. In France the possible flameout and plunge to earth would occur during prime time, perfect for full family viewing, they believed.

10:42 A.M. CST (TULSA)

IT WAS TOTAL AGONY FOR Ron Alcott, the deepest isolation of his life. He sat in his office immobilized by a combination of self-loathing and aversion. Not only was he surrendering his carrier—that was painful enough—now he would be remembered as the only U.S. airline official to bet on the radical 270 design. His name would be attached to one of the worst airline disasters in history.

Ron sat upright at his rolltop desk, the one his father, a grain dealer, had given him when he started the airline. It was the only desk Ron had ever used—from his chilly, back-of-the-hangar days right up to the twenty-third floor of the I.A. corporate tower. Thousands of memories flooded his mind; he wished Lou Walters were at his side, but the chairman was trying to handle his own desolation as he remained helpless in the Trent computer room.

Cap stood by Ron trying to offer an encouraging phrase now and then. Ron hardly heard him; the words were meaningless. The airline president sat in silence, as rigid as a tree in the petrified forest.

Augie Hartman felt that same way. But his response was triggered by anger, not compassion. The young needle-nosed accountant was sweating after he talked to the investment bankers in New York. The day before, his stock had jumped five points in anticipation of the I.A. takeover; now it was off six points as the reports of Whiskey Charlie's predicament began to clog the news wires. A couple of TV sets had been wheeled into corners of the New York Stock Exchange trading floor. Specialists and clerks were sneaking looks at the media splash of Whiskey Charlie's struggle.

"Great show!" one specialist told another. "Like looking in on the Christians and the lions. The poor passengers are even hooked up for sound."

Augie saw the approaching disaster as the end of a deal, not the tragic loss of human life. After hasty talks with his St. Louis office and the investment bankers, Augie tried to settle his nerves. He strode out of the conference room toward Ron's office. He knocked and Cap opened the door about two inches.

"I have to see Ron," Augie said, pushing Cap back and the door fully open as he entered the stilled office. He crossed to Ron and touched his shoulder, trying to demonstrate some commiseration.

"I'm sorry, Ron. I really am. It's terrible."

Ron did not move or edge his eyes toward Augie.

"I think you should leave, Mr. Hartman," Cap said. "We know about those planted stories on the Two-Seventy that destroyed our load factors."

Augie shoved his smooth white hands into his pants pockets and shuffled around the room. "I did not plant those stories. Ron, do you hear me?"

"He hears you," Cap said.

"I forecast a disaster with the Two-Seventy and look what's happening up there now."

Cap reddened with anger. He shouted at Augie, "You know God damned well that the plane didn't have anything to do with this. It was hit. It was a controller error, as far as we know. So don't come in here with a story of being a prophet."

Ron moved. He shook his head and waved his hand at Cap not to shout.

Augie caught the action, and he quickly reached for a side chair, which he pulled up to Ron's desk. He put his hand on Ron's forearm, but Ron removed Augie's fingers and turned toward the younger man with deep disgust.

"What else do you want to say, Hartman?" Ron asked.

"Ron, I've talked to my St. Louis flight department. This Doyle guy has a shaky reputation. He's trying to be gallant and all that shit, but my guys say there just isn't enough time left for the air-to-air transfer. Fuel's running out . . . that plane is coming down the fast way. But look, Ron, we don't have to drop the deal just because of this terrible thing. We can restructure the merger."

Ron frowned and went back to staring at the wall.

"I know how you feel, Ron."

"I don't think you have the slightest idea," the old airline president said slowly. "No concept."

"Of course I do. I'm a sensitive man. Who wouldn't be heartbroken and shocked by all this? But we have no control over events up there. I say we think positively and re-form the deal."

"How?" Ron asked in a low voice.

"Well, first we agree to move every bit of the company to St. Louis. This city is going to be known as the airline graveyard."

Ron gave the man a cold, unblinking look.

"I'm sorry, but facts are facts," Augie barged on. "Then we buy just the assets . . . not the name. It's a bulk purchase. Naturally, we don't want to buy over three hundred lawsuits."

Ron smiled fiercely. "Get the fuck out of here!" he said in an angry whisper.

Cap crossed and took Augie under the arm. He pulled him up and started the South Central man toward the door. Hartman continued to argue.

"Ron, I appreciate your feelings, but we just can't sit here. My stock's slipping fast. Yours is off eleven points. We can do something good, Ron. Please!"

Cap opened the door and shoved the young man out to the hall.

"Will you talk to him? He has to know the value of what I'm saying," Augie pleaded.

"Go back to the conference room and watch it on TV," Cap said.

"Look, if you get him to sign another deal, I'll make sure you stay on as our corporate communications VP, one hell of a job. Name your price, name it and I'll agree," Augie said hastily. He was almost babbling now.

"Hartman, I wouldn't work for you at any price."

"You'll be God damned sorry you said that." Hartman paused, then plunged on. "Listen, I'll even save your unions. I'll put that in writing. I'm not a union buster."

Cap spun around and closed the door quietly without saying another word to Augie Hartman.

10:56 A.M. CST (FORT SMITH, ARKANSAS)

FRANK A'HEARN'S FEAR TOOK the form of stomach butterflies. He was a resolute man, strong and quick-thinking, like Lucky. He couldn't believe he was reacting this way. Frank hadn't suffered such a panic attack since he was a teenager in Australia being dragged out to sea by the backwash of a rogue wave. As he had fought his way in toward the lonely beach, he had felt the heaving of his stomach; now the same feeling was back and more violent than he had remembered. Of all those on the ground end desperately trying to save the flight, Frank was the closest to Lucky and Connie, as close as if they were his own family. And after he heard Lucky's idea of shifting the passengers around, Frank felt optimistic; his butterflies calmed down.

They came flying back, however, when he saw the condition of his tarmac. The DC–6 they were planning to use for the air-to-air transfer was encapsulated in high drifts of snow. The storm had gripped Fort Smith differently from Tulsa. The crystals were lighter and drier; the wind sharper; and through the night, the snow had been pumped into high drifts.

Frank had every one of his sixty men digging frantically at the undercarriage of the DC–6 so they could hook the towbar to the nose wheel. The most powerful tug on the airport stood ready to yank the plane out of the snow. Four generators were shooting hot air into iced engines, and Louie Bonner sat in the freezing cockpit, his teeth chattering, waiting for the signal to crank over the props if the tug didn't work. The prop tips were still buried in the snow. As the minutes slipped by, Frank felt his stomach churn. He yelled into his walkie-talkie.

"Louie, I'll get everyone away. Wind her up and force her out with the props."

"Risky as hell, Frank," Louie answered into his small radio. "The engines are still cold, and there's hardly any traction on the tarmac. This hunk of equipment might get out of control."

"We don't have a choice, Louie, time's running out on Lucky."

"Get everyone far away. I'll try it," Louie said.

When everyone had retreated, Louie hit the first magneto in the start-up sequence. The double-cylinder engines coughed a few times and shot out plumes of blue-black smoke. The spinning props kicked back the light snow, blowing white geysers into the air with huge "rooster tails." With backfires and popping smoke trails, Louie had all four engines spinning. There was not enough time for a proper warmup and Frank yelled into the mike, "Just blast that sucker out, Louie."

Against his better judgment and after testing the feel of the foot brakes, Louie inched his throttles forward. The DC–6 started to vibrate wildly when the throttles were brought almost up against the stops of the power quadrant. The reborn airliner began a rocking motion. So much snow was being shot up that Louie couldn't see a thing through his windshield. With an ear-shattering blast, the nose of the aircraft burst free. It plunged out of the snowbank like a rocket, and a spray of crystals shot high into the deep blue air. As soon as he was free, Louie chopped his power. He tried his brakes to halt his uncontrolled speed. One brake locked and the DC–6 curved its way over the slippery tarmac, heading toward a row of parked planes.

"Louie, hit the brakes again," Frank bellowed into his mike.

"I'm blinded by this snow," Louie roared.

With all the power in his leg, he pounded on the free brake. The rattling old plane swung away from the line of other aircraft and started for the crowd. Everyone dashed in different directions.

"It's out of control!" Louie shouted.

"Get away," Frank yelled.

Louie finally brought the ice-covered DC–6 under control, and it spun to a stop.

As soon as the old bird halted, there was an explosion.

At first Frank thought it was a cylinder head coughing its guts out. Then he saw the airliner sink: a left main landing gear tire had blown.

"Nice job, Louie," Frank shouted into his mike.

"Frank, are you there?" his secretary asked over the radio.

"I'm hearing you."

"You have an emergency call."

"Is the flight down?" Frank asked with paced words.

"Don't know. It's from Sir Ian Pryce-Smith on the second line . . . he says he has to speak to you immediately."

Frank ordered the crew to haul the DC–6 inside, to change the tires and load up. He ran across the glistening ramp, through two hangars, and up a flight of stairs to his office. The weathered Aussie flopped in his cracked-leather Air Force surplus chair, almost afraid to pick up the phone. He felt as if he had suffered through five aircraft disasters that morning.

"Yes, Ian. Sorry for the delay. We had bad problems out back; the DC–Six was plugged in the snow."

"We have had problems on this end, too, I'm sorry to say."

Ian spoke from the conference room. Henry Gibbons sat at one end of the long table with a phone pressed to his ear, and Lou Walters was at a third phone listening in.

"How bad is it?" Frank asked.

"Things are critical."

"Did Lucky tell you that?"

"He doesn't know, but the Two-Seventy is falling apart frame by frame."

"How the hell can you be so sure?" Frank barked.

"We just ran a graphic program on the supercomputer. We plugged in our airframe structural data, plus assumed crash impact loads and other information such as the skin wrinkles, the speed, and weights given to us by Connie."

Frank slumped down in his seat. He knew the meaning of the wrinkles, the frightening clue that there was much too much loading on the battered tail section. Then Henry began, "Very simply, the downward pressure on the stuck elevators is wrenching the jet apart. We're overloading the structure. Turbine vibrations are exacerbating it. As the passengers move forward, the nose comes down."

"Then Lucky was right," Frank interjected.

"No, sir. The more pressure he puts on the nose, the counterbalancing force, the faster the equipment breaks up."

There was a pause and Lou Walters cut in. "Frank, Lou Walters. These people have visual computing, image processing, very realistic. I just saw our flight bust up in midair as if I were watching a horror movie."

"We have digital picture processing here, too," Frank said. "So they re-created the probable airframe failure, now what?"

"We'll have to get on to the flight before Lucky has everyone moved up forward," Ian said.

"I agree. Inform the flight, but why are you calling me on this line instead of talking directly to Doyle?"

Ian glanced over at Henry, who was rubbing his stubby hands through his flopping white hair as if some answer were going to drop out of his head and onto the table.

"You know this Doyle fellow very well, Frank," Ian said. "We're worried about him. That's why I wanted to check with you first."

"Lucky's a solid guy when there's trouble," Frank assured them.

"Doyle's an unpredictable sort of individualist, a malcontent. Will he explode, do something rash, when he hears that he's off on the wrong track?" Ian asked.

"No. He has solid nerves. He does wild things now and then. But the guy is no fool. He wants to live. So what are you saying?"

"Where is Doyle right now?" Henry asked.

"Stand by. I'll check the flight."

Connie told Frank that Lucky was aft by the pressure bulkhead.

"Here's the next question," Henry continued. "Are the passengers being moved?"

"Yes. That was Lucky's plan. The cabin crew told me that the people and seats are being relocated," Connie said.

"Here's what to do. Call back to Lucky and the

cabin crew. Tell them that the people can't be moved. The relocation of the weight will put too much stress on the airframe."

"What do we do?"

"We'll have that answer soon, I hope."

"In the meantime I'm getting a warning light on turbine overheating. I was thinking of taking off thrust on one side to cool the fans down one at a time."

"Not a bad idea. We'll check Rolls-Royce on that, but go ahead. Be careful of the stall. Remember your rudder is gone. You can't depend upon that for directional control."

"I was planning a slight bank into the spooled-down turbine."

"That's it. Be careful. That's a critical move you're trying."

"What else do I do?" she asked swiftly.

"Nothing. Try it," Henry ordered.

When Connie clicked off, Frank said, "I think this whole thing is going to be hit and miss. Trying this or that."

As much as Henry Gibbons abhorred what he called renegade problem solving by wild men such as Doyle, he also knew that a solution to the Whiskey Charlie problem hadn't come from his "white coats" as yet. That made the man wonder if this was going to be a struggle between low tech and high tech. Struggle? He didn't want it to be any struggle, just a solution to bring the 270 down safely.

Slowly Henry was beginning to realize that engineering had its limitations. But what were they? And who was going to come up with the answer here? No longer was Henry worried about the pride of authorship. All he wanted, as they all did, was to save the flight, and in turn, Trent Aviation.

11:04 A.M. CST (Over TULSA)

•

CONNIE QUICKLY PHONED BACK to Lucky.

"I don't have to tell you, we're burning these turbines up," she said.

"I feel the heat. The passengers are dripping with sweat."

"There're frantic warnings on the glass tubes. I'm afraid we'll blow the turbines off the pods if we don't do something."

"Like what?" Lucky asked in a low strained voice.

"I want to shove one thrust lever up all the way and bring the other into normal pressure range. Once I have one engine cooled, I'll try it with the other. Want to come up, or should I give it a try? I called Bristol. They said go ahead."

"Be careful of the fast buffet. You're playing with a quick nose over, love."

"You don't have to tell me."

"Don't worry, I know things are on the shoulder."

"How's it going back there?"

"None of the aft lavatories' doors open. I have the maintenance guys pulling off the side panels around the windows to expose the frames."

"When you get the liners off, what do you see?"

"It's hard to tell by just looking at the frames."

"Alex says there's acute structural failure someplace. We can't tell exactly where yet. And the skin wrinkles are extending, Lucky. I've been feeding reports to England. There's a military chopper right off my left side . . . he's hovering in close . . . giving me clear, detailed information and each damned report is worse. Lucky, we're breaking up from the inside."

"We're getting the same message back here, but I haven't changed the tune. We'll be home for supper."

"Also, Lucky, the Bristol engineers say that we shouldn't bring the passengers forward. The change in weight is going to bust up the airframe faster."

"That might be. But what's their answer?"

"I didn't hear one yet."

"Tell them I'm waiting. And give the cabin gals a call about the passengers."

"Will do."

Connie eased one power lever up to full thrust. As she did that, she dropped the other one off, watching the airspeed indicator to keep it just above the stall. Whiskey Charlie started to turn slightly, and she dipped her wing to keep some directional control.

As Connie was adjusting the thrust levers André came to life again.

"Can I ask you something, Connie?"

"Sure, André."

"What's the background on this Frank fellow? Does he know his stuff?"

"Yes. He flew in World War Two for the Royal Australian Airforce . . . highly decorated . . . went to engineering school in Sydney . . . ran a conversion shop in Calcutta . . . took old World War II birds and converted them into freighters . . . married an Italian woman who died some years ago. That's when he went to Alaska and met Lucky. The guy knows heavy equipment. He's tough and good, just like Lucky."

Lucky entered the cockpit and took his left seat. "Gentlemen, are we all on the patch?" He asked into his mike.

They identified themselves in rapid order, and Lucky said calmly, "Connie told me about the problem. I ordered my crew back aft to halt the weight shift, told them to take a breather. I understand what's happening. I'm ready to help. Whatever you men come up with is fine by me. It's your command. You fellows created this bird, so go ahead and tell us how to get her down in one piece."

"Great, Lucky," Ian said warmly. "Just stand by. We might be needing more information as we run the programs."

"Anything you want," Lucky said. Anyone listening would have thought he was delighted with the arrangement.

Connie was leaning over the seat back as Lucky spoke. When he finished, he released his transmit button and turned to her.

"Connie, what's vital here is passenger confidence. I want you to spot-check back aft. Just move around and say we're catching up with an improved situation. I'll try to figure out something to cool down the cabins."

She slipped a fast kiss on Lucky's cheek, crossed her fingers, and left the cockpit.

Lucky got up, went to the cockpit locker, and took out the emergency kit. Removing the small handheld transmitter, he set it on his seat, winking at André. From the second closet, the hanging locker, Lucky grabbed his flight bag and took out the white cardboard that was backing his clean shirt. He often changed his shirt twice a day to appear clean and totally together for the job. Now, however, it was the cardboard he wanted. He pushed it against the bulkhead and wrote with the heavy red marker that he used for notes.

"WORK ME ON MILITARY FREQ. 346. *NOW.*"

He took the shirt cardboard back to his left seat and pressed the transmit button.

"Military chopper, would you take a fly by my left cockpit window. I want to see if we have skin wrinkles up this way."

"Sure will, Captain. My name's Hoover. Captain Charlie Hoover."

"Okay, Charlie. You might need some binoculars to scan my left windows."

"We've got them, Lucky. You guys are doing one hell of a job."

Lucky then held up the shirt cardboard sign and twisted the frequency dial to 346, used only by the military. He snapped on the small set.

The Black Hawk chopper swished past. Charlie had seen the message; he came right up on the frequency.

"Very clever, Lucky. You didn't want the universe hearing this, huh?"

"Right."

"What do you have?" the chopper pilot asked.

"Listen carefully. We have to take pressure off that tail. There's a wild heat buildup in the turbines. My fuel is half gone."

"Know what you mean," Charlie said.

"Now, you see that we have two elevators on each side, both stuck in the up position. On the inside elevator is the trim tab. Somehow, the bastard is still working. I'll need that to round out for my landing, but the other baby, the outboard flippers, are just hurting us. Is there some kind of gun, maybe an automatic, that you can fire through that elevator? I want to make it like Swiss cheese. If we let the air through, some of the pressure will be taken off, right? Think I'm on line, pilot to pilot?"

"Sure as hell will help. We have firepower aboard. We just returned from an action drill."

"Are the boys accurate?"

"At close range, very accurate. So you want us to pass by and start peppering those outboards?"

"That's what I want. But I'll need to get every other plane far away. I want this just between you and me. The tower can't hear us on this frequency so I'd like to handle this quick. Have to bring the nose down, or we're looking at a spin in!"

"That's great thinking, and it's so simple!" Charlie Hoover was exhilarated.

"Maybe, but do you have a good shot aboard? We can't miss and hit the other elevator because, as I said, I need those trim tabs, and we might have hydraulic fluid sloshing around back there. So we don't want a slug in the tail cone . . . could have a fire."

"Leave it to us. We got your message, Lucky. My boys are good old wild turkey shooters."

"I'll keep this frequency open, but I'm going to tell the other aircraft and those fucking press planes to clear the hell out of here."

"Okay. Just give us the word, and we'll mush up that tail."

Lucky called the tower and told Jack to order the press planes and the chase aircraft to clear the area—he was going to go through some turning maneuvers to test various easy rolls. In a matter of minutes, the other aircraft videotaping the Trent had flown off.

"Good," Lucky said into the emergency unit. "Begin your passes, Charlie."

With the gunner of the Black Hawk chopper aiming an M-23D, 7.62 mm, machine gun at the tail section of the 270, Charlie alerted Lucky that they were making their first pass. As the Army helicopter cruised over the tail section, a burst of shots rattled off, puncturing first the outer left elevator and then the right elevator. The blast of the small weapons fire could not be heard inside Whiskey Charlie because of the high turbine settings. Lucky had to rely on visual reports from the chopper pilot; they came within minutes.

"Got some great holes in those flippers, Lucky. About an inch or a little more in diameter."

"Great! Make another pass, I don't see my speed building up. The nose should be letting down a little."

"Should be. We'll try it again," Charlie said.

They went through four passes, splattering soft lead through the jammed outboard elevators.

It took about seven minutes. Lucky figured that by that time the Trent boys would be back on the air with their finite solution, but the tower frequency remained quiet.

"Lucky, this is about the last time we can make our pass; there's not too much left of those outboards. You have to be seeing something."

"Take it once more," Lucky ordered.

This time the chopper's crew punched out a solid burst of fire through each outboard elevator.

Suddenly, Lucky's airspeed needle inched up. They were at 150 knots and the speed was climbing. Best of all, Lucky thought, the 270's nose had dropped. Now they were climbing at only about forty to sixty feet a minute instead of one-fifty. Lucky drew down on his thrust levers. In less than a minute, the lower pressure ratios cooled each turbine and the blinking red light on the glass panels went to a steady red, a prewarning light, and finally, a few seconds later, it returned to its milky green display, meaning that they were now operating within the normal heat range.

Two other indications of good news followed: The fuel flow meter dropped, and the cockpit became cooler as the turbine heat plunged.

"Very nice, Charlie," Lucky said into his small transmitter.

"Risky, but a damned good idea," Charlie replied.

"It's not over yet," Lucky said, "but we bought ourselves at least two hours, maybe more. The fuel flow has dropped, so we're in normal high-speed cruise, and the climb rate is way down."

"But you're still climbing. We have to lick that one."

"You will!"

"Charlie. I don't want the world hearing me. I might have to start welding inside here. We have a progressive frame collapse."

"How do you start welding? With the gear the DC–6 is transferring? That's like a heavy, time-consuming task."

"Well, the engineers over in England did a good job identifying the problem. They're trying like hell to dope this out, but we can't get weight forward without beefing those frames up back aft. What else can I do?"

"Know what you mean."

"Is there a little surface left on the outboard flipper?"

"A little."

"We might have to blow the whole thing off. Here's my hang-up. You say there's fluid dripping out of the tail?"

"Looks like oil, hydraulic fluid, but some of it might be jet fuel. You got a tank back there?"

"Affirmative. It's for the auxiliary power unit."

"Is there a chance we could get an automatic sniper rifle with very soft heads, so we can do a job on the rest of the tail if necessary?"

"We have heads like that. Sure."

"Charlie, you seem to read this damned thing pretty well. You see the scene back there?"

"Looks like hell. Don't even know how you got this far."

"Let me try something on you. I got shaky vibes about slicing into that aft compartment with all those skin wrinkles, even if we have time. Things have gone a lot slower than I figured."

"Know what you mean. You got failure back there, for sure. The engines at lower thrust levels should halt the vibrating, but touching the structure could start a real collapse. Opening up on those inboards might cause an explosion, and every shot would have to be perfect. You need some trim control. How do we know where the trim jacks are located? We could put a slug through one of them and you'd be lost."

"Charlie, let me clue you into something. Everything we try is a risk."

"I know that as well as you do. That's why we're trying to think this out as well as everyone else."

"Let me give you a geography lesson on this aircraft. Back aft we have an airtight, watertight bulkhead. Up front here the 270 is set up differently than other aircraft. We have a two-level forward compartment with crew bunk space up here behind the cockpit, and then a circular stair leads to a lower level with more bunks and a head. Forward there's the emergency oxygen supply. Underneath, the nose gear well. Aft we have a bulkhead mainframe. Behind there, on the lower section, is our forward cargo hold. This bulkhead is airtight and watertight, like those on a ship."

"So now I know what's inside. So what?"

"In ships they trim off by pumping water from one ballast tank to another."

"I suppose. But you're not a ship. Where do you get the water from, even if you have a watertight bulkhead?"

"Here's a plan. It might not be the final plan, but we have to work with something."

"You do."

"So while my buddy flies tools up here to beef up the aft sections, we get one of those Air Force tankers that I've seen down at the Tinker Air Base outside of Oak City. Instead of pumping us fuel, what if we made an attachment so they could pump water directly into the forward cargo compartment? That would bring the nose down."

"It would. But is there time for all this? I'll get the tankers up here right away loaded with water, but the clock is running. That's an exotic solution."

"It's the only way this flight is going to get down so I can have dinner in Tulsa tonight."

"I go along with you. But start thinking of something else in case this gets to be impossible."

"I never *stop* thinking."

"I'll drop down, refuel, and start things in motion. You tell your man in Fort Smith what equipment you'll need from his local fire department. Hope this works."

The chopper banked away as the cockpit phone rang. It was Connie.

"Lucky, it got cooler in here all of a sudden. What did you do?"

"I just did some fiddling around. A little of this and a little of that."

"Are the turbines cooling off? They don't seem so loud."

"They're cooling. Come on up."

Connie could tell that Lucky had pulled off something, but in her wildest thoughts she never imagined what had taken place during the eleven minutes that she was aft making passenger contact, assuring them once more that Lucky was a man of his word: They would be home for dinner.

11:10 A.M. CST (Over TULSA COUNTY)

●

———————THIS OIL CITY OF SOME 400,000 was a mix of emotions. Some Tulsans were agonizing and sympathetic; others viewed the plight of Whiskey Charlie as a unique close-up of a morbidly exciting event taking place literally before their eyes.

"Where else can you see a disaster of this dimension happening right in front of you?" one TV newsman questioned.

How one viewed the climbing airliner depended, for some, on whether the observer knew someone aboard the flight: a relative, a friend, or a friend of a friend. There were others, of course, who were just out to see a great crash, like the spectators who doggedly follow the fast "Indy" cars hoping for a flaming spectacle.

When the ice-clogged clouds were whisked away, revealing a radiant sky, I.A. 19 could clearly be seen just east of the city. Jet watching either on TV or through binoculars became a sport. Cars jammed the roads leading eastward from the city while radio and TV reported on the best place to catch a glimpse of the slowly climbing jet. Some spectators took along portable TVs so they could see close-ups as well as catching the larger view with their own eyes.

Pete Rosen wasn't about to be congratulated for what he had erroneously created: the hype of a plane headed for outer space. The authorities, one after another, kept disqualifying the "lost in space" concept as dishonest, a piece of slick headline grabbing. Yet people loved to be immersed in what they wanted to believe, true or not, so for many millions, watching the epic drama of the jet creeping higher and higher, the space theory with all its scary wonder still occupied their minds.

Mike Willis, the *Leader* editor who had assigned Pete to the South Central merger story, had worked late the night before. He wasn't due in until twelve that day. His publisher called him at home before Willis had learned of the collision.

"Who is Rosen?" the elderly man with the gravelly voice asked.

"He's a young reporter on my staff, talented, hard-driving sort of fellow."

"Is he our aviation editor? Do we still have one?"

The publisher was thinking of Bumpy, an exbarnstormer who had worked for the paper for years as the self-appointed aviation editor.

"Rosen writes aviation stories sometimes," Mike said.

"Well, he made fools out of us this morning."

The publisher told Mike about the collision and what he'd heard about Rosen's "outer space" bulletin. Then he complained, "We're getting hundreds of calls about that preposterous line. This is an aviation city,

Mike. They think we've lost our heads." He quickly brought Mike up to date on the collision. "Get your ass down there, Mike."

As Mike drove from his home in the southeast section of Tulsa, an area of large homes that formed a sudden contrast with the glassy new high rises of downtown, he noticed something odd about the city. Usually there were large white clouds bellying against the blue sky. Sometimes they floated in from the north, over the upper Great Plains, where all the cold and snow originated. The heat and humidity were Tulsa's pain from the South, where hot vapor was sucked up from the Gulf of Mexico. Either way, some overcast was usually present. But on this day the sky was extravagant. Cloudless. A vast stretch of blue, the deepest Mike had ever seen, arched over Tulsa like a festive tent. The oil city usually had a throbbing pulse, with rumbles and bunches of people moving about. Mike expected to see the fresh snow lacerated, tracked by tire treads. But the sparkling carpet was relatively uncut by vehicles or human imprints. It was as if the city was deserted, or had suddenly been evacuated because of some impending threat.

As he neared his *Leader* building, the strange absence of people was even more evident. The streets were empty, but there was a glow of light through most of the office windows. Obviously everyone was inside, doing something. He entered the newspaper building and found the guard desk unmanned. Mike rode up in the elevator alone, and on the tenth floor, the receptionist wasn't on duty. As he entered the long newsroom through which he had to pass to reach his window office, the mystery of the vacant desks—and of the vacant city—became clear.

Here and there were pockets of people with their eyes glued to one or another of a series of TV sets that had been hastily secured from somewhere. And for the first time Mike's entrance went unnoticed.

He stopped behind a group of people listening to the tense conversations between the cockpit, and the various ground advisers and watching the dramatic close-ups of the Trent 270. It was seeing the appalling pictures in such a context that held the viewer; even Mike was locked in place watching the coverage instead of seeking out Pete Rosen and giving him hell.

The most startling aspect of this media splash—the unbelievable thing—was the fact that the airliner was still up in the air, a flying wreck. The eye and human brain were sending opposing messages: From the look of it, the massive jet should have been splattered over miles of snow. It seemed like a visual trick. How could such a chewed-up jet still be airborne? The sight was there, but it defied human logic. That, the editor realized, was the anomaly. It was brutally real and, at the same time, mythical. Mike didn't even remember how long his gaze was fixed on the TV set: It might have been two minutes or ten, but suddenly he came out of the spell. He had to go find Rosen.

When the young reporter, now the highly quoted "aviation editor," bounced into Mike's office, the editor wanted to chide him about his "outer space" hype. But he realized then that even Rosen's outrageous tag line was bland compared to what was actually happening. Rosen explained what he knew about it.

"The thing has all sorts of side alleys," Pete said.

"Like what?"

"Well, the captain up there sleeps with his copilot."

"Oh, shit. Two gays in the cockpit? Not funny."

"The copilot, as I get it, is a very attractive lady. She's a dazzling young redhead."

"And she's making it with the old captain?"

"He's not so old, Mike. Lucky Doyle is forty-five."

The editor hunched his shoulders in a sign of disbelief. "What's this guy's background? Air Force pilot?"

"No. He flew a bush plane in the Arctic before joining I.A. Used to be a spray pilot. Off duty, he flies an old Waco biplane. They say he's a character around northern Tulsa County."

"So he's going to save the I.A. jet? I just saw it on TV. How can that plane stay up there?"

"Everybody's asking the same question. But Doyle's ideas are stirring up all sorts of controversy. Some experts I called at Lockheed and NASA say Doyle's out of his mind. The flight is doomed! Others say he's so imaginative that he might pull it off."

"How?"

"There're a thousand theories, Mike."

"What are the odds?"

The young reporter shook his head. "Bad! That's how the smart money is betting . . . but everyone's hoping. There's hardly a person in the civilized world who isn't rooting for Doyle."

"And your outer space thing?"

"I put that in as sort of a gag. I didn't know people would take it seriously. But outer space or not, Mike, this thing would have been a media madhouse however you slice it."

"How was the jet hit?"

"That's another whole angle. Why the private pilot hit the jet remains a mystery. He takes off in this storm and there's a mix-up with the control tower. Seems they didn't have the right radar. This guy, who they found north of Tulsa in a million pieces, uses the wrong runway. Before the controllers can straighten things out, bango!"

"All right, keep picking up sidelights on each of the crew members, especially this Doyle. And you'd better call I.A. for a passenger list. Tomorrow, I guess, we'll be printing the longest obituary in the history of this paper."

Pete knew that the bulk of that task would be painful; listing the names, ages, and possibly occupations of three hundred and nineteen dead people. Both newspapermen went solemnly back to the newsroom to watch the brutally close pictures of the crippled jet.

11:16 A.M. CST
(Over TULSA COUNTY)

●

——————WHILE LUCKY WAS DESIGNING his attack on Whiskey Charlie's tail section, Connie had made her way aft. She could see why Lucky had appeared in the cockpit dripping wet. The hot air from the turbine ducts had overwhelmed the two massive air-conditioning units. It was so torrid in the cabins that Connie wondered if the cooling units had not failed entirely and melted down.

The passenger mood all morning had been changing. At first, just after Lucky spoke to them about the midair collision, there were mild outbreaks that ranged from panic to frustration that their travel plans had been altered. These emotions gave way to optimism as Lucky promised everyone that they would be home for dinner. When Tulsa came back into sight, and the order was given to pull up seats in the far aft section and move forward, that seemed to confirm that a positive plan was in action—one that would lead to a landing.

When the cabin started overheating, and the order came through to place the aft seats back on the rails, the passengers saw these conditions as signs that the flight was in serious trouble.

In general everyone remained calm. They did what they were told. But the apprehension level was much higher now. Some people were locked into silence by fear. Others chatted aimlessly to overcome their panic. Still others mumbled prayers. But there was no outward show of hysteria such as wild movements or screams.

The cabins smelled like overcrowded locker rooms after a hard basketball game. When Connie reached the middle crossover galley, Linda grabbed her arm,

"We better PA this. It's getting hotter every second. How long will this last?"

Connie was not as handy with expedient answers, nor as swift as Lucky. She paused and Linda caught the delay.

"I'm not sure. I'll talk to the maintenance guys. Maybe there's a bypass. I'm not sure if we can dump internal heat or not. I'll find out." She was speaking truthfully, but her hesitation unsettled Linda.

"I think you should PA the passengers. Tell them at least we're not burning up."

Before Connie could pick up the PA phone and punch the right button, Alex Anderson reached the galley.

"There's a cutoff bellows in the air duct system," Alex said. "We'll cool this cabin down."

"Ms. Esposito," one of the maintenance men said, "you should come aft, we got this real bad vibrating, the liners are off . . . you can almost feel the problem."

"I will. Let me make a PA first."

"Ladies and gentlemen, this is First Officer Esposito. Up front, as you know, are our chief pilot, Captain Bouchard, and our pilot, Captain Doyle. They are getting ground instructions now on the repairs we're going to make. They're working on this heat problem.

Our air conditioners can't handle the load. The situation is only temporary . . . and although it feels very uncomfortable, the heat is not from a fire. No part of the plane is burning. Try to relax and we should have it cleared up soon."

Connie slammed the phone back on the hook. She knew she wasn't convincing.

Alex tugged at her arm, and they moved along the aisle. She saw the stark looks on the wet faces of the passengers as they eyed her, searching for a slight smile, the kind Lucky wore when he had to. Her smiles were weak and phony; Connie knew it. She kept nodding up and down as if to say, yes, yes, yes, it's going to be all right. That was a hard message to deliver even with facial expressions. Connie was beginning to seriously doubt their lives could be saved. Maybe it was the heat; maybe her exhaustion; or maybe that wide-eyed, terrified look on the faces of the passengers.

When she reached the aft galley, the sight of the flotsam of eggs and bits of airline pancakes, the partially destroyed galley, the leaking aft toilet, the nauseating odor of raw sewage slopping around under them turned her stomach, and she was assailed with a terrible feeling of defeat.

"Feel this, Connie," Alex said. "Here, you can sense what's happening."

It was blazing hot in the galley area—about 108 degrees. But when she touched the bare frames they were icy, the temperature contrast rattled her more. "Cold as hell," she said.

"That's the slipstream racing along the outer skin. Wind chill factor's got to be seventy below. Feel that vibration? Those frames are yanking."

Connie held the frame with one hand, and the long strip that held them together, the top hat stringers and the clips. "I feel the vibrations. I guess I sense the torsion. Is that what you mean?"

"Yeah, there's definite torsion on those stringers and frames. They're deforming," Alex said. "We're coming apart."

Connie agreed with a nod, but she didn't know if she really felt it or whether it was the dismal report from Bristol that the engine vibrations and the loads exerted by the up elevators were literally wresting the aircraft into two pieces.

"Damn it," she said to herself, "this isn't like being killed in an air crash. That's fast and merciful. This is slow death by torture."

Standing in the slopping flow of eggs and sewage, Connie continued to hold her hand on the vibrating frame. Two I.A. maintenance men were also feeling the jet's anatomy. Life or death would be decided in that section of the aircraft. "The vibrations are down!" one of them said suddenly. Connie felt the stringers, the long strips of alloy that held one frame to the next.

Then Alex cried, "He's got the nose down! The turbines are quieter. Pressure ratio's been cut back."

Connie looked up the aisle. Alex was right. She could see that it had leveled out somewhat. And the scream of the turbines was now calmed to a loud purr.

It was then that Connie had picked up the phone and called the cockpit only to hear Lucky playfully saying that it was a "little fiddling of this and that."

"He had to have taken the pressure off those flippers," Alex, a former B–29 pilot, theorized. He was at the windows, where he could see the aft horizontal tail section. He pointed. "Look at that."

Connie moved to the window. "Christ," she cried out. "The elevators are full of holes."

"Hey, Ms. Esposito. Come here, please," a maintenance man said. He pointed to part of the jet's bare frame once more. She felt the stringers. "See, the vibrations are way off now. How did he reduce the thrust?"

"I don't know yet."

She turned and raced forward. A few seconds later Connie burst into the cockpit. Lucky was slouched in his seat. She saw the smirk on his face. He had pulled one off: She knew the look so well. Connie planted a kiss on his wet neck, then on his lips.

"You tricky bastard! I saw what you did."

"Who told you?"

"Alex pointed out those elevators. How did they get holes in them?"

"I ordered the chopper to open fire."

She looked at André, hoping for a response. He smiled faintly. "It was magic." His voice slurred.

Connie wiped her face of beaded sweat, the confluence of cabin heat and fear. Then she slipped into the right-hand seat and shook her head, grinning.

"Well, Lucky, tell you something. I loved you dearly when you were only half bonkers. Now you've slipped *all* your marbles, and so brilliantly."

"But losing my marbles worked," he said proudly.

Lucky punched up the engine condition on the glass panel. Each turbine valve was in the pea-green mode, normal.

But we're still climbing and the tanks are being sucked dry. "What next?"

"Well, I've ordered the army to call for an Air Force tanker. I'm going to pump water ballast down into the forward cargo compartment."

"But I thought adding weight up here would only snap this jet in half."

"It might. But I'm going to beef up the frames with doublers and cross trusses."

Connie looked at the digital clock on the panel.

11:16 A.M. CST (Over TULSA COUNTY)

Lucky had bought them time by taking pressure off the elevators, but, as everyone else had warned him, there wasn't time to rebuild the aft end structure. Foreboding gripped her. There was no way to carry out exotic plans in the minutes left. Connie resigned herself that the end was coming, but she didn't dare show it in her face. Lucky was still clinging to impossible dreams, and she wasn't about to smother his continuing hope, as futile as it appeared to be at that point.

5:18 P.M. GMT (BRISTOL)

•

11:18 A.M. CST (TULSA)

TIME BEGAN TO GRIND ON Ian's nerves. In his heart and head were conflicting emotions. Ian was basically in the same tradition as Lucky Doyle; he was a hands-on, practical man. Usually he left the vast and complicated solutions to Henry and his design-by-computer boys.

The chairman tried to comfort Lou Walters, whose wife had called from Tulsa saying that a cousin she didn't know too well was thought to be aboard the flight. The woman was hysterical; her demand for hopeful answers had only compounded Lou's sense of dread.

"Lou, I'm going outside for a walk. You okay?" Ian asked.

"Guess so. Think those engineers are going to do it?"

"Don't know. Sally, on the main switchboard, said we were getting fifty calls a minute from all over the world offering possible solutions."

"Who should we believe?" Lou asked tossing his hands in the air in desperation.

"Want to know the truth?"

"Of course."

"I just don't know. Nothing like this has ever happened before." With that, Ian moved toward another door which led to the hall and downstairs. "Just need some air, Lou. I'll be on the path down to the first gatehouse. If something comes up, ring me."

Ian was glad that he had grabbed his rumpled coat. As soon as he was outside, he found that the three executive buildings were shrouded in a chilling fog that had tumbled in from the Bristol Channel, not an unusual condition for the last winter weeks in the west of England.

As he ambled away down the cobblestone path, Ian happened to turn around and look back. There were covered walkways between the three buildings so that the engineers could bring their tracings to the main building in bad weather.

When he was a boy, Ian remembered his visits to the works during World War II. The white-coated engineers didn't walk; they ran along the elevated walkways, underscoring the pressure of the war movement. But long after the hostilities, Ian also recalled how the engineers began to amble as the company shifted production to airliners, for which the timetable was no longer so tight.

On this chilly evening, the "white coats" were running again. They were soft-edged in the darkening fog, and their coats flew back as if they were ghosts being chased.

Ian looked the other way. Far in the distance he could see the work lights of the vast apron and beyond were the fabrication hangars, in front of which were rows of completed 270s in their "green states," waiting to be painted in the colors of the airlines who had signed purchase contracts. He wondered whether his 270 babies would ever be delivered now. In every contract there were cancellation clauses, some of which dealt with catastrophic changes in the aircraft's safety record. As Ian continued down the walk, he thought of his father and his grandfather. Both men were flyers, as he was. He recalled his father saying "You can't love aeroplanes a little."

In his father's day almost every man who drew a diagram of an aircraft knew how to fly one. Now he had heard that among the engineers, the brains of the company, only two out of four hundred men and women actually held current flying certificates.

Ian had told everyone in all sections of the Trent Works to stay aboard until released. When he reached the gatehouse, where a crowd of relatives of the Trent workers had gathered, Ian went inside. Old Ned, who had been there when his father ran the Bristol facility, was watching the BBC's second-by-second coverage.

"Oh, sir. Sit down. Been following this bloody thing."

"Terrible break."

"Know how you feel. I've just done up myself some tea, sir, how about a cuppa?"

"Sure," Ian said, slipping into the chair in front of the timekeeper's desk.

"The crowd beyond the gate?" Ian asked, pointing his finger.

"The wives are here waiting to walk their men home when it's over."

The gatekeeper, with his turned-up waxed moustache and his neat appearance could have been a man from the Queen's Own Guard. He had tears in his crinkled eyes.

"It's the worst, sir. I've been listening to it on the telly."

Ian shook his head and turned an ear toward the

BBC Home Service. He knew the aviation expert, a man who had led the Concorde design team for the British end. He was saying: ". . . of course, here we have the direct opposite of the Pan Am terrorist act over Scotland. Heinous groups set out to destroy the Seven-Forty-Seven. What I'm saying is that most aviation tragedies, purposeful or not, begin on the ground, not in the air. And most often it's too late to save the situation."

"That bastard has downed our jet already," Ian cried.

"That's the general consensus, sir. No one gives it a chance . . . as if they're reporting on a funeral. That's the honest but sad truth."

"Do you know what, Ned?" Ian asked.

"No, sir."

"We *will* get that two-seventy down safely. No one will be lost!"

The hunched-up man in the tunic with the double row of brass buttons saluted Ian with a respect a soldier pays to his brave sergeant major. A smile rippled along Ned's mouth.

"Yes, sir, that's the spirit. May I tell them your words at the gate? The folks keep asking me, you know."

"Tell them! Tell them that the word came from me."

Just then the high-handled phone rang with a short burst of bells. Ned answered it.

"Yes, he is with me. Straightaway, sir." He hung up and turned to Ian. "That was the engineering section. You're wanted up there at once, sir."

"Thank you. I'll have that tea with you when we bring that jet down."

Ian ran up the curved cobbles and burst into the conference room. Dr. Kagune was standing there, stiff in his white coat.

"We have people problems," the Indian said.

"Explain that."

"This captain is planning to bring the passengers forward from the last cabin section. When they reach fourteen thousand and depressurize, so that they can bring the cutting tools and generators aboard, Captain Doyle believes that these people are going to pass the masks about in a sane, orderly fashion as the repair work proceeds."

"That's the idea, I guess."

"This pilot does not know the symptoms of the onset of true hypoxia—lack of oxygen. It is terrible, sir. First the peripheral vision grays to the point where only central or tunnel vision is left. And that begins the terror syndrome. Then the fingernails and lips turn blue, cyanosis. The human panic increases. It's manifest in uncontrollable bowel movements."

"My God, man!" Ian said, rubbing the flesh of his neck. "Forget all that business. What's the point of this?"

"Well, sir, when those things happen, there is no order in human behavior. It is a time when man goes down the ladder of evolution, not up. The more he sees the blue lips of his fellow passengers, the deep blue nails, the more he becomes an animal. An animal making raw, desperate efforts to live."

"What will happen?" Ian snapped.

"The strong will fight for the dangling oxygen masks. Women and children and old people will die as the young and powerful take over. You will have a terrible fight among uncontrollable people grabbing for those masks. This is just not my opinion. The human factors engineering section totally agrees. We have talked to other scientists, experts in mass psychology. The plan to supply oxygen on a shared basis will end up killing everyone."

Just as Ian was trying to visualize blue-lipped passengers turning into battling animals, an engineering aide appeared at the door.

"Sir Ian, we have new problems via the computer network line from the Rolls-Royce people."

"We're just finishing this discussion," Ian said looking once more at the rigid Indian doctor.

"Sir, the flight *has* to be down," the engineer said. "I was told to fetch you."

Ian raced toward the door.

"What do you mean, it has to be down?" Ian asked the engineer. "We can see the plane in the air on our television screen."

"We have computer imaging on the network. The turbine people said there was absolute engine failure eight minutes ago."

They ran to the knot of men around the computer terminals. As the group peeled away to make an alley for Ian and Dr. Kagune, one man handed Ian the phone.

"Ian Pryce-Smith here."

The man identified himself as Charles McDufflin, senior engineer for the Rolls-Royce turbine division. "We have network imaging on the tie line. You gave us readouts of compression ratios of those Two-Seventy turbines and the possible consequences of this copilot's cooling methods. The results are on the display."

"I'll look at that," Ian said. "First let me contact the flight." He picked up the other phone, which was open to the tower and to the Whiskey Charlie cockpit. "Lucky, are you reading?"

"I'm on."

"What are the turbine conditions?"

"Still operating."

"Hold on, the Rolls-Royce people say we have trouble."

Ian then signaled for the side-by-side images to be run. Like the pictorial presentation of the jet breaking up from progressive frame failure, this animation revealed a devastating sequence of two explosions of the compressor units, one by constant overheating, the other caused by Connie's alternate spool up and spool down. Both engines became flame red, then white, with vibrating heat, and suddenly the internal parts shook violently. They became one molten white mass that splattered and disappeared from the screen. Ian covered the phone link to Lucky with his hand and talked into the other instrument.

"I just saw that. How accurate is it?"

"The computer cannot be wrong because we programmed the input data."

"It *is* wrong. Those turbines are still operating. I just talked to our Two-Seventy cockpit."

"Sorry, sir. We took the turbine pressure ratios, the exhaust gas temperatures, the time of the spool-up. We see a failure unless something dramatic has changed."

"Stand by," Ian said. He crossed looks with Henry, who appeared puzzled, almost fearful that there had been a vast misprogramming. Ian pondered a second and snapped his fingers as he picked up the phone. He was getting to know the shape, the hidden crevasses of true Doyleism.

"Lucky. Congratulations," Ian said. "You took off some turbine thrust. You agreed that we would work together. When were you going to inform us how you did it?"

"I did wait for your suggestions, Ian, before I jumped in to try something offbeat. We were just about to blow the engines away, and you said there would be a computer or human engineering solution. Finally . . . when none came, I had to act."

"I know what Henry and I promised."

Lucky explained how he'd asked the chopper to fire

into his outboard elevators, making sieves of them so as to let the slipstream surge through.

"Reduction in tail pressure brought the nose down maybe four degrees. With that I could reduce my thrust. That not only cooled the turbines, but we bought us more time to solve things. My flow rate is way down. I won't run dry at twenty after twelve our time, but closer to one-thirty. First I thought we picked up two hours of grace, but it's less than that."

"Good on ya, mate." This from Frank A'hearn, who was monitoring the frequency.

"Fine thinking," Ian admitted. "Jolly good. Now we have other problems that our human factors engineer just told me about."

"Yes, I know roughly what they are. The oxygen supply to the people up front. I was only planning to move them when the aft structure was reinforced."

"Yes. If you shifted weight while the aircraft was nose high, that would bust the equipment in two."

"Frank, this is important. How many more oxygen bottles have you rounded up?"

"Eight. That will give you forty minutes."

"And, Lucky," Ian broke in. "Our Dr. Kagune just told me about the syndrome of hypoxia. It's grim, old man."

"So is freezing to death," Lucky shot back.

"Apparently, the doctor and his staff say that some sort of irrational, ungodly panic will burst out. So you must have the people seated and carry on in some orderly fashion."

"Orderly fashion? I like that word, Ian. I'm all for orderly fashion. You see, the problems are so compounded, I'm afraid there won't be time for equal treatment."

"What are you talking about?" Ian asked, trying to push his thoughts ahead of Lucky's.

"There are going to be rough decisions. There's only so much fuel left. How much time do we give to the passengers? How much to the plane?"

"I'm not certain I understand what you just said."

"Well, we must use the remaining fuel to buy time for repairs. Once we punch the hatch open to take in repair supplies, we can't repressurize the two-seventy. That option is gone."

"Of course."

"So I'm saying that we must conserve the supply of oxygen by our passengers passing the masks around to one another. There must be a sharing."

As Ian heard this idealistic remedy from Doyle, he thought of Dr. Kagune's description of wild, animal-like panic breaking out. A chaos! The final scrambling before the passengers killed themselves!

11:50 A.M. CST (Over TULSA)

•

LUCKY LET THE SILENCE trickle on.

"Have we lost him, Ian?" Henry asked. Just then Lucky spoke.

"I've recalculated. When I brought the nose down, slowed up my climb somewhat, it gave us fuel until after one at this pressure ratio. One-thirty-two Tulsa local is our new fuel exhaustion time unless we bring the nose down farther. I'm reading eleven-fifty, Central Time, so we're looking at one hour and forty-two minutes. As I see it, the first job is to reinforce the aircraft back aft as I've said. I want to hit the mainframe at row one-nineteen with a series of truss braces. We'll need plenty of chrome-moly four, one, three, zero, two-inch pipe. You have that in stock, Frank?"

"We have it, Lucky, plus pipe cutters."

"Good. So I figure on a Warren cross truss to halt the frame collapse. You fellows can refine it, fax it over to Frank. He'll drop it in here with his air-to-air transfer. If my calculations are right, this trussing should halt the structural failure. Now we go back to the second problem. How the hell do we force this big nose down and bleed off altitude? Well, we just changed the tactic a bit. We can't tamper with the ass end, so we pull the same counterbalancing forward. I've called for an Air Force tanker plane. Now get ready. I plan to flood the forward cargo hold with water ballast, just as they would trim up a ship at sea in a storm.

"The forward cargo hold has to be watertight because it's airtight. I want to stretch a hoseline down from the hatch on the top of the cockpit to the forward cargo bulkhead. Now, here're some things I don't know. What kind of a fitting do we need on the hole I'll cut through the bulkhead? Second, how are the trusses fastened? Is it a welding job . . . nuts and bolts . . . is the hose fitting something we fasten with machine screws? Or do we toss in a quick bit of welding there? So what do you fellows think?"

Frank A'hearn appreciated the outrageous nature of the scheme. Water ballast! It was Doyle at his best. Henry and his men felt that the situation was so serious that there was little to be lost by trying anything. Yet Henry felt there was a danger of Doyle's going too far and blowing up the jet.

"That's very interesting, Lucky," Ian said. "Stand by, please, Henry is signaling me. I think he wants to say something."

"That's a terrible risk! There're petrol and other combustible fluids in there. Welding could cause a fire, an explosion. How do we know the fume profile? The flashpoints?"

"Henry, who is our best muckie?"

"A man named Tug Stiles. He's a home aircraft builder."

"Now fetch him quick. Have your structural man design a cross trussing for Lucky."

Ian returned to the phone. "Lucky, Henry is going to design a bracing for your aft main mainframe so we can halt the structural failure. In the meantime, I'm getting one of our production engineers up here to discuss things with you."

Frank A'hearn understood the significance of Ian's suggestion. The Aussie had had no idea of the engineering caste system at Trent, or even the word "muckie." Nevertheless, he caught the need for the new voice. He felt better about it.

Three minutes later the door burst open and a huge, brawny man with blotched skin and a fat, pitted nose strode into the room. His head was too big for his wide body, and his hair was stringy and flecked with dandruff. Ian's first impression of Tug Stiles was of his awkward gait, his odd lumbering footsteps that seemed to go out in uncontrolled paths as if his toes were attached to a puppeteer's strings. Tug wore a russet worksuit with ancient grease stains; out of his frayed sleeves hung the meatiest hands that Ian had ever seen: They were wrinkled, scarred and nicked by age and healed cuts. His fingernails were dirty. He was a true English working engineer out of the Midlands: smart, and proud. He appeared like an aging footballer who'd lost too many hard games in his youth.

Henry explained the situation to Tug, and told him what Lucky wanted to do—the nuts and bolts, the welding options. Then he asked the man sharply, "Stiles, do you know how the hell to solve this confounded thing? We're in dreadful trouble." Tug smiled, the grin illuminating his face.

"Don't have to tell me, sir. I'll give yuh a bit of news. Me and me lads gots the answer. Been hearin' the whole thing on the telly downstairs."

Ian tapped the second phone button. "Lucky, Frank, everyone on? We have our best production engineer ready with the answers, I trust. Now I suggest that everyone start copying what Mr. Tug Stiles has to say."

"Go ahead," Lucky said. "We're ready to copy."

"It's yours, Tug," Ian said, holding the phone out for Tug. He shuffled over to the terminal, pulling a half-smoked cigar from his chest pocket. He struck a wooden match on the thick sole of his work boot.

"There's no smoking in the computer section," Henry said.

"Is that a fact, Mr. Gibbons, sir?"

Lou Walters laughed for the first time that morning.

"First of all, Doyle, I admire what the hell yuh did. Yuh think straight," Tug said into the phone.

"What's next?"

"I want yuh to do just what I say. I'm not *suggestin'*, I'm *tellin'* yuh lads how to get that flying machine down good and safe. Tell yuh why. It's the strongest plane in the air. Any other airliner would be in a million pieces by now. I know, 'cause we engineered that structure far beyond the certification requirements. And another thing, if we get her down, we'll have so many orders that we'll lay on two thousand more men. And that airline of yours will operate without an empty seat. Everyone's goin' to realize that they hired the best pilots in the world.

Okay, my commercial is over. Now then, the controlling point is the size of the hatch that you're goin' to pop out. It's twenty-two by thirty inches. Everything has to fit through that opening, with, say, an inch to spare. That's the main constraint. Understood so far?"

"We got it," Frank said.

"Right. Now here's the order of things. First yuh

send down about eight more standard oxygen bottles, the large tank size."

"We have them," Frank cut in, "I was just told that."

"Yuh rig those on the racks under the cockpit . . . so instead of eleven minutes of oxygen delivery, yuh got now thirty minutes. Doyle, forget about pulling those seats off the rails. Put them back. Have everyone seated. I think I heard you're doing that. Now yuh was askin' about bolts or machine screws for the cross pipes? Yuh don't got enough finger space for bolts with gloves on. They're thick, huh?"

"Five ply," Lucky answered. "Frank's Arctic suits are good down to ninety below. By the way, they have to come down first, before the oxygen."

"It'll be almost a hundred-fifty below zero Fahrenheit when that slipstream air comes in. It's goin' to come in like five of your hurricanes. We'll deal with that later. About the waterhose connections: A'hearn, you get on to your fire brigade. Have them take a torch and cut a coupling off those big input fittings, the ones that go from the water supply to the pump system."

"How do I fasten the couplings? With a weld?" Lucky asked.

"No! Don't like weldin' goin' on when you're deliverin' oxygen. Make things easy. Use the pull-type cherry lockbolt. That's the fastest way to tighten up your structure.

"Yuh major problem is the division of yuh time. How much for this . . . how much for that. Not everything can be done."

"That worries me real bad. We can't take enough oxygen aboard. We don't have the manpower or the transfer time. So some things are not going to happen, are they?"

"Of course not."

"Now who's goin' to be in charge here? You, Sir Ian?" Tug asked.

"I'm the chairman of Trent. I'm responsible, so I'm in charge."

"Good. The human factors group should start blockin' out the air flow pressure and temperature comin' in that cabin hatch. And I hope you knew what Doyle was tellin' yuh."

"About the couplings?"

"No, sir. Doyle was tellin' yuh that some people are going to die 'cause there isn't time for everything and everybody. What he's askin' in his own way is a very hellish thing. Which way do we let them go? Which is easiest? A chill-off or death by lack of oxygen."

Ian was miserable at what seemed a heartless approach, but he knew that the production engineer was merely saying it the way it was. Tug was the best of Englishmen, the sort of man who had traded his iron-working tools for a gun when necessary and gone out to fight and often die. The Tugs did knotty jobs without asking too many questions. And they were good at them. Ian, patting Tug Stiles's shoulder in its coarse work suit and smiling, suddenly looked past the muckie to Dr. Kagune standing behind Tug. There was something cold and frightening in the Indian's look.

12:10 P.M. CST (Over TULSA)

●

WHISKEY CHARLIE BEGAN TO represent much more than a critically damaged airliner trying to land while climbing higher and higher every minute. The tragedy became an archetype of everything that was wrong with the new course of civil aviation. It turned into a forum for embittered air travelers who had suffered fare increases, flights canceled, lost luggage, unexplained delays, poor service, and a hundred other complaints not all arbitrary or insubstantial. It was a rare time to be heard because everyone was listening.

"This can't go on," a caller from Atlanta phoned NBC. "Engines fall apart . . . parts of wings and fuselages just rip away . . . anyone can smuggle a plastic bomb on a plane. What the hell is happening?"

Those familiar with aviation, the mute insiders, knew exactly what had happened and why. A wealthy inexperienced pilot had been licensed too quickly. Doug bought a five-ton plane that was much too complex for his level of experience. Then on a day when he should have waited for improved weather conditions, he misused an autopilot that he barely understood. Thus the collision.

High-time pilots and air traffic controllers realized that there were thousands of "squirrels" like Doug threatening the entire airways system. When the public discovered that the controllers at the Tulsa tower could not see the entire field because they lacked ground radar, that rattled the very roots of American aviation. As expected, the initial calls to networks came from aeroengineers, pilots, airframe mechanics, hobbyists, model airplane makers, aviation ditherers, and shouting crackpots. Everyone had a better solution than Lucky Doyle. CBS alone counted four hundred fifty-six calls suggesting that parachutes be dropped into the Whiskey Charlie hatch instead of tools and oxygen.

Airline executives—the real pros, not the Augie Hartmans—snickered at those solutions. They knew that the fear of flying was trivial compared to asking a passenger to put on a parachute and jump out, even when faced with the ultimate alternative of death. After these wild card solutions ran their course, the tone and texture of the phone calls began to take on a solid dimension.

Clearly, an airline consumer revolt was starting.

It was highly emotional and primitive. Nevertheless, the depth and fury of it jarred Washington officials and lawmakers as well as airline executives. This sudden spontaneous grass-roots protest was similar to the rebellion in the movie *Network*, in which Peter Finch implored TV viewers to go to their windows and yell out their feelings. The feeling here was a blend of passenger fear and anger that the nation's aviation policy, or the lack of it, would expose passengers to preventable crashes. The greed of and manipulation by airline officials was also a well-defined target.

Airline authorities knew and understood the boiling

anger. They'd heard it all before. The elite executives were smug, depending on the fact that railroads and buses were no longer alternatives to the nation's business travelers. Then the complacency faded as the phone calls took off in another direction. What should we do about our aviation crisis? A live interview with a leading consumer advocate, shared by all the networks, had a crushing effect. The president stiffened, lawmakers didn't miss a word, and airline executives saw their position seriously threatened.

"What's happened today," the consumer advocate said during the interview in a flat, objective voice, "tells us that there are numerous 'flying squirrels' out there —people flying planes who shouldn't be, and who are a danger to everyone else. It tells us that at least one major airfield—and who knows how many more—is not adequately equipped with radar and other safety devices. And *that* tells us that it's time for a new cabinet post: a highly qualified Secretary of Aviation."

At once calls poured in to the network, suggesting Chuck Yeager, John Glenn and others.

An airline pilot for a major carrier said, "A cabinet secretary or a czar is a must . . . someone we can look up to . . . respect. Right now the system is rotten. I don't fly with the ease that I used to. I'm disgusted. The other pilots I know are confused . . . job-threatened. The flight deck morale slips a bit each year. That's not how big airliners should be flown. What's happening today is a warning. We'd better listen to the message, now!"

The maintenance men also went to their phones. One said, "You really want to know what we do? A lot of us paper the airplane. We make God damned good log entries; progressive maintenance, fixing things. But half of them aren't done. We're supposed to change the tires after so many landings . . . same with the brakes.

We just don't have time for each job. Management says, 'Keep the equipment flying. That's all. Delay whatever repairs you can.' So we write it up to make it look like it's done. The FAA inspector comes and looks at the books. He pats us on the back . . . and says that we're doing great. Know what, we even got a safety award last year. Here's the truth. I got nine widebodies flying up there today with brakes that are papered, tires that are papered. Too many cycles on them. There's some landing gears that are retracting slowly. They're papered. We'll fix them eventually. In the meantime the log says that they already have been fixed. It's a world of neat papers, all in order."

A male flight attendant phoned the Canadian television network to say that he had seen pilots drinking only a few hours before their sign-in time. He also knew five others who kept company with drugs, and that's why he had requested a transfer from flying to ticket writing.

Pete Rosen, by devious means, had procured a copy of Doug Halsey's logbook from the newly widowed Mrs. Halsey. To Pete's amazement, the new log showed only two hundred and sixty hours of total flight time, from the first day Doug climbed into his two-seat trainer until his last business flight before the crash. The log also revealed that Doug was properly licensed. He had a private ticket with both a twin-engine and an instrument rating.

Pete called Mrs. Halsey to ask her where Doug bought the turboprop. She remembered the broker's name at Jones Field, across the Arkansas River from Tulsa. Pete phoned the aircraft broker, who had been watching television all morning. Obviously he had a particular interest in the situation as the one who had sold Doug the sophisticated turboprop. Harrington knew two things. There wasn't one single navigational instrument or electronic device missing from Doug's cockpit. He remembered very well that his client had spent an additional $77,000 for gadgets to enhance safety for the one-man cockpit: weather radar and the latest autopilot with all the features of an airliner. He also realized that Doug was an intelligent man and that he had missed only one question on his written test for his private pilot's license and only two on the much tougher written test to become instrument rated. Doug was trained by an instructor who had 20,000 hours in his book. There was nothing, the broker had told himself all morning, that he had not done or provided for Doug to become a safe, competent pilot. True, the architect's training period had lasted only a limited time—after spending over three hundred thousand dollars to buy the richly appointed turboprop, Doug had wanted his wings fast—but every law and obligation had been fulfilled.

"I have Doug's logbook here in front of me," Pete said.

"I see. How did you pick that up?"

"I have ways. I'm reading here that Halsey had a total of only two hundred and sixty hours in the air. I added the figures at the bottom of each page."

"Halsey was perfectly legal to fly today. He had the right licenses and a damned good plane. I sold him a solid package, a real low-time turboprop that had always been hangared, owned by a corporation with a top pilot and a qualified right seater. Those guys ran a good operation. Professional all the way. No shortcuts."

"You said a right seater. A copilot?"

"That's what they had. Those boys flew the equipment in here and turned it over to me."

"But Doug flew the plane alone."

"Yeah. The equipment is under the twelve thousand, five-hundred-weight rule, not a pure jet, so you don't need a type certificate or a copilot. That's the FAA rules. I didn't make them."

"But didn't you feel strange about putting a new pilot into that sort of plane? Jeez, it was a small airliner!"

"My business is to sell aircraft. He asked for the best instructor I could find. I got him that."

"Did you suggest a copilot until he got used to things?"

"He told me he wanted to fly alone. The plane was certified for a one-man cockpit. We upgraded his autopilot. It was what they call a flight director. . . Lessens the cockpit work load. Doug even had a moving map. Could see where he was every second."

"Who was his instructor . . . The same man all the way through?"

"The same man. Good fellow. Used to fly for American. He told me that Doug was a sensible pilot. Cautious about things. I knew that because Doug always talked about safety."

"Didn't work, did it?"

"Not for him. It's real terrible. Worst I ever heard. Guess Doug had it on the autopilot when he should have been flying himself."

"Sounds like it. When he was training, do you know if they went into actual cloud conditions, or did they just use the hood to simulate clouds?"

"You don't have to fly in the clouds to become an instrument pilot."

The logic of it was missing. How would a student build confidence to tackle clouds when he never flew in real clouds during his training? Pete asked himself.

"Who was the FAA examiner?"

"There wasn't an FAA man . . . just a designated examiner."

"Who was that?" Pete asked.

"The instructor."

"Are you telling me that the man you hired to teach Doug Halsey was the same guy who signed him off?"

"Yeah. There's nothing wrong about that. It's legal. He went by the book."

"It seems to me that the book is terribly wrong."

"Maybe it is. But as I told you, Mr. Rosen, I didn't write the thing. I just obey it."

"But this collision this morning has to have an effect on you and our entire aviation policy and procedures."

"Of course it does. I feel terrible about it. But, Mr. Rosen, I've sat here with my stomach aching all morning trying to ask myself, how could it have been prevented? I knew Doug. I cared about his safety and that Trent up there is Tulsa-based. So I'm right in the middle of this tragedy. Don't think I'm unaffected or detached. Hell, no. If I sound that way, it's not because I'm trying to get out of anything or cover up for something I did wrong."

"I'm sorry," Pete said slowly, realizing that he was giving Harrington the impression that the broker was a link in the events that caused the collision. But Pete felt that the broker was being completely open. He had one more question.

"Mr. Harrington, in second-guessing this air-to-air crash, what was missing that could have stopped this from happening?"

"On the equipment or human side?"

"Both."

"I've thought about that ever since I tuned in the TV this morning. I tried to piece together the probable cause."

"Were you able to come up with answers?"

"I think so. I've talked to maybe fifteen people connected with aviation this morning. Here's the consensus.

The tower should have had ground radar. Then both Doug's aircraft and the Trent should have had collision avoidance equipment."

"Is that available?"

"In a limited way. It will be on all airliners in a few years, but the technology was there perhaps five years ago. The system works."

"Then why don't all airliners have it?"

"It's not cheap, Mr. Rosen. And civil aviation is a giant game of politics and bureaucratic manipulating. Safety costs money. It cuts down profits . . . makes the government deficit look worse than it is."

"So that crash could have been avoided if they had had one or both pieces of equipment?"

"Absolutely."

"What did Doug do wrong?" Pete asked.

"He took off."

"Did he break flight rules?"

"No. That's the sad point. We taught Doug everything to equip him to handle that plane like a pro. Still, he was a newcomer to aviation. What we can't teach is judgment, Mr. Rosen. Doug should have just looked out of the window and said, 'I think I'll wait an hour or two until things improve.' "

"Then the rules for large aircraft operations are too weak?"

"Much too weak."

"Give me specifics for my story."

"Here's just one example. Under the Federal Air Regulations, Part Six-One-point-Five-Five that deals with the second in command of a large aircraft. The copilot doesn't have to be type-rated in the equipment —doesn't even have to have a commercial pilot rating. All the person needs is a private ticket with an instrument rating, and to be familiar with the aircraft, and to make three takeoffs and landings to a full stop. So under

U.S. law you can have an eighteen-year-old with around two hundred hours of flying time who can act as a copilot of any big jet airliner, a seven-forty-seven in fact. That's one of the most lenient laws of any country."

Pete Rosen was shocked.

"Does that happen?"

"No. The airlines wouldn't hire such a person. They could, but they have much higher standards of experience."

"I have a deadline, Mr. Harrington. So I have to sign off here, but I'm shocked at what you tell me."

"You should be. Everything that happened today or is going to happen is preventable. Print that."

"Last thing. Do you think this Doyle will pull them out?"

"I don't think so. I'm sorry. But facts are facts."

12:16 P.M. CST
(Over TULSA)

LUCKY CALLED AFT, TELLING Alex and the maintenance people to get the fire axes. The liners had to be ripped off in the area where they needed to truss the collapsing frames.

Confident once again that he had things covered, Lucky reached into his second flight bag and took out a fresh white shirt. He dug further into his flight bag for a shaving kit and left the cockpit.

André shot a quick look at Connie, who hadn't stirred. When she didn't react, the chief pilot flung off his restraining shoulder belts and followed Lucky out to the lavatory on the left side of the bunk area.

"What are you doing, Lucky?"

"What does it look like, André? I'm going to shave, clean up, and change my shirt."

"Why?"

"Because I always do on these flights. At about twelve o'clock, when we get into Chicago, I use the large lavatory off the operations lounge, shave and change into a fresh shirt. Then Connie and I have lunch in the

Tower Club. Usually a good lunch, too. What's wrong with that?"

André was pop-eyed.

"This isn't Chicago, if you haven't noticed."

"I know that, André. You don't have to remind me. We're over Tulsa making very slow circles. I always clean up about this time, so I'm doing it here instead of O'Hare."

"Shouldn't you be aft with the work crew?"

"I'm going there in a few minutes. I want them to see me looking together. The visual image of authority is important, André. It's the whole thing. Once they see the skipper losing it, you have problems. How I look sends a direct message."

"Like what?"

"It tells them I'm not concerned, not going gaga."

"But you *are* concerned, aren't you? You know what's happening, right?"

"Of course," Lucky said as he stripped off his soiled shirt and ran the warm water for his shave.

"Just wanted to make sure. You seem so casual."

"André, underneath I'm as stretched as anyone. But you heard me. Did I offer a solution or not?"

"You did."

"What do you think of it?"

"Don't know."

"Come on. You're the chief pilot, a former fighter ace, whatever. You must have some feeling. Do you understand my approach?"

"It's hard to put together."

"What is it that you don't understand? We're trussing the cabin frames and stringers to stop the creeping failure. Do you get that much?"

"Yes. Of course."

"After that we'll take on a load of water from the tanker plane into our forward cargo compartment as ballast to pull our nose down. Lowering our nose will give us more air time as we come back on thrust. Then on final, at the precise moment, I'll use my trim to pitch the nose up for the landing. That should give us our flare out to set this bird down nicely."

Lucky came out with a white beard of shaving cream on his face. He leaned into the cockpit. Connie turned around and winked, not affected by Lucky's pause for shaving. She knew that Lucky would not abandon that routine now: He did things by design, what he deeply felt was right for his façade, for *his* way of cockpit management and problem solving. She also knew Lucky's minor quirk of never flying a plane without a tie. He had hundreds of pictures of early airmen on his walls; under each leather jacket they wore a shirt and tie. One of Lucky's memorabilia pictures showed Igor Sikorsky's May, 1940 helicopter flight in his VS-300. He not only took off in a shirt and tie, he wore a dark business suit with a dark hat. To Lucky that was genuine class.

After checking the cockpit, Lucky returned to the lavatory to finish his self-polishing job.

The emotional damage, the attrition of both time and the airport slipping away from them, was rapidly eroding passenger confidence. The cocksure businessmen in first class who had come on board immaculately turned out and who had continued to tap buttons and write on their yellow pads for a long time after the collision, were now disheveled from the forty minutes of blazing hot air pouring from the air ducts. The seats were being replaced on their rails; to the passengers, that revealed indecision, which was further unsettling.

As Lucky returned to the cabins looking like a new man to talk with his work crew, he had to thread his way through a forest of outstretched arms and anxious questions. His shaped-up face and shirt did not temper the rising concerns.

"We still going to make this, Captain?"

"How we doing?"

"We're getting there," Lucky said with a fresh smile.

When he reached the first galley, Lucky signaled for the men to halt their work. Along with the flight attendants, he gathered Alex and his work crew around him.

"Bristol likes my new plan. I'm talking to the right guy at last. But I have to tell you that there're risks working in temperatures worse than those in the Arctic. You might lose toes or feet, or even your lives if the cold drops your body temperature by twenty degrees."

"We don't have much choice, Lucky," Alex said.

"Not much. If we don't pull the nose down, then we're all going in the fast way. So, if any man wants to sit up there with the passengers, go ahead. No problem. I shouldn't be asking any of you to do something that the others aren't doing."

As Lucky spoke, he caught sight of the young flight attendants hovering about Linda Glen, their eyes wide, as if she were the experienced symbol of protection. The mother figure. Lucky could see her open fright. This was the first time that he had mentioned losing limbs. The word *death* shook her. Why was she so shocked? Lucky asked himself. What did Linda think would happen when they punched out an escape hatch?

"Linda, do you know what happens when you open a hatch at about fifteen thousand feet?"

"Not exactly. The oxygen masks come down."

"Yes. But let me run you people through this so we understand what we're facing. The aircraft is pressurized now. This means that the pressure per square inch inside here is about what you would have at an altitude of around six thousand feet. But the outside air has much less pressure. The higher we climb, the more the pressure drops. If we didn't equalize the pressure between the inside and the outside, a hurricane of air would rush out. Very dangerous."

"And the outside air wouldn't have much oxygen." Linda added.

"That's the misconception. The ratio of oxygen, about twenty one percent, to nitrogen, remains the same up to about seventy thousand feet."

"Then why do we drop the masks in an emergency?"

"Because the air pressure has dropped at high altitudes. The constant water vapor pressure in the lungs takes a much bigger bite out of the available air pressure. So the lungs need supplemental oxygen to clear the carbon dioxide out of the blood. That's why the masks come down. It's not the lack of oxygen outside at high altitudes, it's the lack of pressure on the lung sacs. Does that make sense?"

"Yes. But what will happen when the hatch is opened? What will it be like?"

"A glacial whirlwind will slice in here. Temperatures fifty to seventy degrees below zero. The cabin temperature will drop unbelievably fast. Our trouble is this. We won't have enough emergency oxygen. Usually, when a decompression happens, we dive for lower altitudes. But today with the elevators jammed, we can't dive until we restress the aft end of the plane and pump water ballast up forward."

Lucky could see that those standing around him in the galley understood why oxygen was needed at high altitudes without a cabin being pressurized. What was not understood was the total impact of what was coming, the horror wasn't understood. Some people would have proper protection, most wouldn't. There wasn't enough emergency bottled oxygen for everyone; people would die. Lucky was trying to tell Bristol that, hoping that they would offer the solution he had been waiting for all morning—that Tug Stiles or somebody would get back to him and say, "We got it. There's a way we won't lose anyone."

Lucky returned to the moment and bellowed like a hardened field marshall. "Let's move it!

Lucky walked over and picked up the galley phone.

"Connie, that little portable transmitter. I don't want everyone hearing all this. Work them on three four six. See if we can patch England through on that frequency. We're down to bad stuff here," he whispered.

"I think I know what you mean," she said.

Lucky then made his way back through the empty last coach section. He felt the exposed frames and stringers in the litter of the last galley. The stench was stronger now, and he seemed to feel the vibrations without even touching the guts of the 270. When he did touch the icy structure, he was alarmed. Now it seemed to be moving in two directions. The throbbing was running lengthwise as well as surging up and down the frames. He turned and saw Alex Anderson standing behind him.

"Didn't see you, Alex. You feel something different back here?"

"I picked it up before."

"What the hell do you think is happening?"

"I think the elevators are pulling one way, thrust another, and I smell jet fuel. The crash broke the APU fuel tank back there."

"Let's get up to the cockpit."

The two threaded their way up front through the passengers and their questions that Lucky acknowledged with short meaningless phrases. When they entered the cockpit, Connie was speaking into the emergency transmitter.

"They can give us a patch, Lucky. What's the new problem?" she asked, seeing him slump down in his seat.

"Things are going belly-up. There're additional vibrations back by the aft galley for one thing. Passenger morale is further down than ever. Is the patch through?"

"Yes, the tower has the military frequency."

"Lucky, that transmitter is going to give out. There's no recharger up here with us. I'd go back on the other frequency, so we can save that one in case of a real emergency," André said, making his first helpful comment of the dreadful day.

"What do you think, Alex?"

"I agree."

"We'll tell them to go back on the departure frequency," Lucky said. "I don't know what I was hiding anyhow. There's no sense anymore. The trouble here is new problems all the time, and time is what we don't have."

6:20 P.M. GMT (BRISTOL)

•

————IN BRISTOL THE MAIN WORK was now centered on how many pounds of water had to be pumped into the forward cargo compartment, the profile of the chill factor, and the air pressure that would surge into the 270 cabin, displacing the turbine heat, when the escape hatch was opened.

Ian was still haunted by the tragic look he had seen on Dr. Kagune's face when he was called upstairs. Kagune's office was where the engineers who worked on human factors carried out their odd experiments, in SHM, Spatial-Human-Management, or how much room does it take for a fat woman with arthritis to move about in an aircraft lavatory?

As soon as the chairman entered the department, Dr. Kagune pointed to his office. They entered and closed the door. Ian was apprehensive; he sensed what was coming, what had to be said and decided.

"You have a very forbidding look on your face, Dr. Kagune—or should I say 'foreboding'?"

"True. We are going to be faced with deadly decisions, Sir Ian. I can give you alternatives, but it is you, sir, who must decide who lives and who dies aboard the jet."

"Do we have that much predictability?" Ian asked, not really wanting to know.

"That Doyle fellow is rather keen, like Stiles. He was asking you for the death sequence. Did you know that? Did you catch the very implications of it?"

"Yes, he said they did not have time for everything."

"He was asking you how to handle things. He expects you to choose the manner of death."

"You're mad!" Ian burst out.

Dr. Kagune punched up his computer terminal. The inside display of the aircraft began to form, with each passenger represented by a red cube.

"Before I show you the death sequence . . ."

"Must we talk in those awful terms, Dr. Kagune?"

"Yes, we must. Because we have been forced to take on the role of executioners and humanitarians at the same time, a frightful cross-duty, I'm afraid. This chap Doyle has a fast mind for practical things, like this pumping water aboard, but he has only a scarce knowledge of physiological effects and predictions. He was trying to tell you that. Shall I explain where we are, sir? If you would rather not hear it or take part, I shall fully understand. But you must give me the authority with full immunity."

Ian knew he had to hear it and accept the total responsibility, as hard as it was. He nodded.

"I'm sorry to confront you with such brutal realities, but we must bring that aircraft down safely for a hundred reasons. Saving lives is the prime motivation, of course."

"Just get on with it quickly, Dr. Kagune, please."

"Hypoxia is the lack of sufficient oxygen to keep the brain and other body tissues functioning properly.

Our greatest difficulty is the wide variation with respect to hypoxia's susceptibility. There are many unknowns. Carbon monoxide from smoking, certain drugs, alcohol, extreme heat or cold, plus anxiety increase the body's demand for oxygen. Age is a factor. Some people will experience deterioration at ten thousand feet, others at sixteen thousand. So there are too many unknowns to predict behavior and physiological tolerance. We are left rather meandering about in the darkness. The same is not true for hypothermia. We can plot, almost in precise curves, what each degree of body temperature drop will do. The death sequence is quite predictable, whereas hypoxia still remains something of a mystery."

Dr. Kagune rose to his feet and dimmed the light so that they could view the screen. Ian stood, also moving away from the terminal, but really wishing to scramble from the office. The doctor pressed a button to run the death-by-freezing program. A flow of blue rushed along the side of the 270.

"The air outside the plane is about ninety below zero, with a speed of one hundred and sixty miles an hour. The cabin temperature will be raised to one hundred and fifteen as a heat barrier; even this will fall hastily, as you shall see. The wind-chill factor is somewhere near one hundred and fifty below zero. Now the cockpit escape hatch is off after the aircraft has been depressurized. Even the closed doors will not seal off that much of the icy inflow of air. The blue air rushes in as the clock on the bottom of the image ticks off the time passage. Now in two minutes the cabin temperature drops to ninety. And look what happens in eleven minutes. It is five below in the cabin and dropping five degrees a minute. The cold has become our killer. See how the color of the cubes change from red to pink? The passengers are feeling the initial stages of frostbite. The pink goes to yellow. The acute stages. They desperately suck at their oxygen masks. Now the light blue begins. Notice how fast it darkens. Their pain is unbearable. In nineteen minutes you are looking at three hundred dead people. But before that happens, we predict a mass panic, something on the order of what I told you before. Some will leave their seats and rush for the men who are wearing their thermal suits transferred from the rescue plane, the old DC-six. These men will represent the foe, in a way. Those suits might be ripped off. There will be mass terror. This is not the way to terminate the passengers who are too old or weak to live."

Dr. Kagune spoke with dispatch and distance, as if he were referring not to human lives but merely to animals put up to die in an experiment to determine acceptable killing: the most effective manner.

"I don't understand how the people will die. The hatch will be plugged after the supplies are taken on. So the temperature will go up again. But pressurization will never be regained. Supplemental oxygen will be vital."

"True. What is likely to happen is this. There is little pain associated with the lack of oxygen. As we said, the masks will have to be shared. Doyle told us that there isn't enough oxygen to go around. As the passengers see their nails go blue, they will associate that with freezing to death because they are experiencing the pain of a sudden, acute drop in temperature.

"As I said before, Sir Ian, the human instinct for survival takes over. The masks will not be passed around in an orderly way. Panic will prevail. Panic will lead to death. They will die from the lack of oxygen. But the passengers will think they are freezing to death. They *are* slowly freezing, but the critical element is oxygen, the lack of it. That will be the prime killer. Some heart attacks, some violence by the strong trying to rip the thermal suits off the work crew, but that will not account for the major cause of death. I am sorry, sir, to talk in these objective terms. I couldn't feel more terrified by what is about to happen; still, sir, it is my duty to tell you the probable sequence of events so we can make it easier on the three hundred or so passengers up there."

"Yes. I understand. It's no easier for you to speak this way than it is for me to hear it. Ghastly!"

"Very few compassionate people have ever been faced with such decisions, sir.

"Would you step out to our mock-up lab? I will show you a much surer solution. More humane."

Ian followed Dr. Kagune to a small room off the main Human Factors Laboratory. Inside was a duplicate section of the 270 flight deck and the bunk area built on two levels. This was constructed with precise accuracy so that they could arrange the equipment racks below the cockpit without wasting space.

"I never thought I would use this mock-up to arrive at a manageable death program," the doctor said.

For the first time, Ian noticed a flash of humanity behind the Indian's dark, inscrutable eyes.

"For the dreadful reasons we saw on the computer imaging—how mass hysteria could very well bring the whole flight down—I have devised another plan that is safer and far less painful. Notice up there. The escape hatch over the cockpit. I recommend that we release that one.

"Doyle may have decided that already."

"What's the reasoning behind that idea?" Ian asked.

"Several reasons. They can drop the tether rope and water hose in much more easily. The opening is larger. It is a straight drop. You see, it's a much shorter distance to the oxygen racks directly below. It will save many footsteps. More important, we don't chill off the passengers quite so hastily. The air blast enters where the men are wearing protective gear, after they break open the first transfer net. We begin oxygen delivery in a relatively warm cabin. There are two doors separating the inflow of icy air from the cabin. The men go aft and truss up the frames in question. Then the work crew retreats behind the door to the bunk area, and they block it with cross pipes so that it won't be bashed down. Once we deliver the water ballast to the cargo compartment, we take a door that has been pried off the galley buffet, and with a hydraulic jack pushing up on a pipe with a plate welded on each end, we press this against the opening. But don't think we have repressurized. That's impossible. Unfortunately, we are delivering less and less oxygen. As I see it, there will be only twenty minutes of minimum flow until the craft gets down into the fourteen thousand feet area, where some passengers will recover."

"How many might be lost?"

"We are predicting over a hundred deaths, sir. The work crew and the flight deck people will live."

"And the cabin attendants?"

"They will probably be sacrificed."

"Who will know this?"

"Only us."

"We must tell Doyle."

"Then you are informing the world of our plan."

"Is it really murder?" Ian asked.

"Call it necessary elimination. Triage. The oldest of nature's laws, sir. The sacrifice of some so that others may live. It will be understood. There is no culpability. We will have saved many, many lives."

Ian shook his head. He was drenched in sweat. Dr. Kagune crossed to him and put his arm over the chairman's shoulders.

"You should not bear the responsibility. If this does come out, sir, I will say that it was my design. My death program. But it is a life-saving idea. If we let a panic develop, no one will live."

It took Ian a moment to grasp his senses. "Appalling."

"But necessary. We must take a firm grip on the survival program."

"How?"

"I was coming to that. You see the model here. There are two sets of pipes coming off the oxygen bottle system, but the model doesn't show it. Anyhow, the larger of the two pipes feeds the cockpit, bunk area, first class and two of the coach sections. The smaller but longer oxygen line feeds the far aft coach section. By turning this red valve, the entire oxygen supply is fed to the forward areas."

"And the last coach section has *no* oxygen supply?"

"That is was I am saying. Those sitting there will be just breathing ram air from the vent system."

"But they'll think they're getting oxygen when they're not."

"That's about it."

"They will die?"

"Correct, Sir Ian. But it will be fast and not too painful. I doubt whether we will see a panic."

"Even as their lips go blue?"

"They will start to pass out before they can exert physical force. Remember, it is the old and the ill who are sitting there, not the young and strong."

"Who decides?"

"Doyle."

"Does he know he's making life and death decisions?"

"No. A person has only so much emotional and physical stamina. He has his hands full getting the nose down, halting the structural problems. He could not take this on in addition to his other complex duties. Those he created for himself."

Ian was shocked at how objectively, how coolly he was speaking with the engineer, as if they were discussing something as casual as when to plant the spring flowers or to clip border grass.

"Do you think Doyle is dumb enough to buy this? I find the man rather keen. The same sort of expedient, basic thinker that Stiles is."

"Yes, I do believe we have two of the same kind there. But to fully address your question, sir, we will tell Doyle that he must select the oldest passengers, those with illness, and seat them in the very far aft of the plane so they are the warmest. Remember, we are now going to direct Doyle to open the cockpit escape hatch, not the one over the wing. It will make perfect sense to the man and to the cabin attendants."

"But he'll realize that no oxygen will reach the last cabin."

"Not at all, sir. I have another scheme for that one. I will direct the first officer, Ms. Esposito, to go aft with Captain Doyle. Left in the cockpit is the chief pilot, this Bouchard gentleman who doesn't appear to be a strong leader."

"That's so. Lou Walters said he hasn't actually flown for many years."

"Then we will use him to turn the valve. I will get on the wireless patch as the flight surgeon. Make sure to tell Doyle that's who I am, the doctor who saves people, if you will. At the proper moment I will ask the chief pilot to go down and turn the red check valve all the way to the left."

"So he is the executioner without knowing it?"

"If you choose to look at it that way, yes. He will carry out the plan. There is no other way. I showed you the alternatives. You either lose less than half of the passengers or all of them, to be perfectly blunt."

"How many people up here know this?"

"You and I, sir. I do not confide in my engineers on matters such as this."

Ian, to stall his throbbing headache and his pervasive fears, began to pace up and down on the green plastic-tiled floor. He shot somber glances toward the full scale model: It had a theatrical quality, like a high priced movie set, for even the muted lights of the glass cockpit glowed with richly hued colors. The assembly was so real that Ian thought he could climb in and take off. He pictured Lucky and the others filling the plush overstuffed seats.

"Sir Ian, are you all right? You seem ill," Dr. Kagune was asking.

"I'm sorry."

"I regret, sir, that I had to tell you of this plan to save people. I wish you would consider it as such, not as a scheme for killing. One can see a glass as half-empty or half-full, as they say. We are taking the half-full side. If we don't, there will be no water at all in the glass. No one will live even if they somehow land safely."

"I don't think this Doyle can carry out what he plans. There isn't time," Ian said.

"Quite right. We have been timing functions up here, and frankly there is too much going against him for a solution. Of course, I hope I am in error. I never wished to be so wrong."

"What is your impression of this man?" Ian asked.

"He's perplexed our entire department. We have twenty-nine aviation behavioral scientists up here with advanced degrees and heavy experience. This Doyle has them whipped."

"Are you speaking in negatives, Dr. Kagune?"

"Doyle, on the surface, has poor flight habits," Kagune replied. "He's everything a pilot should not be. For instance, he is antiauthority, impulsive, invincible in his own mind, macho, and maybe even deluded that he can bring this flight down. Yet, with all that's going against him, he seems to function in strange ways. He might be telling us that we should return to basics, that the glass cockpit must be taken with a huge grain of salt. What have all those electronic systems done for us today? Nothing. The same is true for our supercomputer. It's stalled and helpless. To me Doyle is proving that common sense is not that common. He has assumed new pilot roles."

"Are they valid?" Ian asked.

"I can't say. If the plane crashes, his actions will be studied for years. If he lands the Two-Seventy, I hope you give us the opportunity to study this man's mind for years."

"His heart, too," Ian retorted.

The phone rang. "Dr. Kagune here."

"This is Stiles. Got Doyle on the other line . . . wants to know if we should serve the passengers a small lunch. Is the chairman with yuh?"

"He is. Just a minute."

Dr. Kagune walked away from the phone, taking Ian by the arm.

"It's Doyle. They're serving the passengers a modified lunch. I'd suggest that we tell him now."

"What?"

"The switch in plans. Why we want certain people in the far aft section."

"Who tells him that?" Ian asked with a faltering voice.

"I will, sir. I'll take the responsibility, as I offered."

Ian felt a renewal of strength. He went to the phone quickly.

"Lucky, this is Ian. You're serving lunch?"

"It'll be just a few things to eat. Whatever we have in the center galley."

"Good. Now, Lucky, I think you said before that there isn't time for everything. The implication was that some of the passengers might not make it. But you promised that they would be home for dinner."

"Yes, but that was before I knew that we had acute structural problems."

"Of course. Well, I came upstairs to our Human Factors Laboratory. That's where the flight surgeons are. A most compassionate Indian doctor from Calcutta is in charge of this department. Dr. Kagune thinks he has a way of saving everyone if you and Stiles can keep that aircraft together."

"We have some new vibrations aft, but I have a standby plan and the choppers are all around me now. The tanker plane is about to take off from Oklahoma City."

Ian could sense the new brightness in Lucky's voice.

"Excellent."

"Stand by."

Ian handed the phone to Dr. Kagune, wondering how well and how easily Lucky would adopt the doctor's death scenario—what he'd know of it.

"Hello there, Captain Doyle."

"Hello, Doctor," Lucky answered.

"Fine work so far, Lucky. Shooting bullets through your elevators. The water ballast. Keen thinking."

"Thank you, Doctor."

"Now my department might have found a way to bring everyone down. First, we're showing a very poor survival rate as soon as you open that midsection hatch. You sensed that too, because you asked us to work out temperature gradients."

"Right. I've flown in the Arctic for years."

"That's what I understand. So you're sensitive to

vast temperature drops once the aircraft works above sixteen thousand or so. Now I'm going to offer you an alternative. Would you agree, sir, that the farther one is away from the slipstream, the warmer it will be?"

"Of course," Lucky said.

"Very well. I suggest that you pop the hatch over the cockpit."

"I was thinking about that all the time."

"Good. You'll have a much shorter route to the oxygen bottle storage area. And the tanker plane will be able to force the water nozzle down quicker. Most important, there will be two doors blocking the direct inflow of frigid air to the cabins. They won't be airtight by any means, but we show an acceptable pattern of temperature in the cabins. Some hard chill up forward in first class, but as we move aft, it becomes much warmer. Now, since you are using water ballast as your primary tool for gravity displacement, where the people sit becomes of little importance. Do you agree, Captain?"

"Yes. Everything you've said so far makes sense. The weight of the water replaces my original idea of moving passengers."

"Glad we agree. Then, sir, what we need to do is to protect the old folks and those who are ill. You must make a humanitarian selection. Seat the ones in greatest danger toward the rear where it will be warmest. That will save them."

Ian buried his head in his hands.

"The chairman and I have talked about this."

Ian was handed the phone. He had to work through the tight dryness in his throat.

"Yes, Lucky. These men up here have found the answer, I believe. And there is one more feature to the forward hatch idea. As soon as you take on the water ballast, Dr. Kagune wants you to have a buffet door ready, one that can be stripped from the galley."

"A door, how come?"

"Pushed up against the open hatch, it will cut down on the inflow of air. Not enough to repressurize, but it will help you and your work team."

"That's simple enough, but how the hell do I get that door to stay up in place?"

"For the upward pressure you'll need one of those scissor jacks. A'hearn must have one . . . we'll check. We feel this plan will fetch you at least twenty extra minutes so that you'll be able to drop down to lower altitudes where the oxygen level will be sufficient for total survival."

Lucky was filled with joy. That was the idea he needed.

"Thank you, Ian, thanks from all of us."

As soon as the phone was replaced on the cradle, Ian said, "Those were the most dreadful decisions of my life."

"But, sir, they had to be made."

"I wonder. Should we have told him the truth?"

"No, it would have affected his work. The man would have been destroyed."

12:29 P.M. CST (Over TULSA COUNTY)

THE TV AUDIENCES HAD swollen to more than a billion. In many ways the world had stopped; the air drama over Tulsa was that riveting. It was full of twists and turns, new ideas, fresh threats, and the longer it dragged on, the more magnetic the crisis became. From the very start, viewers had felt that there was a sound basis for Lucky's actions, even though some of the aviation experts sitting beside the TV commentators of the world questioned the soundness of the arctic pilot's decision-making. Others assumed that transferring tools and gear to a crippled jet and the splashing of water ballast into a cargo hold had happened before.

When they learned that it hadn't, the facts added yet another dimension of excitement and speculation to Whiskey Charlie's plight. The aviation historians rushing to their archives and libraries swiftly discovered that there was no other incident that even remotely matched the Lucky Doyle survival plan. Water ballast to upset the design center of gravity was a first; transferring tools and equipment to a crippled jet loaded with passengers had never happened before. They all agreed aviation history was in the making—or unmaking.

Tulsans were out by the thousands, edging into every available position to see the landing or the crash. The airport had been sealed off for hours, but many would-be witnesses had broken through the barriers to cheer and to pray for Doyle's triumph over the impossible. It was their hometown aircraft, with hundreds of Tulsa people aboard.

In Fort Smith, Arkansas, during the first two hours of the catastrophe, TV viewers did not realize the significance of what some aircraft repairman was doing over at the end of the municipal airport. As soon as they learned of Lucky's water ballast plan, thousands of spectators rushed toward Frank A'hearn's conversion shop where the thirty-seven-year-old DC–6B was on the ramp, props turning, the last of the equipment being stuffed aboard. The roads to the airport became long, thin parking lots, but no one cared. The sun was out, the new snow was beautiful, so they just abandoned their cars and talked in groups while they waited and watched the sky for a single sight of the lumbering old DC–6 on its way to help Whiskey Charlie.

It was coming up to the three-hour mark since the collision. Fuel was below the one-third mark. As yet nothing had accomplished positive results except blowing half the elevators off. All other ideas were negative actions that were not taken for fear of an inflight breakup.

The two men who knew Doyle best were Frank A'hearn and his test pilot, Louie Bonner. They had been through years of tough going up north with Lucky Doyle. Now they sat in the cockpit of the reborn DC–6B, watching the highly dramatic coverage on a portable color TV.

"Do you think this is all for nothing, Louie?" Frank asked.

The beat-up aged man who looked as reddened and shredded as an Aleut Indian, agreed with a nod. "Yeah. I can't see how they can make it. But then I didn't think they would last an hour, and that was over two hours ago, so what do any of us know?"

"Tell you what happened. Doyle had these ideas, maybe they were workable, we'll never know. But he messed up on one thing."

"The time element."

"You got it, Louie. He never understood how much time it takes to pull off a great trick. Everything has to go right. Can't be one false move. You never get it the first time. The poor guy in his will to live lost sense of time. Reality."

"When I helped cut that coupling off the fire engine, I went inside for a weigh-up. Seventy pounds. They won't attach that to the cargo bulkhead. Too heavy. Not enough time or manpower."

"They have less than an hour now," Frank sighed. "It's a pure Lucky Doyle dream. We're going up there for a folly. Think we should try it or not? Ah, shit. What am I saying? We don't have a choice."

"But how would you have handled it?" Louie asked.

"Don't know," Frank muttered.

Back aft, the cargo nets had been loaded and arranged in order of their drop sequence into Lucky Doyle's cockpit hatch. Each of the twenty-three man work crew was bundled up in Arctic thermal suits. They wore safety harnesses with heavy mountain-climbing line that ran to cargo attach points along the inner side of the hull. The mammoth load door had been cut off, and the crews would be working in the rush of the slipstream air roaring in through the 8-by 14-foot cavity.

The lead crewman, seeing that everything on the manifest sheet was aboard, spoke into his voice-activated mike attached to the sides of his headgear, a thermal version of the space helmet.

"Frank, I went over the list three times. We have everything aboard. Let's wind her up."

"Pull everyone away from the cargo opening and keep low and attached at all times."

"We have it."

Frank signaled for the wheel chokes to be pulled. When they were clear, he edged his throttles forward and they taxied out to the main runway packed twenty deep with cheering people. There were good luck signs, balloons, even banners for causes such as saving the whales and antiabortion messages. Anything to catch a slice of the world TV coverage.

"They're making too much of this," Louie Bonner said.

"You're right. When we return after it's all over, I wonder how many will still be here?"

"Depends on how it ends," Louie said without emotion.

"I think we know that, Louie."

"I'm afraid we do."

They taxied out slowly, going through their pretakeoff checklist. When the tower told them to taxi into position and hold, Frank slapped Louie's knee saying, "Let's tell ourselves this is going to work."

"You got it."

They ran up each of the four "Pratt" engines, checked the magnetos, and pulled the props through their exercising. All dials were in the green on the panel, and Frank said to the tower, "Ready."

"Cleared for takeoff," came the reply.

Slowly, Frank brought his throttles up to the stops, and the heavily loaded cargo plane began its takeoff run, a slow, long process. Finally, after chewing up almost 4,900 feet, Frank pulled back on his yoke and the plane lifted slowly. As they climbed out, they looked down at the thousands of people jamming the access roads. They could even see people waving, and beyond, on a slight rise of a hill near the runway threshold, a group had dribbled out green paint on the snow to make a huge sign.

"GOD BLESS YOU. GOOD LUCK."

"If they only knew how slim the chances are," Frank said, feeling the worst desolation of that day. "Shit! I promised I wouldn't think of those things."

Dr. Kagune and Ian were watching the takeoff from the conference room off the computer section.

"How do we handle this?" Ian asked.

"We want Lucky and Connie Esposito out of the cockpit so we can speak to André privately."

"It won't be private. The whole world is eavesdropping on the tower frequency."

"I've thought of that. For a while Doyle was using the military band, wasn't he?"

"True. But they went back to the regular frequency. Their portable transmitter works only on batteries."

"Is the power low, or were they saving it?"

"The latter, I suppose."

"Here's how I'd suggest we implement the plan. We tell Doyle to come up on the military frequency. The tower will switch us over. I don't want someone on the line coming back at us if they find out what the red valve does."

"Won't the chief pilot know?"

"Not unless he goes into the manual. I doubt if he'll do that. Why would he doubt us? We designed and built the jet."

"Doesn't Lucky have to PA the passengers so the division of seats can be made?"

"Of course. I'd tell him that now. Then I'll get on and talk to him about going aft with Ms. Esposito."

Three minutes later, after Ian suggested the PA, Lucky picked up the cockpit phone.

"Ladies and gentlemen, Captain Doyle again. The flight surgeon in England, one of the group that built this aircraft, has made an excellent suggestion. As you know, we are going to open a hatch to take on tools for the repair job. You can see helicopters surrounding us now. Soon you'll see a couple of Air Force tanker planes. One will transfer water to our forward section to bring the nose down for the landing.

"For your comfort, it has been suggested by the British flight surgeon that the last cabin will be the warmest because we will be opening the hatch up here on the flight deck. Some cold air will reach into the first and second cabins, and I am asking you to dress warmly, putting on your hats and gloves and overcoats. The last cabin will be the warmest. Unfortunately, we cannot all gather there because of seating restrictions. Now will the elderly, plus those with illnesses, please make themselves known to the flight attendants so that you may be seated in the warmest section of the aircraft. We will start to reposition ourselves immediately. We are now estimating our landing back in Tulsa to be about one-thirty. Again, we are sorry for these problems, and I must congratulate every one of you for your courage and cooperation. Thank you."

"How do you feel about things now, Lucky?" Connie asked. "I'm still jumpy as hell."

"I am, too. A lot could go wrong. But at least the passengers aren't going to freeze to death. I've seen that happen up north. It's a bad way to check out."

"Painful?" André asked.

"At first. You think you can't stand the aching any longer in your hands and feet. Then all of a sudden it goes away. You feel nothing. That's when you know you're in deep trouble. If that happens, it's seldom reversed. A leg or an arm goes. If the body hits about eighty-two degrees, you're dead."

Then Dr. Kagune started with his suggestion.

"Now, Lucky, the success of this operation depends to a great extent on passenger attitude. They must be assured that you and your copilot are optimistic about solving the problem. The way to accomplish this is by visual reinforcement. By that, I mean your presence back aft with Ms. Esposito. Within a short time you will be starting your work. I would strongly suggest that you and your copilot go aft for the last time in your uniforms. The next time the passengers see you, you'll be in one of the arctic suits. Captain Bouchard can handle the cockpit and call you if a problem arises. So would you two get on to that right now?"

"Sure," Lucky said. "I'll have Captain Bouchard slip into the left seat here."

Dr. Kagune waited about two minutes. In that time he glanced over at Ian, who was sitting slump-shouldered at the end of the conference table.

"If you have second thoughts, sir, I could cancel what I am about to say."

"I've been thinking it over. It's necessary. But I wonder if this should be kept from Doyle?"

"I think so. He has too much on his mind, as I said before."

"Thank God," Ian said.

12:29 P.M. CST (Over TULSA COUNTY)

The doctor pressed down the button on the telephone and said,

"Captain Bouchard, would you stand by on the military frequency?"

"Will do."

After a minute Dr. Kagune asked, "Are you alone?"

"Yes."

"Fine. Just stand by, André."

"Ian, would you please get on the other phone and ask Tug Stiles to come in here."

The chairman caught the move on Dr. Kagune's part. He did not wish the "muckie" to hear what was being said. The doctor was not afraid of Henry's monitoring it. He was certain that the main design group had not waded deeply into the various elements of the 270, such as the emergency oxygen system. That was detail design, a first-floor job. On the other hand, Stiles was just the one to know the system.

"Ian, tell me if you see Stiles coming down the hall. Go outside, please, and make up something to halt him for just a bit while I get word to Bouchard."

Ian quickly moved to his feet and left the room. He didn't want to hear the death order anyhow.

"Now, André. I'm back on the line. Lucky Doyle has a great deal on his mind. For him and his copilot to be effective, I want to give you some of the responsibility for the systems. I think it would be much sounder if you did not bring this up with Connie or Lucky. It would only introduce a new factor for them to worry about."

"I quite understand, Doctor."

"Now when they are aft trussing up the bulkhead and we drop the oxygen masks, I want you to leave the cockpit for just a few seconds. You'll be on the autopilot anyhow."

"That's correct."

"You are to go down the stairs to the lower bunk area. Behind the row of oxygen bottles, you'll see a red valve. You have to reach in back. I want you to turn it all the way to the left. This will direct a stronger flow back to where the older people are sitting."

"Couldn't I do it now?"

"No! We must test the whole system once we take in the new bottles. I have a checksheet here. I will tell you when to turn the valve."

"That's easy enough. Anything else?"

"I want you to be our countdown man. Keep track of the time to fuel exhaustion. Give Lucky the information. We're trying to establish certain units of time for each task—taking the bottles in, the work on the truss, and the water delivery. So you are rather the timekeeper. Do you understand that?"

"Yes, sir."

"And we will not inform Lucky of your task with the valve."

"I understand."

"Or that you are officially keeping time. It might be offensive to the man."

"Of course. I see your point."

Two minutes later Charlie Hoover in the military helicopter worked the flight with a cracked voice. "Lucky. You on?"

"This is André Bouchard. I'm chief pilot."

By this time Ian was back with Tug Stiles.

"Get Doyle up there right away. I think the skin wrinkles are gaining on us," Charlie said. "I'm ordering all the press planes away. Anything could happen here."

André felt a hollow feeling overtake him as he phoned back for Lucky to return to the cockpit.

Tug picked up another conference room phone. "This is Stiles. Just heard that, Bouchard. Have one of those camera planes get in there with a close-up lens. We want to see this."

"Right away."

Jack Haverly, who now had an Area Supervisor on the scene, took over. He asked the CBS camera plane to slide in for close-ups. Lucky entered the cockpit, changed seats with André, and Connie followed, sliding into the copilot's seat.

In the computer section, Henry had called up the structural model on the mainframe terminal. A programmer pushed himself up to the keyboard as Ian and Tug joined them.

"A'hearn, where are you now?" Tug asked.

"In the air."

"We have new problems," Tug said.

"I heard."

"We might have to switch plans, might need different tools."

"Just for your information, we have about every damned thing you could possibly want."

"Are you sure the right plane is moving into place, the one that's feeding the BBC?" Henry asked.

"Of course," Tug said. "That's right, isn't it?" He asked the control tower.

"I'm the pilot of the CBS plane, we're supplying the satellite feed. I'm almost in there. We have the door off on the left side, but I can come around and they can shoot out of the windows for the opposite view."

"Give us a picture of the left side first."

"I wish I could see this," Lucky said.

"Maybe it's good you can't," Tug Stiles said to himself, as he watched the first dramatic close-ups of the skin wrinkles appearing on the screen. Tug covered the phone with his hand so that Lucky wouldn't hear him.

"Oh, shit! We got progressive frame collapse! The

butt straps and stringer clips are going. How the bloody hell did that happen? I figured takin' the juice off those turbines would halt the vibrations. You want to tell Doyle what to do, or do I get on to him, Gibbons?"

"What's your idea?" Henry asked in a whisper, making certain that the words didn't reach the cockpit.

"I want those liners off. He's got to measure the time and distance of the frame movement. Without that, we don't know a thing."

"I agree. Tell him that."

Tug put the phone to his mouth.

"Lucky, go back aft and start ripping off more liners. Tell the people back there to find seats up front."

Dr. Kagune, who was watching the TV in the conference room with Lou Walters, stood up, shaking his head. He dashed out.

By the time Kagune entered the computer section, the CBS Cessna 414 had moved around to the other side of Whiskey Charlie. The same pattern of skin wrinkles was creeping up past the aft galley door and heading for the wing root.

"There're even more wrinkles now," Tug exclaimed.

"I don't want those people displaced out of the last cabin," Dr. Kagune shouted.

"What the hell do I care what yuh want?" Tug said. "Got to move 'em. How the hell do yuh think we're goin' to get the liners off? Got to derail those seats."

Tug again talked to Lucky, "You hear that, Doyle? What I was just sayin' to Kagune?"

"Heard it. There's no way we can open up the back end with those people sitting there."

"But I want them returned to those seats when we open the hatch. They're positioned for safety," the doctor said. "If those passengers aren't aft, you're going to be looking at trouble. We'll pick up casualties."

12:29 P.M. CST (Over TULSA COUNTY)

"Doctor, I'll deal with that when I get to it," Lucky said.

"I still request that the passengers be replaced in the last cabin."

André Bouchard couldn't help but hear how adamant the doctor was on the point. It was far more critical, he thought, to halt the structural failure. If they didn't, it would hardly matter where the passengers were sitting.

Lucky ran through the cabin. When he reached the last crossover galley, he signaled for his crew and told them to derail the seats in the aft cabin.

"The skin wrinkles are gaining on us," Lucky said.

Alex Anderson shook his head in frustration. As an experienced airframe man, he knew what that meant.

"Ladies and gentlemen, please give me your attention," Lucky said, standing on a seat in the last cabin. "We have been informed that we might have to make our repairs in a different way. We were going to screw in some pipes across the back frame there where you see the liners off. Now we've been requested, as a precautionary measure, to remove more side panels, those plastic sections around the windows. So I'll ask everyone to please move forward and find your original seats in the other cabins. Then you will return to this section before the forward hatch is removed."

Some passengers could see the set look on Lucky's face.

"We have a new crisis?" one elderly man asked.

"Sort of. Please unfasten your seat belts, and the cabin attendants will show you where to sit."

As soon as the seats near the windows, rows of two, were removed, Alex picked up the fire axe and started hacking away at the liners. Others stripped the material from the frames with their hands. They clawed away as fast as they could. Some knuckles became bloody, but the I.A. maintenance men did not stop. They sensed what was going on behind the insulation panels and their throats tightened. When enough was stripped away on one side, Lucky and Alex moved in to study the frames.

They were canted backward on a slight angle.

"We're looking at catastrophic failure! The bearing stress valves have been exceeded! You guys, don't just stand there. Hit the other side, quick. Pull those liners off!"

They hurdled over the middle seats and started to derail the seats on the opposite side. While that was underway, a huge young man who looked like a professional linebacker started to swing the axe, wildly chopping away more of the liners toward the front of the last cabin.

Lucky moved in to feel the frames.

"They're twisting now. We have some buckling. Connie, got that marker pen?"

"Right here," she answered, stepping up to the exposed frames and stringers. "Draw a line along that frame. And start your timer."

"It looks like shit, Lucky," she said.

"Don't tell me. How many monkey wrenches can this fucking thing have?" Lucky asked. They watched as the shaking frame slowly covered the blue line made by the pen, creeping forward at about a sixteenth of an inch per minute.

"Make a note of that, Connie."

"I got it."

"Time it up front there where they have the other liners hacked away."

Connie moved up five seats. Again she drew a blue line on the inner skin, using the frame position for a guide.

Alex felt the frames again with his hand. "We're

lookin' at a plane with a broken back. Cross piping won't fix it."

"You're right. We gotta go lengthwise and fasten these frames together, like putting a splint on a broken leg."

"But it's more complicated than setting a splint. The pipe will have to be screwed into each frame," Alex said.

"That'll take a lot of material and time. And I'm scared of the time element."

"Me, too," Alex said. "And if we're getting wrinkles here, they have to be on top also."

Lucky agreed and dashed to the galley phone to speak to André. "Ask Bristol to run a program. Take the strength properties of the alloy pipe or whatever Frank has, and draw them in on the structural imaging. You know your primary structure. That should tell us how many pipes or alloy strips we'll need."

"Lucky, there isn't time to rebuild the whole plane," André said.

"I know that, but we have a mess back here."

"Lucky, you got the same problem over here," Connie called. "Just about a sixteenth of an inch per minute, but I'd say it's more like one thirty-second. Just under a sixteenth."

"I'll phone that up to André for a repeat. See what's happening on the other side."

Lucky ran aft. He picked up the phone and repeated the data to André for relay to Bristol.

"Lucky, they just asked if the stringers are deformed."

"Tell them the elastic limit has been reached. We're beyond the proof stress number. Have Bristol run the program with the two-inch tubes, connecting the frames aft of the last mainframe. I want to know how many and where to put them. Also, ask Frank what the lengths of his tubes are, and see if he has a whole bunch aboard."

When Lucky left the aft galley, he crossed over to where Connie was marking up the exposed frames on the far side of the aircraft.

"Bad break," he said.

"Is there a chance to stop this?" she asked.

"Of course there's a chance. But André just reminded me of the clock. We can't be laying in tubes back here and getting the couplings ready for the water ballast. I bit off more than I could chew. Much more!"

Alex heard Lucky. He could feel the panic mounting among his men, and he crossed to the captain.

"Maybe we should ask ourselves what's causing this," he said.

"I know. It's the tail pressure. The flippers are pushing down. Frames are being stretched by the weight back there. Turbines are moving us forward. There's a counteraction going on. So we know. So what?" Lucky asked.

"You solved it the first time, Lucky. You had the chopper open fire on your outer elevators. What about hitting the inner ones?"

"I thought of that. Frank's sending me down big CO_2 bottles. But go back there, Alex. You can smell the jet fuel and hydraulic fluid sloshing around in the tail cone. So he puts a slug through the inner flipper. What if a spark ignites an explosion? It'll take the pressure off, but we won't have a tail!"

"I don't think there's a buildup of fumes."

"Then what am I smelling? It's not perfume, Alex," Lucky barked back.

"You're smelling raw kerosene. There has to be air rushing in there. Part of the horizontal stab is off. Rudder's gone. Air must be funneling in."

"So what are you saying?" Lucky asked, abruptly running out of patience.

"I doubt if you have the conditions for an explosion. An ignition? Yes. You might have a fire. That can be contained."

"You can't tell me that there's no chance of an explosion."

"No one can say that without getting in there and measuring the fumes. That's impossible."

"I'm *not* going to ask for more bullets until everything else is exhausted."

"Well, Lucky, I've been in aircraft engineering for forty-two years and flew B–Twenty-Nines in the Pacific, so I have hands-on experience. Fastening these frames together is a big job. We have good strong guys here. They'll do anything, but only six of them are real sheet metal boys."

"I hear you, Alex. I'm just not anxious to open fire on that tail. But it could all end with one bullet. You know that. And we could lose the trim control."

"And it could all end just as fast if those frames collapse!" Alex said.

"We're fucked one way or another! Shit! I just can't win here," Lucky wailed.

André's information had been fed into the Bristol computer. Tug Stiles told the programmer to establish the bracing tube profile.

"It's already in, Mr. Stiles," one engineer said.

Tug's face lit with a secret smile. In all his years at the facility, not one person had ever addressed him as Mr. Stiles.

"I'll draw in the tube connections. See what it does on the imaging," Tug ordered, as he sketched in the pipes with what he called his fantasy stick. "Run that."

The animated imaging revealed the elongation

without the pipes, connecting each frame. Then with the new function entered, the tubes in blazing red flowed in, connecting one frame to another. It retarded the failure. Tug drew in more lines to represent additional tube connections. The vibrating and the stretching eased off and stabilized.

"That'll do it. Now go and optimize that tubing," he yelled at the programmer. "We got to give Doyle the proper spacing."

As the programmer tapped in different placements of the tube sections, Tug picked up the phone.

"How many tube lengths yuh got aboard, A'hearn?"

"Fourteen. Twenty-footers. That's what you asked for, old man."

"I know what I asked for."

"What about the turning radius, once we drop them in the forward hatch. I don't think you want them that long."

Tug handed the phone to Henry Gibbons. "Hold this. Kagune, you fly upstairs and give me the maximum turning radius that can be handled through the cockpit escape hatch."

The doctor paused a second, shooting a long look at Ian. "But let me say one more thing to the flight."

Tug handed the phone to the Indian doctor.

"Captain Bouchard, I want this stressed once more. As soon as the structure is reinforced in this new manner, I demand that those seats be placed back on the rails and that the elderly passengers resume their prior positions."

"I'll inform Lucky of that."

But an alarm went off in the Canadian's head. He was troubled by Dr. Kagune's overinsistence on returning the passengers to the rear cabin seats. André picked up the massive 270 operations manual and turned to the section marked "Emergency Procedures." He ran his finger down the column to the oxygen delivery system. He read for a while and then froze as his eyes found the words:

THE OXYGEN MASK DELIVERY SYSTEM IS REGULATED BY A FORCED DELIVERY. IN THE CASE OF DEPRESSURIZATION AT HIGH ALTITUDES, THE SYSTEM CAN BE SEGREGATED. IF THE LOAD FACTOR PERMITS, THE CONTENT OF THE OXYGEN DELIVERY MAY BE CUT OFF TO THE LAST CABIN AND DIRECTED FOR A LONGER DURATION TO THE FORWARD PASSENGER SECTIONS. TO CARRY THIS OUT, A CREW MEMBER SHOULD GO TO THE EMERGENCY OXYGEN RACKS IN THE ELECTRONIC BAY AREA UNDER THE COCKPIT, AND TURN THE RED VALVE COUNTERCLOCKWISE. THIS WILL ELIMINATE OXYGEN DELIVERY TO THE LAST CABIN WHILE INCREASING DELIVERY TIME BY ABOUT NINE MINUTES TO THE FORWARD PASSENGER SECTIONS.

12:39 P.M. CST
(Over TULSA COUNTY)

•

CONNIE AND LUCKY ENTERED the cockpit with shortened breaths. André could see the tension beginning to grasp these people; he felt his own heart beat wildly. They were less than an hour to fuel exhaustion; he wondered if he should mention the red valve at this point. The chief pilot was about to open his mouth as he slid from the left seat, giving it to Lucky.

"André, did you get the information to Bristol?"

"Yes, they have it, Lucky."

"What did they say?"

"Good news. The idea of connecting the frames together with alloy tubes appears to stop our structural problems."

"It will work, then."

"That's what they say."

Lucky punched the transmit button. "We have to pick up speed. We're out of fourteen thousand nine hundred. Air speed's holding on one-forty knots. Fuel flow as before. Stand by."

12:39 P.M. CST (Over TULSA COUNTY)

Connie was recalculating her fuel flow.

"It's still about one-thirty, Lucky, give or take a minute. But our rate of climb has picked up."

Lucky passed the fuel flow information along to Stiles. As he did, he felt a sharp tap on his shoulder. André had decided to speak.

"What's the matter, André?"

"I must tell you people something," he said urgently.

"Can't it wait?" Connie asked. "We're in deep shit, André. Lucky doesn't think he has time to lay those tubes in."

"Bristol is planning to kill all the passengers in the last cabin!" André said, his voice rising to a shout.

Lucky spun around. He looked at Connie to make sure she did not have her finger on the transmit button.

"What are you saying? Kill them? How?" Lucky asked.

"Dr. Kagune told me to go below and turn off the red check valve for the last cabin."

"What the hell does that do?"

"I read the manual, Lucky. It detours the flow of oxygen to the forward cabins. Eliminates service to the last cabin. That's why he wanted the old and sick people back there. It had nothing to do with keeping them warmer."

As he said that, André handed Lucky the 270's manual. The pilot's face became livid as he read. Blood vessels stood out from his temples.

"Those fucking bastards!" he raged. Connie had never heard him so wild.

"Holy shit!" she said. "You sure of this, André?"

"Yes."

"Who else told you?"

"That Dr. Kagune."

Lucky was still consumed by anger. He had asked Bristol for a solution, not an organized death plan.

"What do we do, Lucky?" Connie asked.

"I've got to know whose idea this was."

He knocked on the transmit button.

"Tower, switch us over to the military frequency."

"Will do."

Lucky piled up the small portable transmitter and pressed the rocker arm on the side. "Get Tug on the line," he snapped.

A second later the "muckie" responded.

"We're working on the tube layout now, Lucky."

"Listen, you fucking bastard! Why didn't you tell me about the check valve?"

Tug looked around the computer room. Ian's head was bowed.

"What check valve, Doyle?"

"Bouchard just said he was asked to turn off the oxygen service to the last cabin with that valve in back of the tank rack."

"Calm down. Who said that?"

"Kagune, the guy who asked us to divide the passengers. He was going to kill them with quick hypoxia."

Tug glanced around the room. Everyone was silent. The message traffic was now on a speaker phone that they had rigged up in the computer section. Tug could tell that Henry Gibbons knew nothing of this. He was just as shocked as everyone. Tug moved over to Ian.

"You knew about this, Sir Ian?"

"I did."

"You approved it?"

"Yes."

Before anyone could reach Tug Stiles, his fist was streaking through the air and crashing on the upper jaw of the chairman. Ian was hurled back. He collapsed into a heap at the base of the computer mainframe. A group of "white coats" started toward Tug. The titanic footballer reared back and held up both fists. The engineers halted as if a whistle had gone off.

"Get Kagune down here, Gibbons. Or I'll get him," Tug bellowed.

Henry picked up the phone with a shaking hand. In the background, Waffles raced out of the room to call the Bristol security people.

"Dr. Kagune, would you please step down here straightaway." Henry spoke swiftly. It had become clear to everyone in the computer section that only the human factors engineer and the chairman knew about the death plan.

Several "white coats" helped Ian up and into a chair. He was bleeding from the nose and mouth, but he managed to say, "I'm sorry. I was going to tell you."

Tug didn't answer. Instead he picked up the phone.

"It's true, Doyle."

"It's the worst thing I've ever heard," Connie burst in. "What were they thinking?"

"Kagune had better have an explanation. If he doesn't, he'll be talkin' to the Bristol detective superintendent, he will!"

Dr. Kagune appeared at the door and Tug started toward the gaunt Indian. Henry and four "white coats" ran in front of the tall engineer. Tug reached him first and the "muckie" clenched his massive left hand around the white collar of the petrified doctor. He dragged him to the phone by the computer terminal. The human factors engineer saw the blood dripping down Ian's shirt and he knew what had happened.

"This death plan your idea, Kagune?" Tug growled in his face.

"It was," he said stiffly.

"Yuh get the bloody hell on that line and explain it to Doyle! Don't leave a thing out. Doyle, I have a very shaky Indian doctor about to tell yuh why he did this."

"Better be damned good," Lucky said.

"There was no other way, sir," Kagune started.

"I'm the captain of the aircraft. You don't call the shots, fellow. What the hell were you thinking about?"

"I was trying to avoid a panic. You were about to kill everyone because of oxygen starvation. We worked it out. There was no way you were going to deliver enough flow through the emergency bottles for more than a half hour. If you directed the entire supply to the first three cabins, you had a chance of saving maybe two hundred if the jet could have been brought down quickly enough. If a panic had broken out, the entire flight would have been lost."

"Why didn't you tell me? My passengers have rights. It was their decision where to sit, not yours."

"There had to be an expert authority, Captain Doyle. You are not trained in altitude sickness or mass psychology. I am."

"Don't give me that bullshit! There's no way that you could say what people will do."

"There is. The will and fight to live are fundamental. There're hundreds of papers on this. You cannot expect the plane to be repaired and reach acceptable oxygen levels by emergency delivery. You would have to spend all your time delivering bottles to the racks. I ask you, sir. How would you work on your water ballast and repair those frames back there? I would suggest that you rethink the plan."

Ian, who had shaken off his dizziness, took the phone from Dr. Kagune.

"Lucky, Ian. This was my fault. I talked it over with Dr. Kagune. The man might be right, but concealing it from you was dreadfully wrong. I should have spoken to you. I'm sorry. I guess Tug Stiles taught me a lesson."

At that point, four security officers with Mr. Waffles appeared at the door.

"It's all right, Waffles, gentlemen," Henry said. "There was just a bit of misunderstanding."

"Ian, I accept your apology," Lucky came in. "My point is this. I promised my passengers that they would all get home to Tulsa for dinner. I'm going to make sure that happens."

"Of course, Lucky. As poorly as we acted on this end, Dr. Kagune still has some points worth thinking about. You said it yourself. There isn't time for everything. You can't risk an inflight breakup while you're trying to save the passengers. All of you will die. Dr. Kagune drove that point home to me. It's the most awful decision of your life. From now on, it's all yours. The total responsibility is up to you. If you can land safely with everyone alive, God bless you. If you don't, God bless you, too!"

Tug came up and extended his hand to Ian who took it. "Lost me head. I deserve charges, sir. I'm sorry."

"I understand," Ian said.

They both looked at the large clock on the wall. According to the fuel flow calculation, there were fifty five minutes remaining for Whiskey Charlie.

"Tell me truthfully, Tug," Ian asked. "Doyle is a keen one. But he's out of time, isn't he?"

"I'm afraid he is, sir. I don't think it matters where anyone sits anymore. I'm terribly sorry to say that but I must, sir."

"What went wrong here? I mean why did Doyle's plan fail?"

"For two reasons, Sir Ian. Doyle understands much more about aircraft structures than any pilot I ever spoke to."

"He studied engineering many years ago in some junior college in Florida. He had time as a crew chief in the Navy. That was the information passed on to us. Why was he so off base? Why didn't we tell him that over an hour ago?"

"Because we didn't come up with an alternate solution."

"You seem to be contradicting yourself."

"No, sir. Doyle knew that in a stressed skin–type structure, if a part, or many parts are in compression, and calculations suggest that there will be buckling under extreme loading, then it is usually possible to add some stabilizing axillary structure to halt the major problem. That's why Doyle called for the two-inch tubing. He was planning to add additional stringers on the inner side of the frames. The idea was sound."

"What happened?"

"Doyle didn't know the other missing elements. He never built planes on a fabrication floor. And I don't think he carried on major airframe repairs on the carrier. He didn't realize just how long all his repairs would take."

"Why didn't someone here tell him?"

"Well, when Doyle took pressure off the tail, we thought the situation would improve. It might only need a few new stringers, or none at all."

"What was the other missing element?" Ian asked.

"There was no way Doyle could have known the extent of the tail damage. The structural integrity back there was obviously in much more danger than we realized at first. The jet, sir, was barely being held together. The aircraft designer is faced with weight reduction. But this Two-Seventy was slightly over-designed. We put a little more meat and potatoes into the structure than we needed to. Still, it wasn't enough for the aircraft to survive the forces of the collision."

12:39 P.M. CST (Over TULSA COUNTY)

"So Doyle did everything he could?"

"No man could have done more. He read the situation right. He kept his head. That was his greatest contribution."

"But it's all over."

"There's always miracles," Tug said slowly.

Ian looked at his engineers. He asked, "Does anyone have an idea?"

There was only silence in the computer section.

12:47 P.M. CST
(Over TULSA)

•

———-———-——WHEN THE CHOPPER UNIT AT Tulsa first called for Air Force tankers by way of the Pentagon, the commanding officer, Colonel Jeff Goodwin, had scoffed at the idea. For one thing, running water through the pumps and fuel lines aboard a KC–10 would probably damage the delivery system beyond repair. Goodwin was batting for a gold shoulder star. When the request reached his office that Friday morning, he wondered if he wanted to be associated, even indirectly, with disaster. Around the Tinker Air Base, bets at twenty-to-one odds were being taken against the 270 rescue. It wasn't that anyone wished a crash with a high death toll, but the former Arctic flyer wasn't taken seriously. His ideas were beyond Air Force comprehension: The flight was too far gone for intervention. That was the feeling among the pilots at the Tinker base.

Jeff was about to contact the Pentagon once more for consultation when he saw his air base on television. CBS had already said that the Air Force was cooperating. The president, a former aviator with a pilot's heart, had offered all possible military help, and everyone watching TV associated the helicopters incorrectly with the Air Force. In reality they were Army choppers.

When Dan Rather phoned Goodwin on the air, the ambitious forty-two-year-old commanding officer pledged not one Air Force tanker but two, the second serving as a backup. Not only that, the colonel told Rather that he was still certified in the KC–10 equipment and that he would personally fly the mission. There were younger, perhaps more qualified men at the base, and they saw Goodwin's offer as a slide toward instant recognition in the Air Force sport of "star reaching."

As he took off later that morning in one of the tankers heading for Tulsa, Goodwin secretly thanked God that he hadn't completed the call to the Pentagon expressing his concern. As he looked down just after the tanker's wheels were retracted into the wells, the colonel saw crowds of people standing beside their cars. Similar to the scene at Fort Smith, thousands had left their TV sets to be there when the tankers took off to help Whiskey Charlie.

12:58 P.M. CST
(Over TULSA COUNTY)

•

IN THE FIVE TO TEN MINUTES beginning around 12:47 P.M. that day, the terrible truth started to emerge all around the world. Lucky Doyle had become an instant aviation hero. He had kept his head, as Tug Stiles put it, and offered wild but apparently workable ideas on how to land Whiskey Charlie safely. Lesser airmen, the buttonpushers, would have been rocked off their bearings and given up long ago. Lucky continued to feel that he could bring this bird back home in plenty of time for dinner, as he so often repeated. At the start of this extraordinary effort—what seemed like years ago—most people held no hope for Lucky or his plane. Few shared his faith that the impossible could be possible.

The lesson Lucky seemed to be teaching to the millions who were viewing the megadrama was that fear, panic, and surrender were the true enemies, not necessarily the predicament itself. In that sense he had become a victor. No one disagreed with the man's unflinching tenacity.

But just before one o'clock, serious doubt began to

eat at the public's confidence—and that of some of Lucky's friends as well. In the DC–6, cranking out the air miles from Fort Smith to Tulsa, Louie Bonner said to Frank, who was flying the heavily loaded supply plane, "You watching the clock?"

"I am."

"We worked as fast as we could."

"It wasn't fast enough," Frank concluded with a long sigh.

"Poor bastards. And after all that. Too bad."

Connie sensed the implacable disappearance of their precious minutes just before one o'clock. She looked from the cockpit window. The tanker planes had not appeared yet, and Lucky was sitting silent, expressionless, waiting for the air drop. She saw a slight shaking of his head. At the start, she had been sure she was going to die. Then Lucky spread hope around. Now, as she looked at the fuel gauges, her first fears returned, and they were worse than before. She could tell that Lucky was losing hope. He was giving in to the inevitable. They had all pegged it correctly. Time had just run out on them. Where the hell did it all go? she asked herself.

Back aft, Linda Glen came up to Alex Anderson.

"We're not getting out of this, are we?" she whispered.

"I don't know."

"Yes, you do. I can see it in your face. Look at the mess back there, even I can see that this jet is coming apart little by little. Why don't you just tell me it's all over? I'd rather know."

"I have faith in Doyle."

"God damn it! There's only so much one man can do, and we're low on fuel. Even Lucky has admitted that. See . . . see! Look at the passengers' faces. What do they tell you?"

"They're waiting."

"Sure they're waiting. Before they were waiting for something to happen to get this fucker down. Now look at their faces. They're waiting for death. They know it's coming."

"Don't give up, Linda. Lucky needs us."

"And don't be a goddamned fool!"

"What do you want me to say? We're going to be killed. Does that make you feel better? Does it?"

"It might. At least I'd know."

"Lucky wasn't jerking you around. He believed in what he could do."

"Listen to yourself. You just spoke in the past tense. It's all past now. There's nothing left, Alex. Over and out."

Up front Connie was about to say something along the same lines. Then Lucky sat upright and a certain smile replaced the resigned look on his handsome face.

"André," Lucky said with freshness to his voice, "you could be a great help here."

"Anything, Lucky."

"Get your coat on, pull up your tie, and go back aft. Introduce yourself as the chief pilot. Say things are coming along fine."

"They're not, are they?"

"At this point, no. But I plan a turnaround here."

"How?"

"I have something in mind. But I'd like you to establish passenger contact. Tell them that things up front are in control."

"But they're not."

"I just have to pull out a few creative adjustments."

"Lucky, I must say, you've been damned creative, but your ideas just aren't workable. We'd need days to patch this bird up. We're falling apart. It's that simple."

"André, I'd like you to take a walk while I think this out."

The chief pilot jumped off his observer's seat, pulled up his tie, pasted on a smile, and moved toward the hanging closet. He put on his custom-tailored captain's coat and turned toward the instrument panel.

André left the cockpit, and Lucky continued to stare ahead.

"I never asked you, Lucky."

"What?"

"Are you afraid of dying?"

"No, just getting killed when it's unnecessary."

"What's the difference?" she asked.

"Plenty. I'm afraid of premature death if you want to know. That's why we aren't pulling a deep six today."

"Still getting home for dinner, is that it?"

"That's it. Because I love you more than ever, so I'm not letting all that disappear."

He flipped up his shoulder straps and slid out of his seat.

"Where are you going?"

"To the lower bunk area. Want to see that valve."

"Lucky, before you allow yourself too much time, look at the altimeter. We're out of fifteen thousand feet and climbing."

"And you look at that airspeed."

Connie was so mesmerized by the two clocks, the countdown to a spin-in, that she hand't noticed what else was going on in the glass cockpit. The airspeed had climbed to 165 knots.

"You forgot some basics," Lucky said, with a grin.

"Fuel burnoff. Lighter load. The air's less dense up here," she said with a leaping smile, as she flicked back her long red hair.

"You got it," Lucky said. "Quick. Get some heat off those turbines and recalculate."

Connie eased back on the two thrust levers. Just at the slight shake, the onset of the buffet and stall, she inched them forward again to obviate the deadly warning of an upset. When the new fuel flow was established, she called up the engine data on the glass panels. With a flick of another button, Connie called up the ultrafast solution on a computerized glass window.

"We *are* going to make it," Connie said.

"How do you know?" Lucky asked. She then pointed to the glass panel. The computer had taken the turbine pressure ratios, the new fuel flow, pounds remaining, the density altitude, and the reduced weight. The result now popped up in scarlet on the screen.

"See, the fuel exhaustion time is now about two-fourteen instead of one-thirty. Get that to Bristol," Lucky said, as he picked up the portable transmitter and left the cockpit.

"Where are you going?"

"I told you. Want to see the valve. Those bastards! Haven't forgiven them. Doubt if I ever will."

Lucky stood with his body slouched against the cockpit door, looking almost smug. She had seen this omnipotent gaze before, always with a wink tagged on to say, "Not bad but I can even improve it." The look frightened Connie. Was he in some kind of fantasy world that defied harsh reality?

"Get that look off your face, Lucky!" she demanded. "I detest that look. I hate it! God damn you, do something. I dare you!"

His odd smile became a grin. He pulled Connie to him and kissed her passionately. Suddenly she felt fortunate. The fear of death seemed to be banished as his warm embrace continued.

"Hang on. The fat lady hasn't sung yet. The old gal hasn't even arrived at the theater."

Then he was gone and the cockpit door was left open.

When Lucky reached the lower level, he quickly looked around. Something was wrong. He felt different.

It was not a panic attack, when a million immersed alarms all surfaced. He had a grip on his nerves, or almost, he thought; yet things seemed different.

The lower bunk area appeared much larger, as if the entire rest area, the bunks, the folddown table in the center, had been infused with yeast. He moved to one of the bunks to feel the soft outer blanket. It looked twice as wide as he remembered. Lucky pushed his arm slowly across the bunk surface so he could feel the side on the hull liner. His approach was very sluggish. What if he couldn't touch it? In his mind he knew that the width of the bunk could be no more than thirty inches at most, well within the reach of his outstretched arm. He feared not being able to touch the liner with his hand because the distance looked so vast to him.

When his hand finally made contact with the plastic liner on the side, he realized that his eyes had been deceiving him; the bunk was just the width it should have been. But something was wrong. The door to the forward electronic bay seemed forty feet away. He knew better. It took nine steps for Lucky to walk to it; he counted them off. He entered, looked at the rows of oxygen bottles, all hospital green, all standing at attention just as before. He thought for a second that he was seeing forty bottles lined up instead of nine. He reached behind the rack and felt the valve. His disdain for Ian came back. He looked at his watch, shook his head, and spoke directly to the grim reaper.

"Fuck you, buddy. You're not grabbing me yet!"

Returning to the bunk area, Lucky forgot about the odd malfunction of his vision and concentrated on the problems at hand.

1:06 P.M. CST
(Over TULSA COUNTY)

•

———-———-——ONCE AGAIN LUCKY REACHED across the bunk to feel the liner. His impression of distances was still askew. He tried to imagine what was happening to him. The aircraft was still fully pressurized; he hadn't been suffering from a cold or an allergy, taking medications that sometimes exhibit side effects that are more pronounced in the air than on the ground. It was nothing like that. So what the hell is happening to me? he asked himself. Having no answer, Lucky just chalked it up to nerves. Maybe that was it.

Lucky had come down to the lower level to face alternatives: death or a new idea. What a fool he had been, he thought. He had misled everyone and himself by thinking that they could restress the aircraft before the fuel ran out. Maybe the folly of that idea was pressing on his nerves? Or was it the lie he just told Connie? He had been playing a game. His smug look in the cockpit was merely a cover-up, and the fat lady story—that was nothing but sick humor to keep up the confidence level, his own and Connie's. Now it was white-knuckle time. Lucky knew he didn't have a new idea. Worse, the old ones had failed. What had he been doing all morning? Playing a fantasy game with himself and all the others? Now it was all over. But what other idea could he have presented? Had anyone in Bristol or elsewhere offered a workable solution to save Whiskey Charlie? No. Why not, he asked himself? Maybe the whole thing had been beyond hope from the start. As these thoughts were racing across his mind, he felt that he was losing faith in himself and he still felt odd. Not scared, just different.

Then Lucky's eyes focused on the deck. He noticed the flush hatch that led to the nose gear well. It was the only hatch in the aircraft that could be opened and then resealed to an airtight condition. The hatch had been designed in the Trent 270 so that the crew could inspect the nose gear visually if they picked up a warning light on the panel indicating that the gear was not down, or down but not locked. Lucky pressed the side of his transmitter which he was holding.

"Charlie Hoover, you on?"

"Reading, Lucky."

"Charlie, I'm down by the forward hatch to the nose gear well. It's a pressure hatch that we can reseal."

"You thinking of taking in supplies that way? How do you hoist pipes and bottles up? You don't have a winch in there. And water doesn't flow up hill."

"Right. But listen to me. I might have something."

"Better make it fast, Lucky, or you're going in."

"Charlie, I know all that. Here's where I'm coming from. We just bought ourselves a little more time . . . took off some thrust. But the whole repair job, I mean my entire plan, lacked one element: simplicity. Good old simplicity, Charlie."

"It was complicated all right, even with plenty of time on your hands. But it was the best you could do. Now what?"

"I have a more basic plan. Stay with me a minute. Some years ago when I was getting my multiengine rating in Florida, I used to tow banners up and down the beach for some suntan oil. Now, the drag and weight of the banner would pull the tail of my Piper J–3 down."

"Of course, we've all seen those banner planes with their tails low."

"Now why couldn't we pull our nose down the same way a banner tugs at a tail?"

"Don't get it."

"This is going to sound totally bizarre, but then they say I'm in that corner. But right now there's nothing to lose by going completely off to never-never land."

"I'm sorry to say that's about where you are now . . . damn close to a fatal spin."

"What if you send me down some heavy cable in the form of a large loop. Like a giant lasso. I grab it from the top escape hatch in the cockpit. I haul it down here to the hatch that leads to the nose wheel bay. I open that and drop the cable down, securing one end with shackles where the strut and side braces tie into the fuselage structure."

"Yeah. So you have this great big lasso of cable hanging down. What does that buy you?"

"Now listen and don't laugh your ass off."

"Don't worry, old buddy. No laughs now."

"All right. We have two tankers coming with water. We should see them any minute now. I have one of them slide into the lasso up to the guy's wing root. We have the two jets attached."

"It's crazy, but go on."

"Not entirely crazy. What we're doing is pulling the banner towing trick. The jet below me has to yank my nose down, the same way the banner pulls the tail of the small plane down."

"You're right. I think it would happen that way if everything went right."

"Now both aircraft are descending. I don't have the hellish problem of oxygen."

"Right."

"As soon as we reach warmer air, we have the other tanker get the stiff hose into the top hatch. They shoot water down into the lower bunk area. That will weigh tons. Now the bottom tanker slows its speed and slips out of the lasso. We're in a nose-down attitude . . . say two or three degrees."

"That would be hard to control, Lucky."

"I know. But it's possible."

"How do you land? I mean, you might hit the runway with a three-degree down angle. How about the flare?"

"I knew you'd ask that. Listen to this. When we have the airport made, we open the forward nose gear doors, the water flops out by the ton. What happens? The nose comes up. Right?"

"In theory, yes. Your flippers are jammed up. With the water dumped, the nose has to come up. Clever as hell, Lucky. But I don't have to tell you. One mistake and you're in a million pieces."

"I know but I'll be in a million pieces if I do nothing. What's there to lose?"

"Nothing. You're right about one thing. It's simple . . . I mean the idea won't chew up time like transferring tools and trying to rebuild the ass end there. So what do we do?"

"Where can we get some cable quick?"

"There's a crane company in Tulsa. They use that sort of cable for high-rise construction."

"I know that company."

"One problem, Lucky, you might have structural failure on the tanker. You'll be putting one hell of a pull on that fuselage. What if the cable just tears into the skin and ribs?"

"Don't think it will if we work it easily."

"Yeah, you might be right. Okay, Lucky, let's hit it. I'll call them below."

"Call the fire department. While they are rushing that cable over, they can be attaching the connectors.

"Will do. I'll drop down and refuel. Mind if I ask you something, Lucky?"

"Go ahead."

"How the hell do you come up with these ideas?"

"When you're down to zero, nothing is too wild. Listen, Charlie, are you married?"

"Why?"

"I'm inviting you and your wife over for dinner tonight after we land."

"Lucky, before we talk of dinner plans—and thank you . . . I know my wife wants to meet you—why don't we get that birdie down first."

"Sure, back to the problem. What else is on the list?" Lucky asked.

"I'll have my commander talk with the tanker planes. Ought to see them any second."

"We'll work Bristol . . . ask for the numbers. They should get on to McDonnell Douglas for structural confirmation on the tankers."

"Good. Which frequency?"

"This little set is weakening," Lucky said. "Batteries are going. We'll hit the open frequency. Doesn't matter who hears us now."

"You're right. We have to go for it."

Lucky dashed up to the cockpit. "No one's going to die. I have it!" he bellowed.

"What?"

Lucky slid into his seat and banged on the transmit button. "Tug, pick up your pencil and take notes."

"Go ahead, Lucky. We're all on," Tug replied from Bristol.

Lucky went through the entire lasso routine with Tug while the others listened, stunned.

After ten seconds of rapid thinking, Tug sang out, "What a helluva concept, Doyle."

"You guys work the McDonnell Douglas engineers in Long Beach, California. Program in the tanker data and the loads we'll be exerting. Don't want to pull the guts out of my nose wheel support or break the tanker jet in half. I have an idea that we won't exceed the ultimate stress limits if we work it step by step. Damned carefully."

"I heard that, Lucky," Frank said. "Might make it. Where's the cable coming from?"

"There's a crane company in Tulsa that has heavy-strand stuff."

Frank and Louie broke into smiles. Connie couldn't say anything. This was the breathtaking Lucky Doyle she loved: the complete wacky wizard with a flare and humor all his own.

"Did you guys hear that?" Ron Alcott asked the other I.A. people who'd arrived at the control tower.

"That Doyle is something. Will it work?" Cap asked.

"It might. Sure it will. And I play golf with Rich Sims." Ron moved to the phone and called his golfing friend at the Sims Crane Company. After he explained what they needed, he turned to the others, with a bright, authentic smile.

"Sims just heard the transmission to England. He's already laying out the cable. Has two fire trucks on the way. He's right near the field, over on Pine Street. He's going to try to shackle in a soft pad on the loop of the cable so it doesn't tear into the Air Force tanker."

1:19 P.M. CST (TULSA, I.A. CORPORATE HEADQUARTERS)

•

EXCEPT FOR THE OPERATIONS department, who were working on the other I.A. flights that day, and the quiet reservations section, everyone in the office spewed out to the parking lot to start for the airport. Twenty-one stories up, Augie Hartman watched from a window.

"Will they save the flight?" he asked the South Central men behind him.

"It's a crazy solution," someone said. "Could work."

"Mr. Hartman, everyone's heading to the airport. Should we be there?"

Augie turned and looked at the men around him. They stared back with hostility.

"Why's everyone staring at me?"

At the far end of the conference room, near the door, the company lawyer, a rangy man with a pock-marked complexion signaled Augie to him with a wiggle of his finger. Augie left his group, who continued to regard him angrily. Once outside, Augie rested his aching back against the wall. The lawyer folded his arms and glared down at the younger man. He looked as if he was going to speak but only sighed deeply. Finally the words arrived,

"Just came over the Dow Jones broad tape."

"What?"

"The whole shit safety story you designed and planted."

"Do you think the two-seventy is a safe plane up there in the air with half its tail hanging off? Do you?" Augie demanded.

"Yes, and so does everyone else. It has to have iron balls to stand up to that pounding."

"I did what I had to do."

"Augie, you're finished. They found out about you, discovered what you are."

"How can you say that? You're on the team."

"No longer, Augie. You broke too many rules of this business."

"Just because I was warning the public about a dangerous jet? It should have another engine, two more."

"You're not an engineer. You're not even an airline president."

"I'm right. I know it."

"Augie, you turned against something that's as old as airlines. One carrier never uses the safety factor against another. It's the first law. You knew it. You broke it."

"Listen, fellow. Don't climb up on a horse too high for your own good. When that jet comes down, my stock will hit seventy-five. I hope you were listening to the latest from that asshole captain up there. Did you hear it or not?"

"I did."

"Hanging a loop out of one jet to be snagged by another. When Doyle talked about it, we all had a hard time to keep from laughing. I saw you grinning. You don't think they're going to land in one piece, do you?"

"I hope the hell they do."

"So do I. But be realistic."

"I'm out of South Central, Augie. I don't want to see your face again."

The beanpole man walked away from Augie. Forever.

1:22 P.M. CST (Over TULSA COUNTY)

•

7:22 P.M. GMT (BRISTOL)

EVERY AIRCRAFT COMPANY in the world had been monitoring the message traffic between Whiskey Charlie and Bristol. The engineering department at McDonnell Douglas had come to a halt long before. Their chief engineer for the Commercial Division, Claude Cooper, had requested a computer call-up for the fuel transfer systems on their KC–10 tankers from the database. The "hit" was immediate. Claude had also asked for the entire structural program from the direct access storage. The lasso idea would be placing additional proof loads on the tanks, pumps, and flow lines, since water was much heavier than jet fuel. When the call came through from Bristol, the program was already imaging. They had monitored Lucky's request to England, and like the helicopter manufacturer, the McDonnell Douglas company was proud to assist in the Whiskey Charlie rescue.

The maximum permitted takeoff weight of their KC–10, the military version of DC–10, was about

590,000 pounds, or just over a hundred tons lighter than the Trent 270. What had to be determined was the breaking strength of the two-inch cable: Those figures were phoned in by the Tulsa crane company. The weight needed to overcome the pressure on Whiskey Charlie's up elevators was only forty tons, less than twenty percent of the entire tanker's gross weight.

The engineers at the crane company had thought out the problem. Eleven of them were riding on a Tulsa fire truck attaching a heavy four-inch-thick bridle pad to both ends of the cable. With this arrangement, the tanker would rest on a soft fabric pad, the pressure being well distributed. The cable would not dig into the jet's structure. The pull would be soft and wide.

Then the report came in from McDonnell Douglas. "We looked at our working loads for certification of the DC–10. Then, of course, we took the abilities of the materials first and multiplied those values by the proof factor. The end result, the proof load, I mean, seems to be within the ultimate stress envelope," the McDonnell Douglas engineer said to everyone via the tower patch.

"Then this will work from a mechanical and load point of view?" Lucky asked.

"But there's a red flag," the McDonnell Douglas man said.

"I have one too," Frank A'hearn added.

"One at a time. Go ahead, McDonnell Douglas," Lucky said. "What do you have?"

"Well, there's wind gusts down there in Tulsa according to their last Terminal report. You're on the back side of a deep low pressure with gusts to forty knots. Do you confirm, Tulsa Tower?"

"Yes," Jack said, looking at the anemometer. "We're gusting forty now and then."

"That puts added loads on both structures."

"But we'll be below our rough air entry speed," Lucky assured them.

"I know. But there's a gust load factor."

"What's the risk?" Lucky asked.

"Hard to say. It's there, but limited," the McDonnell Douglas engineer said.

"What's *your* red flag problem, Frank?"

"The temperature in that wheel well is going to be like the South Pole on a windy winter day. Let's handle it this way. First, get some thermal gear down to Lucky from the chopper to halt the acute body temperature drop. Then I send down the real heavy-duty survival gear a bit later."

"I'm reading you," Charlie Hoover said. "I'm on the ground refueling. We have exposure gear and nets. We'll get them down via a cable drop."

The pumper truck pulled up with the bulky coil of thick cable; the crane company engineers showed Charlie and his chopper crew how to fasten the shackles. Charlie Hoover looked at his watch. It was 1:21, fifty-six minutes to Whiskey Charlie's latest projected fuel exhaustion time.

As he eyed the chopper being loaded and the dark spec of the Trent 270 climbing higher into the azure sky, Hoover's commanding officer came over.

"You and this Doyle seem to communicate well, Hoover."

"We do, sir."

"I was monitoring it. You did one hell of a job."

"Thank you, sir."

"Tell me, off the record, is this Doyle half a nut, or half brilliant, or what? No one around here can quite figure him out."

"There's a way to nail this guy down. He has, sir, what they call old-fashioned field expediency . . . making it all up as he goes. Doyle's not into the flight manual but that's okay. What he's facing isn't in the book."

"He's writing his own book."

"That's all he *can* do."

"You pull out all the stops. Tell you one thing, this Doyle is the coolest guy I've heard about."

"Yeah. One idea after another. Never gives up."

"Are they going to make this?" the officer asked Hoover.

"I'll be damned if I know, sir. All I want to do is help."

"And I'm damned proud of you, Hoover. Good going."

The new Lucky Doyle idea so stunned Bristol that no one dared to speculate one way or the other.

At that point, Mr. Waffles and two of his assistants rolled in a tea trolley piled with cups and small trimmed sandwiches that the chef in the executive kitchen had made.

"Tea is served in the conference room, Sir Ian," Mr. Waffles whispered.

"Thank you," Ian said. "Tug, Lou, Henry, perhaps some good Bristol tea and cakes."

"I want to run some numbers on the load pull," Tug said. "But thank you, sir."

The three men stepped down the hall to the engineering conference room. Thoughtfully rubbing his jaw, Ian searched the trolley for his favorite, cucumber sandwiches. He was delighted to see that Mr. Waffles had also laid on Irish cut glass goblets and a bottle of twenty-year-old Fabersham Scotch.

"That was a terrible thing Stiles did to you, Ian, hitting you that way," Lou said. "He shouldn't have lost his temper like that."

"My fault," Ian said quickly. "Mistake in judgment."

Henry's thin voice cut through the exchange. "Frankly, I don't know what this so-called prophet, Doyle, is doing. Water ballast! Hah! Then pulling that airplane down with a cable."

Ian poured himself a Scotch and padded about the room, talking as he moved. "I wonder if we'll ever get to meet this strange man, this Doyle?"

"I doubt it very much," Henry said.

"Drawing our Two-Seventy down with a cable is no more outlandish than the roof of a seven-thirty-seven peeling off, or the side of a United jet just falling away."

"I think you're right, Lou. When I meandered down to the gatehouse for a bit of air, I wondered if we hadn't become slaves to high tech. We can't even solve a simple problem. We can design spaceships with fine precision, yet we lose the simple skills to fix a few skin rivets so the fuselages will stay together. It's men like Doyle and Stiles who still have the basics." As Ian muttered on, there was a knock at the door.

"Yes," Ian called.

"Sorry, sir," Tug said, dipping his big head into the conference room.

"Come right in, Tug. Have a tea or a nip," Ian offered.

"Have to run me numbers. Just wanted to inform yuh, sir. I talked to the lads on the first floor. They've been very much into it, they have. With all their hearts and heads, they had a real go at things."

"I'm certain of that," Ian replied.

"They don't see why Doyle's ballast idea and the down haul can't work. There's plenty to be answered yet. But it's comin' along. It is."

"Grand."

"Just wanted to bring up the good news from the base floor, sir."

"Thank you, Tug."

The old footballer closed the door.

They all sat there quietly. One by one, they'd come round to share the thoughts that Ian had introduced. Each man thanked God that Doyle had not lost his head. And if he was a bit odd by today's high-tech standards, thank God for that too. Each man felt that Doyle represented common sense at its highest level. He was showing the world that a plane still needed a pilot: In the end, it all came down to human strengths and human courage.

But in all their minds the fate of Whiskey Charlie had been written at last. At that point anything and everything had to be tried, but very few thought the cable proposal would work. Many aviation authorities, especially the design engineers, didn't give it a chance. They were saying to themselves and to each other, "This is insane. You'll have two big jets down, not just one. Why is the Air Force allowing this? And why would the crew of the KC–10 risk their necks like this?"

1:28 P.M. CST
(Over TULSA)

"THERE THEY ARE." LOUIE Bonner pointed off to his left. Frank A'hearn twisted his neck up toward the halo of the sun; he saw the huge canted jet moving so slowly that at first he thought it might have been stapled to the sky.

"Makes me ache to see it," Frank said as he tapped his mike button.

"Lucky, we're in sight."

"I have you, Frank. Thanks for everything."

"I've always made house calls. You okay?"

"Not bad! Not bad! You hear the message traffic about my sling idea?"

"I caught it."

"Any suggestions?"

"Don't think so. It's the damnedest thing we've ever heard of. Louie and I were talking on the flight up here. We can't see any reason it wouldn't work, but tell that Air Force guy to go gently. There're wind gusts. So take it real slow."

"Lucky, this is Louie. Can I ask you something?"

"Sure."

"How in hell did you think up that sling idea?"

"By banner towing."

"What's that?"

"You know. Planes fly along beaches towing advertising banners. I used to do it. I noticed that the weight of the banner pulled my tail way down. So I figured the principle had to work for the nose of a plane as well as the tail. Weight on the end of the loading arm is critical!"

"That's true. But it's a complex theory."

"I know that but it's the same concept as the coin collectors. When aircraft weight gets out of the envelope, things happen."

"Lucky, the gods watch after you, I hope," Frank said. "I'm going to fly by your tail and take a look at the mess. We'll be ready to drop the thermal gear and CO_2 tanks . . . I have six nets of it. Then as I understand it, the tanker plane comes and lets the water ballast go."

"But that's not until we reach much lower altitudes. There'll be some time in between."

"Good luck! I knew you'd pull out of this!"

Frank A'hearn clicked off and Louie Bonner looked at him, accusation on his gnarled face.

"You're a liar, Frank," he said. "You never gave this a slim chance."

"I know. But what the hell do you say to a guy who's riding a high. Hear his voice?"

"Yeah. He really believes all this."

"He has to. What else does the poor bastard have?"

"Ladies and gentlemen," Lucky started, "soon we are going to drop the oxygen masks. The cabin attendants will show you how to hold them. We are working on a way to bring our nose down and you will see an Air Force jet, the military version of the DC–10, under us with a cable attached. Then the oxygen will be terminated as we reach lower and much warmer altitudes. We are well on our way to solving the problem. I know it has moved much slower than we expected, but things are looking better than ever. We will be back to Tulsa long before dinner."

Lucky then told five of the brawniest oil field workers to edge into the cockpit along with Alex. Then he turned around to face them.

"Here's the drill. Number one. I want Connie and André out of here behind the closed cockpit door."

"I'm staying up here," she said.

"Hell you are! We're going to be popping the escape hatch and there'll be a whirlwind in here, . . . a tornado of icy air. Now, the chopper will hover directly overhead, . . . drop down thermal suits, . . . not the heavy gear that's aboard the DC–six but good enough to protect us as we yank the cable below. That will come down next from the chopper. So as soon as we grab the net, we open the door to the bunk area. We jump into the thermal suits, . . . we come back to the cockpit and grab the heavy cable."

"But why are André and I out of the cockpit?" Connie asked.

"In case the cold gets to me too quick, we'll need backup pilots."

André agreed. He opened the door and left the cockpit.

"Charlie, you hear me?" Lucky said into the mike.

"We have you. Go ahead."

"Now, this is important. As you hover right over us with the net in place, we'll pop the hatch. We'll have to pick up your first load quickly. I'm reading sixty below outside air temperature. We won't last long in that temperature plus the wind-chill factor. The guys will have to grab that net within a minute or we're finished. I'll drop the oxygen masks as soon as you are in position. We'll start to depressurize."

"You'd better start that a couple of minutes before you pop the hatch," Charlie said. "Just let me maneuver for a while to make sure we have the net directly over you."

"Go ahead."

The chopper slowly worked into position about ten feet over the upper portion of the glass cockpit. Each of those inside were bundled up with scarves wrapped around their faces. Alex then handed out nine small bottles of oxygen that were carried on the Trent for cases of passenger illness such as heart attacks.

"I'll reach out for the net," Lucky said, pulling on a pair of heavy gloves that had been sent up to him from a passenger.

"Here we go. The masks are coming down."

Lucky pressed the release switch, and hundreds of yellow objects dangled down like swarms of wiggling goldfish. The passengers put the masks to their faces as Lucky started to decompressurize the jet. Three minutes later Charlie said, "I have my position figured out. Okay, let the hatch go. I'll slip sideways so it doesn't crash into my tail rotor."

The chopper dipped away as Lucky popped the hatch, which flew clear of the chopper. Charlie brought his machine into position. The loaded cargo net was unreeled toward the opened cockpit hatch.

The wind tore into the cockpit with such force that everyone was knocked down in a heap by the blast of air. It was so wild and chilled that it stung the flesh right through the layers of overcoats. Lucky pushed to his feet and, held up by five young men, he reached toward the bottom of the plump net. With a jab of his hand, Lucky jammed a finger into the rope cargo net. Two other volunteers clinched other ropes with their fingers. In one move, they all pulled and the net edged through the hatch as they passed the portable oxygen bottles around for swift inhales through the masks. When they had the net inside the cockpit, the crew opened the door to the bunk area, and once more a barrage of wind ripped in so hard that Connie and André were hurled down on the deck.

"Get into these quick!" Lucky yelled over the scream of the wind tearing into the jet's forward section.

They ripped open the net; nine thermal suits were spilled out, and each person changed as fast as possible. They began to suffer from the rapid fall in temperature: Their skin stung, and breaths were shorter and frosty white.

"Everyone okay?" Lucky yelled up against the squeal of the slipstream that was sailing through the cockpit door jamb.

"We're with you, Lucky! Everything hurts but we're all right," Alex yelled. "Keep those oxygen bottles going around, everyone."

"Now we have to go back for the cable," Lucky ordered.

They opened the door to the cockpit, and again the icy torrent of wind blasted them; they had to push each other forward into the cockpit. This time the slipstream did not have quite the lethal effect of glacial air moving at more than a hundred miles an hour. The thermal suits helped but only to a point.

"Cable next," Lucky yelled into his mike.

Through the open hatch Lucky looked up into the azure sky as the slipstream continued to slice in at them. A dark outline moved into place. Their eyes were watering and their vision was cut down to simple patterns of light and shade. The end of the heavy cable lasso slowly dropped through the open hatch with an ear-shattering clang. They grabbed it and opened the door to the bunk area, pulling the stiff cable through and down the circular steps to the lower level.

In the bunk area, Connie was so busy pulling out the thermal gear that she did not realize how painful the subzero wind was that was tearing into her skin. Everything was a dazzle, a frantic swish of movement for a few moments as they climbed into the gear. Gloves and face masks were put on with such speed that there was no time to realize the barrage of frigid air that was invading them. Then the realization. The torture. With the wind-chill factor, it was about a hundred degrees below zero, and this blast ate through their protective garments as if they were made of tropical netting.

Connie had always believed she could take anything that the elements had to deal out. For nights on end she had suffered through icy nights. Her job had been to fly canceled checks around in single-engine planes with heaters that hardly worked. The penetrating chill in those tiny cockpits was almost killing. She was proud of herself for handling those flight conditions, bundled up as she was in double gloves, a ski mask, fur boots, and as many sweaters as she could slip over her slim body.

But this was something else. Far worse. She had to suck in oxygen at the same time. The stream of air was so sharp that it tore deep into her. She had the feeling her skin was burning up. Yet no one complained. Forget pulling this fucking plane down, Connie said to herself. We're not surviving this cold. And maybe the whiffs of oxygen were not enough. Each person up front had the same thought. Lucky seemed to be the least affected. He knew Arctic air, he thought.

Even though the door to the passenger section was closed, the temperature there was dropping by about three degrees a minute. Linda Glen could tell, because the passengers started to wave one hand while holding the oxygen masks to their faces with the other. Each of them had been bundled up with all the coats, gloves, and hats they could find, but the air seeping in around the cockpit door was sharp and cruel. The Trent's heating system was useless.

"Miss, is it going to get colder?"

"Yes," Linda said. "They opened up the cockpit hatch to take in the cable. It will get colder before the air becomes warmer. But please don't talk. Keep the mask to your mouth. Breathe normally."

"But I can't stand this cold!" a woman up forward in first class cried. "I've got to get up and move about."

"No. Stay where you are. Breathe through the mask. Don't move!" Linda said, taking a breath of oxygen herself. She had seen Lucky Doyle take command of things, and she suddenly gained a spurt of new courage and determination. She went to the telephone and made the sharpest PA of her life.

"Ladies and gentlemen," she said, "my name is Linda Glen. I'm the senior cabin attendant. I've been with this airline for many years. I know you are suffering from extreme cold and it will get worse. Keep the masks to your face. In a couple of minutes the cable will be dropped under us, and a plane will pull this jet down to warmer air. The captain needs everyone seated in order to balance the plane. Please understand one thing. It's all coming down to these few moments. You will *not* freeze to death! It will be painful! But you will live. You will die if you get up and move around without breathing through the masks. Stay where you are and put up with the cold for a few minutes, or it will be all over for you, me, and everyone aboard. You must obey orders!"

"Lucky? You reading this?" Charlie said.

"I'm with you," Lucky answered.

"You'll see a big pad that the boys attached to the cable ends. That goes on the bottom of the loop so the tanker can slide in there without damaging the skin."

"Good thinking."

"How are you guys holding up?"

"We're freezing our asses off. These suits stink!"

"As soon as you pull the entire cable assembly down, we'll get out of here and let the DC–six send you down the heavier gear, but be careful, it's more than sixty below zero."

"Don't tell *me*."

When they had the entire cable aboard Whiskey Charlie, the chopper moved away and Frank A'hearn edged his DC–6 into place.

"Here come the heavy suits, Lucky," Frank said.

Another cargo net started down. Two of the oil field workers reached up through the hatch. The wind slammed their arms against the hatch coaming, almost breaking their bones.

The second net was hauled inside and down into the lower bunk area where it was warmer after they closed the cockpit door. Connie returned to the flight deck to check the glass panels. She realized that no one was going to be able to stand for long the freezing air that was blowing into the cockpit.

"Frank, we're going to have to rig some sort of a temporary hatch. The air in here is hell! I can hardly feel my fingers and I have these orange gloves on."

"I thought you were told by Bristol to get a buffet door and jam it up there with a scissor jack."

"Then send the jack the hell down! This cold is much worse than I figured."

"Have a few guys get in the cockpit to grab it."

Connie felt dizzy now. She pulled herself out of the cockpit seat, took a whiff of oxygen, and yelled down for a few of the oil riggers to help her with the hydraulic jack. She had to scream over the siren sound of the wind to tell Lucky what had to be done. Then Connie called Linda, telling her to have the rest of the maintenance guys rip off a buffet door.

"As big as you've got. We have to seal off this air flow," she said.

"It's getting cold as hell back here," Linda added. "I have passenger problems."

"It's not the tropics up here."

Lucky entered the glass cockpit in the heavier gear, looking like a padded polar bear. He sent Connie down below to dress in the new survival gear that Frank had provided. Within five minutes, a galley buffet door was slipped up to them in the bunk area. Lucky told Frank to lower the jack, which swung free of the 270 hatch and then crashed back against the fuselage.

"Sorry about that," Frank said over the transmitter.

"Forget it. That's the least of our problems."

Lucky and two others finally grabbed the large ungainly jack and tugged it inside the jet. Within five minutes, the galley door was being scissored up to close off the opening. Air still ripped in around the edges, but the main stream had been sealed off.

"That helps," Lucky said to Frank.

"Good going, buddy. We're moving off now. How much fuel time left?"

Lucky quickly scanned the gauges.

"About twenty-five minutes."

"You've put up one hell of a fight, Lucky."

"It isn't over yet."

7:39 P.M. GMT (BRISTOL)

•

IAN, WATCHING THE TRANSfer of equipment to the 270, first from the chopper and then from the DC–6, pulled Dr. Kagune and Henry aside.

"What do you men think of this?"

"The most extraordinary thing I've ever seen," Dr. Kagune said. "For one thing, Sir Ian, I don't know how the bloody hell that crew is getting by with the chill factor, just taking a few whiffs from portable oxygen bottles. I can predict this with certainty. There are going to be cases of acute frostbite, maybe loss of limbs."

"You, Henry?"

"Oh, I'm sorry, Sir Ian, I wasn't listening. I've been at this all day, seems like a lifetime."

"All of us feel the same way. It's like days under dreadful pressure."

"But think of what all those on the flight must be feeling and experiencing."

"Yes, indeed," Ian said. "We should be the last to complain. But Henry, just as old friends and fellows together in this aircraft business, what's the odds of this working?"

"Slim. Very, very slim. Time is running out. Well, it's been running out all day. But now we're down to the last turn to the wire, as they say on the turf track. In straight talk, Ian, the odds are terribly against Doyle. But what a valiant effort, I must say. Hours ago, I thought we had the fool of fools on our hands. Now I've come to admire the man with all my heart. We didn't come up with another solution in spite of my thinking we could find one. I've been very humbled by this. So have my engineers."

"We all have."

"Agreed, Sir Ian," Dr. Kagune said.

"They *are* going in, aren't they?" Ian asked Henry.

"I can't say for sure. Truthfully, I thought I would be home now telling my wife that Trent Aviation was a failed company, and that the largest loss of life in any one American air crash was our fault somehow. But I'm still here. The flight is still up. You ask if this will work. Honestly, I don't know anymore. The whole thing, these cables between aircraft, is so unprecedented and off the charts, that I have no answers. I've been useless all day. Will this do it? It's anybody's guess right now. Doyle is on to the right engineering principle, but there are too many things that could go wrong. You might as well ask the local tapster if it will work. His prediction is as good as mine at this point."

"I understand," Ian said. "About this frostbite, it might be all academic, but what is it, Doctor?"

"Well, severe cold constricts the blood vessels. This reduces the warm flow of blood to exposed tissues. The skin appears flushed red at first. Then white or grayish yellow. In extreme cases swelling and bleeding will take place because of fluid accumulation after thawing. This is a setup for gangrene. In most cases amputation is called for."

"I see. But that's the least of the problems right now, isn't it?"

"The very least," Dr. Kagune said, and Henry agreed with a dip of his head.

1:49 P.M. CST
(Over TULSA COUNTY)

●

———————AS THEY OPENED THE PRESsure hatch in the lower bunk area, another blast of frigid air erupted into their masked faces. Lucky ordered the wheels lowered via a telephone connection to Connie. There was a hum that could be heard over the whistle of the wind. The hydraulic system was feeding power to the nose gear actuating linkage. The whole massive assembly of huge forgings: the main strut; the side braces; along with cylinders; torque tubes; the drag link, and two giant tires on their axles and brake pads, curled out of the well and locked into place with a deafening clang!

Lucky then straddled the torque tube as the frosty gale rushed up at him. He signaled for the end of the cable with the eye splice to be dropped down. He circled that around the landing gear side brace. Even though the Arctic suit was guaranteed down to ninety below, he felt chill penetrate the layers of insulated fabric. His work gloves were so bulky that they surrounded the thick shackle that was handed down. He knew what he had to do. None of those looking down into the wheel well realized Lucky's daring and the high risk he took, because they had never had to work in an Arctic icestorm. Lucky knew what might happen to him, but he took the chance. He knew that if he kept his gloves on, he would never thread the shackle and take up on the bolt head, or push the safety wire through so that the bolt wouldn't back off. It all had to be done with bare fingers.

Lucky didn't have the gloves off for a second when he knew he had blundered. The feeling in his fingers went as if his blood had instantly drained. But he continued, realizing it was the only hope they had now. Somehow, without actually feeling the shackle, he snapped it around the cable's eye splice, jamming in the bolt, taking up on it as hard as he could. He signaled for the safety wire, and it was almost torn from his fingers by the blasts of the curling slipstream. Without that safety wire, the bolt might work loose. He took it in his teeth and used that pressure to feed it through the eye of the bolt. He twisted the wire tighter and tighter until the torque limit was reached.

Alex could see that Lucky was in trouble. He dropped into the well, and holding the bungee cylinder, he grabbed his friend by the armpits. It looked as if Lucky had been about to fall through the well and out of the Trent to the white carpet over 16,000 feet below them.

Lucky was wavering. He was wobbly in the head because he hadn't taken a dose of oxygen in two minutes. All this was made more difficult because there was no sense talking or even yelling. The piercing whistle and tear of the wind was so fierce that no one could be heard.

Finally, Lucky had the bolt safely wired, and he motioned to be hauled out of the well. He wasn't sure that the bolt was as tight as it could have been, but he had done what he could and time was slipping away again.

When Lucky was hauled back into the lower bunk area, they pushed the oxygen mask to his face, then dropped the cable down.

The loop spilled from the bottom of the jet and waved about like a giant hangman's noose in a gale of wind. The cable's undulating path was only about fifty feet below the underbody of the 270. Charlie peered up as the KC–10 inched up on the swaying bridle.

"Think I can work my nose into it?" Colonel Goodwin asked his copilot.

The colonel had taken the left seat in the tanker jet, and he let everyone know it. But under his calm facade, Jeff Goodwin was frightened. The large loop seemed like a dangling threat: a snare that could hold him and kill him. Somehow a waking nightmare engaged the colonel's mind. Once he had maneuvered his tanker's nose into this noose, he imagined that it would tighten up, the huge Trent 270 would take over. Something would happen, control would be lost.

They would go in together just as some experts had predicted.

The colonel tried not to dwell on that possibility, for in front of him the cable loop seemed to be opening. He eased his trembling fingers forward on the three thrust levers while his copilot looked over and noticed his shaking knuckles.

"There we go, sir. Inching up now. Very nicely. Slowly does it."

They were about twenty feet from the loop when suddenly, and for no reason, the entire cable rig flipped into a giant figure eight, closing the opening as fast as a snappy dog clamps his teeth shut.

"Shit!" Goodwin cried. "Have we got to fight this?" He backed off on his thrust slightly. His nose fell. He figured out his mistake. The right action would have been to nose up to retard his forward motion while tickling in a bit more power.

"Don't worry about that," the copilot said. "It'll open up again. When it does, go for it quick."

"You're doing fine," Lucky said on the phone as he looked below. "It's opening. Lower your nose and give it the juice."

Goodwin followed orders as if he were a first-day student pilot. As soon as he saw the figure eight unwind, the colonel pushed the yoke forward, coming in with power but far too much. There was a hollow-sounding explosion as the thick cable whipped the side of the Air Force tanker. The cable continued to pound the fuselage with an ear-shattering rattle like the continued blasts of fifty machine guns at close range.

"Take off thrust, sir!" the copilot bellowed. It was too late. The cable loop flung aft and collided with the wing root with such force that the entire tanker shook, first pitching up and down, then rocking violently as the new force, an alien one, was plunged into the delicate balance of the aircraft's lift. Goodwin pulled up his nose slightly to ease the pressure on the pounding cable. Once more he pulled the wrong move.

"If I may suggest, sir, I would take off thrust. In that way, you'll settle into the padded part of the sling. I can see it far below us."

The colonel pushed his nose down again and without saying a word, he came back on his thrust levers. The tanker plane settled into the sling. The cable slapping against the KC–10's skin eased off; only an occasional bang could be heard.

"Very nice, sir," the copilot said.

Goodwin looked up at the jet above him. It was so large that the midday sun was blocked out, casting a dark shadow over the entire tanker.

The cable stretched out of the 270 bay, becoming taut. Lucky knew he had his pull. He raced up the stairs to the cockpit, pulled the door open, and entered.

"We got it, Connie! The tanker has the loop! Come on down, you bastard, come on down," he yelled delightedly.

André slid from the left seat, letting Lucky replace him. Lucky hit his sidestick button but his fingers missed. Connie could tell what had happened: Lucky had lost all feeling in his hands. She reached over and held the button down for him.

"Should I take off thrust? I see my nose coming down," Lucky said into his mike.

"My descent is two hundred feet a minute," Goodwin reported.

"Want to take that to three hundred? I am already out of seventeen thousand," Lucky yelled out.

"I'll try my spoilers," Goodwin said.

The tanker jet had pulled Whiskey Charlie's nose down to a point at which the airspeed picked up to almost one hundred eighty knots. Lucky signaled that Connie should reduce thrust, to idle. The fuel flow plunged.

"You got too much drag in there for me," Goodwin yelled.

Frank A'hearn broke in. "Lucky, go to twenty degrees of flap. Your nose is down enough. You won't stall now. You have to move exactly the same way as the tanker below you."

Connie pressed the flap handle.

"Lucky, it's working," Charlie said.

"So far."

1:49 P.M. CST (Over TULSA COUNTY)

There was a knock on the cockpit door. "That bolt on the shackle is going, I think," Alex reported.

"Can't do anything about it now. I want to see if we can get the nose down even further. Keep an eye on the cable assembly, Alex. As soon as I'm into twelve thousand, I'll call on the phone and you can cut off the oxygen flow." Shivering, Alex left the cockpit, taking a drag on the portable oxygen tank in his gloved hand. Connie felt Lucky's stiffened hands.

"I've got bad frostbite," he said.

She started to remove his gloves slowly. Lucky felt nothing: That's when Connie knew it was serious.

"I'll be okay." Lucky said. That, she thought, was the true rarity of this man. As bad as things went, from horrible to deathly, he still managed to punch a smile on his face.

1:58 P.M. CST
(Over TULSA COUNTY)

●

"FRANK, WE'VE GOT PHYSICAL problems!" Lucky said into his mike. "I picked up a bad case of frostbite. There're six others who might have it to some degree."

"How bad did it hit you, Lucky?"

"Very. But forget it. I'll need the large hose."

"We have three lines aboard," Frank answered. "Plus the fittings from the Fort Smith fire truck."

"There isn't time to drill them in, Frank. The guys are half out of it. Our fingers are stiff. I'm going to start hitting that tail with soft lead. Charlie, you still have those turkeyshooters up with you?"

"Sure do."

"Wait a minute," Tug Stiles cut in. "If you start on those inboards, Doyle, how yuh goin' to round out? You'll destroy the trim control. How you going to pick up that nose once the Air Force plane backs out of the bridle? You have to have some control on the landin' or you'll bust it up completely."

"I know, I know. Listen a minute. When we release

the cable at around six thousand, the tanker above us will shoot water into the lower bunk area. It's an airtight hatch. Has to be."

"It is. I designed it," Tug said.

"All right, then I'll have maybe five tons of water slopping around under me. That will bring my nose down."

"But you'll be broken in half, Doyle. Yuh got flipper pressure one way, water weight another. Those frames won't hold yuh together."

"I know that," Lucky shouted back, starting to lose his temper. "I'm giving up the flippers. Charlie will blast holes in them to take the pressure off."

"Then yuh got explosion possibilities back aft."

"I called for choppers with CO_2 pumps and tanks. Frank, did you load the large CO_2 tanks in case we have to fight a fire from the inside?"

"Just like you asked for, Lucky."

"Then after they drop the water hose, send down those CO_2 tanks," Lucky said.

"Lucky, Tug asked you a question. If you pound those elevators with lead, you'll lose the trim control. How do you pitch the nose up for a landing? You can't go in with a down angle."

There was a pause as Connie caught the full thrust of Frank's question. She put her arm around Lucky, rubbing his arms up to his elbow, trying to bring his circulation back. Lucky's face was clearly devoid of blood; he looked ancient, as if this struggle had not only robbed him of his hands but years of his life.

She saw him swallow twice before he spoke. His voice was hoarse and broken.

"I thought of this before. We have a load of water below us. We're on a nose-down final approach. I'll send someone below to flip the lever on the hatch. The water flows out into the wheel well with some leakage. So when I want to get my nose up, I drop the gear. The water plops out. The nose comes up, just enough for me to drive this baby on in a flare. I can do it in steps. Gear down, gear up. I have some control of the water ballast, right?"

In Bristol, Tug Stiles moved toward Ian. The "muckie," a practical home aircraft builder, and a flyer, was for the first time in his life totally confounded. "Never heard of anythin' like that. Will it work, Gibbons?" Tug asked.

Henry peered at his men and the computer terminal. There was nothing they could say. Nothing they could do.

The stillness at Bristol was repeated around the world. The aircraft expert assisting Dan Rather, a former Douglas senior engineer and test pilot, looked vacant. "Captain Ranson, how would you assess this latest idea? Or is it bordering on desperate dreams?" Rather asked.

The white-haired engineer pushed back in his seat on the CBS set. "It's so far beyond the envelope of our aviation experience, I can't even guess if it's real or a desperate attempt at grabbing straws. Doyle's mechanical logic is sound, but there are so many variables—the wrong displacement of water, electrical shorts, and a hundred other bugs. If he submerges his electronic racks with water, he'll be left with shorts and no electrical systems. He'll lose some capability. Elements of the hydraulics are electrically actived in that particular jet. And what if the nose gear doors can't stand the added weight of the water ballast?"

Henry and Tug realized the same thing. Tug reacted first.

"The doors are beefed up. But an electrical failure is the problem. I've got it! Doyle should cut around the main electrical circuits. Just like that heart operation, bypass surgery. Go right to the emergency power supply so the electrical jungle in the lower bay will be dead by the time the waterfall hits it."

"Tell him that," Ian ordered.

Tug repeated the procedure to Lucky.

"Beautiful," Lucky said.

"What's your fuel time when you spool up?" Tug asked.

"Nineteen minutes," Connie said, looking at the numbers on the glass panel.

"Say altitude?" Tug asked.

"Thirteen thousand. . . . We're losing six hundred feet a minute," Lucky said. "Tug, do I let the water flow into the nose wheel bay with the hatch open, or do we close it after we drop the cable?"

"Keep the hatch closed. That water pressure in the nose wheel bay could bust through the landing gear doors."

"You afraid that water might interfere with the hydraulic system on the gear?" Lucky asked.

"No. We worked on that a long time. It's all watertight because a lot of snow and runway slush gets kicked up into the nose gear well. But I'd get set for yuh drop from A'hearn straightaway. Forget the oxygen bottles. You're low enough. Won't need them. The fire fighting equipment? Hell, yes. Yuh goin' to have trouble back aft. Don't like shootin' up that tail, Doyle."

"What else can I do? I'm fuel critical! You tell me I shouldn't shoot water in here with the elevators exerting back pressure. We'll pull that jet apart. That's what you told me."

"Take it easy, Doyle. I know what I told yuh. You're doin' a good job. Just don't want to see your arse blown off after all this."

"One of the I.A. mechanics aboard thinks there's enough air getting in there so it won't explode. A fire, maybe. Explosion, no."

"Hope he's right. Have to give it a go," Tug said with little conviction.

"I'm right above you again." Frank said. "Pull your guys away from the opening after you remove the temporary hatch."

Louie Bonner was flying the DC–6. Frank and his crew in Arctic suits were attached to its cargo hold structure by harnesses and ropes. Frank, on his stomach, inched toward the wide opening of the cargo hatch. He tossed out the coiled rope with the heavy monkey fist on the end, playing it out until the hemp bounced along Whiskey Charlie's top skin.

"Give me an inch more throttle, Louie," Frank said into the boom mike off his fur-lined helmet.

The DC–6 inched forward. When the knotted ball was just above the hatch, Frank let it drop and one of Lucky's crew grabbed it.

"We have the ball," Lucky said into his mike.

The DC–6 crew pushed over a distended cargo net packed with fire fighting gear and clanking CO_2 bottles. Thinking about the choppers laying bullets into the 270's two inboard elevators, Frank's stomach butterflies returned: The Aussie agreed with Tug. There was a good chance of an explosion; it could not be predicted one way or the other. But if they didn't blast holes in the jammed elevators, the weight of the ballast water forward would pull the jet in half; there was no doubt about it. The threat of breaking up the 270 jet by an explosion or by a hull separation was about equal.

"I'm scared as hell of this," André said to Connie.

"What the hell is he supposed to do?" She whispered. "He has to take a chance on those elevators."

"So goddamned primitive."

"Come up with another solution."

"There isn't any."

"I haven't heard of anyone outdoing Doyle today," she said with a snap.

"You know something? I have the feeling that Lucky's a ghost."

Connie pulled back and looked at the sallow face of the chief pilot, thinking that the pressure on this man had pushed him over the edge.

"A ghost?"

"Lucky's from another age. People just don't do things like this anymore. It's yesterday stuff. This cable, . . . pumping lead through elevators, . . . water in the forward hold."

"You ought to be damned glad you have a ghost, . . . a yesterday man. Figure he came back from the dead to let you live. He's just the sort of ghost who's going to get us the hell out of this. So shut up!"

"You're right. If he's a ghost he's a God damned imaginative one."

"The only kind, André. The others are not worth having around. What did all this technology do for us today?"

"Nothing."

As Frank retrieved the line to lower the fighting equipment, he wondered how the hinge attachment on the elevators had lasted as long as it had. When one of the aviation experts commented on the same aspect of the freakish incident, he said that the Trent 270 definitely had more structural beef than any other commercial airliner ever built. Others in the industry realized the same point: The once-condemned airliner was now drawing solid praise.

"Everyone all right down there?" Frank asked.

"We're fine. The guys feel better. Some of the blood's beginning to flush around their arms," Connie said.

"What about you, Lucky?" Frank asked.

"Not picking up much feeling. I popped some skin off. I'm bleeding."

"How bad? Can you still handle the sidestick?"

"I think so. If Connie works my thrust levers."

"Now, Lucky, you make sure you have those tanks ready back there. If you get combustion, you'll have to shoot the CO_2 in fast so it doesn't get out of control. Don't waste the stuff on smoke, just fire."

Lucky phoned back aft to make sure his crew was positioned with the CO_2 nozzles, ready to head off the fire that he knew was coming as soon as the chopper opened up.

The last load from the DC–6 contained a six-inch rubber suction hose. Alex, exerting all his energies, flopped one end down into the lower bunk area as he hacked away at the liners around the opened hatch. A shaft of slipstream air continued to surge in. Taking part of the tether line from the drop rope, Alex looped it around an exposed stringer. He tied the end to the hose coupling.

"Hand me the phone. Want to PA the passengers for the last time."

She placed the phone by his mouth. He drew in a deep breath. Weakly but calmly he spoke, with pauses between the words.

"Ladies and gentlemen, as you can see, we're much lower now and the cabin will be warming up soon. To the left is the airport, which I'm going to have foamed for us. You will see a helicopter pass our tail several times, . . . you might hear the rattle of a machine gun. What we are doing is blowing small holes through the elevators to take off some of the pressure. When we detach the cable from the Air Force plane that is drawing us down to much safer altitudes, we will flood our forward area with water. Things have worked out well so far. You have seen some of the volunteers moving past you with fire fighting tanks. We might pick up a fire within the tail cone.

"You might smell or even see smoke. But the fire, if any, will be contained in the far after section, since there's an airtight pressure bulkhead back there that would prevent the flames from spreading forward. When the crash occurred, it ruptured the hydraulic lines that operate our control surfaces. Also, I'm afraid the impact ruptured the four-hundred-gallon fuel tank that supplies the aircraft's auxiliary power unit, a small jet engine located in the tail cone.

"We are now estimating a landing around two-fifteen. How smooth—or rough—it will be will largely depend on the action of the water ballast. You will feel certain unusual up and down motions of the jet. Our angle of descent will be steeper than normal. At a point near the runway, when we extend the landing gear, we plan to let the forward water ballast go. The water will flow out. The nose will come up and by that time we will be on the ground. The landing will be much rougher than usual because most of our pitch control is gone. At least we will be there in plenty of time for supper. It's been a long flight for all of us. We've had some things go poorly. Other ideas for a safe descent proved better than expected. Again from all of us, thank you for your bravery and good cooperation."

When Lucky clicked off, he tried to move his fingers and wrists. All feeling was gone.

"Connie, we have to find someone to dive down in that water and open the hatch."

"You've found him, Lucky" André said. "I was

on the McGill varsity swim team, and I'm a scuba diver."

"Think you can do it, André?"

"I'm sure I can. These Oklahoma guys aren't exactly swimmers, but I can handle myself underwater."

"You have it then. It's going to be a chilly dive, and for God's sake make sure you don't go out the hatch with that load of ballast water."

"Frank sent you plenty of rope," André replied. "Just get a line around me. We'll use that as a signal. When you want the nose up, just give it a yank and I'll open the hatch."

"Sounds good, André. Another thing. You were listening to that Tug Stiles. He was afraid we'd blow the tail off. Alex, tell André what you think."

"I told him that I thought conditions for a fire existed when the bullets start hitting our elevators. But to set up an explosion, you'd need trapped fumes. I don't see that. Some of the horizontal stabilizer is off. The rudder is gone, snapped off at the hinges. Those ribs and verticals are not airtight. Ram air must be shooting in there."

"But you can't be certain," Connie interjected.

"It's an educated guess. That's all. There's nothing certain about anything in this screwball situation," Alex said.

"But Tug seems much more concerned about it than you do," Connie said. "What does he know that you don't?"

The I.A. maintenance man rubbed his face. It was a telltale clue: He would not say there would be no explosion with bullets sailing into the control surface. Even a small amount of trapped fumes could cause a detonation that would certainly blow the tail off in a chain reaction of kerosene explosions.

"Well," Alex began after thinking it over, "we both know that the science of detonation isn't totally understood. Some planes explode in a crash. Others don't. It's never been sorted out."

Connie could see that Lucky was feeling pain as some blood returned to his lower arms—a good sign. His face was screwed up in thought. It was, she knew, a super tough decision. Should he risk the bullets kicking off a deathly explosion or not? It took him a few seconds to speak. When he did he said something that Connie never thought to hear Lucky say.

"We need the computer. It's a *necessity*! We have to grab a prediction on structural failure." Lucky signaled Connie to depress his transmit button. "Is Gibbons there?"

"I'm on," Henry answered. "You want Stiles or me?"

"You're the computer ace aren't you?"

"I do my best."

"I have the worst decision to make now. I'm afraid of an explosion back there."

"So are we."

"There're several opinions. Is there enough air shuffling around in the tail cone to prevent a blast?"

"No one can answer that," Henry said.

"That's what bugs me. Things I can't get hold of."

"It's dreadfully nagging to us also. We're damned both ways."

"Things are going okay for the moment. Fuel is being saved. The tanker below me is pulling us down nicely, . . . no structural problems on either end. So I don't want to pop my ass off now."

"Of course not. We see the good progress on the telly. No one would have believed this, Lucky. I didn't. I think I know your next question," Henry said.

"What if I didn't call for more shots and left things as they are? I'll have water slopping all around below me, about thirty tons of it. . . ."

"We estimate twenty-five," Henry interrupted.

"How fast would my structural breakup occur? Would it be gradual, the way it is now? Would I have enough time to reach the runway, or would the computer show a fast breakup in the air? Can your computer take the variables and give us a sequence of events? With a time database?"

"That's what it can do, as long as the proper information is entered. We have a solid database now, . . . your frame movement, . . . the engineering loads on the structure as built . . . failure limits. We can program the weight and position of the water. As a matter of fact, we have three men working on the program now. Stand by, we'll see what happens here. It might take five minutes, perhaps eight, to provide some reliable forecasting."

Jeff Goodwin heard the transmission in the air tanker and said, "If that tail blows, I want to get out of here, Lucky."

He had hoped that no one in the Pentagon would lose sight of the dangers in this mission: one jet attached with a two-inch cable to another.

"Jeff, let me ask you something," Lucky said.

"Go ahead, Lucky."

"You saw that sheared-off horizontal stabilizer back there."

"Sure, what about it?"

"Think there's air blowing in?"

"I heard your conversation. I'd say yes, if there're lightening holes in the tail ribs."

"There are," Tug answered. "We know there's some air gettin' in, but is it circulating enough so we don't have fume pockets? All yuh need to kick off a detonation is a pocket of trapped fumes. That changes the flash point of other trapped fumes. There're all types of explosions, . . . one big blast . . . a series of small ones, . . . the delayed action kind. Any one of them will tear off that tail. It's hangin' up there by a deformed structure. Wouldn't take much to crack it off!"

All Goodwin wanted to make sure of was his tanker's freedom from the 270 long before they started to eat into the tail section with soft-leaded bullets. If there was to be an explosion, he wanted his tanker out of the noose and far away. In all his years of flying, Jeff had never experienced such a dread of air work. An aircraft, by definition, is designed for emancipated movement in any direction: to have that scope restricted by a thick cable shackled to a jet three times the tanker's weight seemed to upset every theory of free flight. It was weird, Jeff thought.

If he had seen the uncanny TV pictures of his tanker slowly edging the nose of the much longer Trent lower and lower into friendly air, the colonel would have been even more rattled. With the huge jet positioned over the smaller tanker, an almost perverse visual effect was generated. It looked like a balancing act full of threats. What if something went wrong and the mighty 270 stalled and merely fell on the tanker, taking it to earth and crushing it as flat as a runover tin can?

"I would have never believed this, Lucky," Frank said. "Only you would think up that idea, but the tanker's pulling you down nicely."

"I had to go for it, Frank. I miscalculated the time for the patch-up job. It was a two-day job, and I thought I could pull it off in an hour."

"How are your hands?"

"No feeling yet."

"Frostbite can be handled. Don't worry about that. Just get that flying machine on the ground. You're very close now."

"Thanks. I'll see you soon."

"I'm going to slip off and land. See you down on the runway."

As Frank A'hearn banked away, he took a last look at the two jets, connected with a cable, slowly descending together.

"If I hadn't seen that with my own eyes, Louie, I would never have believed it."

"It's about as whacko as you can get. But that's how Lucky always liked it. The tougher, the better."

"He never played around with things like possible explosions and dumping water out to get his nose up for a landing. That's really going the hog," Louie added.

Chris Ranson, sitting beside Dan Rather in New York, called the final stages of the Whiskey Charlie episode "the ultimate imbroglio of aviation problems. Unimaginable."

Rather said that there were hundreds of calls to the network from airline pilots saying that their aircraft would not react in the same way the Trent 270 had. Ranson offered the explanation that the new English jet was a different breed of aircraft; its structure and systems were different from other widebodies. Yet the principles of flight and mechanics were the same.

The TV viewers understood the explanation: The Trent was a special bird, but what eluded almost everyone was the Doyle plan. What would happen when the cable was let free and the tanker plane started pouring water ballast into the 270? Chris Ranson, using a blackboard, brought immediate clarity to the scheme with drawings.

"It's actually very simple," Chris said. "All morning

Doyle has used the fulcrum concept. That's been threaded through his entire thinking in many different ways."

Ranson drew a seesaw on the blackboard.

"If someone can understand the principles of a seesaw, then Lucky Doyle's idea becomes simple. It's at the very far ends of the seesaw where the weight really counts. In aviation we call that the ends of the loading arm. On TV it looks as if the smaller Air Force jet is pulling the huge airliner down toward earth. But how can this be? It appears backward. The heavier, much larger jet should be on the lower end. The big guy should take the load. What's really happening? All planes have a center of gravity around the midsection. On each end of the seesaw, the weight has much more force than it would in the middle. So we look at the cable. It's attached to the nose gear of the airliner, far forward. All they are doing is changing the direction of the nose. It's gravity that is pulling both jets down. The Air Force tanker is doing nothing more than directing the angle of the descent. That's the principle Doyle has been using.

"So once they're in warmer air, the tanker plane will slide out of the loop. At that point, the nose of the Trent will pitch up again. Then Captain Doyle wants the Army chopper to take some pressure off the tail by shooting holes in the elevators. He knows that this will not bring his nose down enough for a landing. But without intervention they'll just start climbing once more until his fuel runs out. So what does Doyle do? He replaces the pull of the Air Force tanker with the added weight of water dumped into his forward hull. Now the jet's nose is down once more. It's pointed in the right direction for a landing. But he can't land just like that. He'll drive the nose into the runway. They'll crash! So he's come up with a unique concept. Just before he flares, brings his nose up for the landing, he drops his landing gear, the water pours out, the nose comes back up, just then he takes off his power, and the jet falls on the edge of a stall. He hopes it won't fall far because the runway will be right under him. Doyle's gone back to the playground, to kindergarten, for a fundamental concept. It's super low tech. That's why his logic frustrates us; his whole line of reasoning flies over our heads. It's sad. We can no longer think of seesaws."

"I think we understand the process Doyle's using. But something horrendous is still hanging over the man's head," Rather said. "Yes, indeed. If just one of those bullets hits trapped fumes, it doesn't matter how brilliantly the seesaw effect works."

The ex–McDonnell Douglas test pilot drew something else on the blackboard: the outline of the Trent 270. He then stroked flash lines coming from the tail section to represent an explosion.

"If there's an instant ignition, this will happen." Ranson then took his blackboard eraser and wiped the tail off his drawing. "If that happens, they won't have a tail section. As goes the tail, so goes the jet."

2:08 P.M. CST (Over TULSA INTERNATIONAL AIRPORT)

———————"OUT OF SIX THOUSAND FOR five thousand," Lucky said, "What do you have, Bristol? What's the verdict?"

"We're experiencing a bit of trouble calculating the free surface of the water you're going to pump in. It'll slop around. The weights will change," Henry said.

"Of course," Lucky said. "But there must be a constant figure."

"We plugged in as many variables as possible. We'll image it and get back to you fast as we can."

Tug, who never trusted computer resolving any more than Lucky did, edged closer to the large terminal.

The passengers were warm now, and the oxygen valve had been turned off. The airport, just below them, looked like a safe haven, the scene of a homecoming, the proof of the captain's promise. While passenger confidence rose again, their lives or deaths were being decided by a supercomputer more than 4,000 miles away. Henry's programmers had piled up the 270 database, the structural models, the frame failure rate, and the timetable, which was updated once more by Connie. She had moved aft to mark up and time the frame movements. The deformation was increasing. She phoned the bad news to the cockpit, and then ran forward ignoring the barrage of questions from the passengers.

The new data were entered, and the failure pattern was aligned and programmed. A core of information was beginning to mount. Henry ran the imaging two ways: What would likely occur if the elevator was *not* opened up by chopper fire, and what would happen the other way?

The imaging crept across the screen in dimensional animation. The outer skin was presented in light pink. Whiskey Charlie's scenario was picked up at the point where the tanker plane had worked itself loose of the downhaul bridle. Now, as expected, the 270 assumed an eight-degree up angle. On the computer, the turbines' levers were inched forward to prevent the stall and spin. Although the plane and delivery nozzle were not imaged, the entry of the water at the flow rate, which had been radioed in to Bristol by the tanker, was represented by a spate of blue entering the lower bunk area through the six-inch suction hose.

A digital clock showing minutes and seconds and geared to a selected time mode clicked along the baseline of the graphic imaging. Two minutes went by as the first five tons of water gushed into Whiskey Charlie's forward section. At the ten-ton level, the frame collapse picked up. At four minutes and ten seconds, with about twelve tons of blue slopping around in the lower hull section as realistically as if it were wet to the touch, the frame buckling became more apparent. A split in the skin section began to develop just aft of the trailing edge of the wing root as the pink outer skin warped. The nose of the aircraft came down about four degrees as predicted. Suddenly, without even the fractures elongating, there was a confused intermingling of all the structural members. Two seconds later, Whiskey Charlie split in half with its shredded parts strewn out, a blinking geyser on the screen. Even that deathly breakup had its own computer surrealism. The two halves fell away. Then the terminal went black. Total time to failure: five minutes and forty-one seconds in actual time, speeded up to twenty-nine seconds in computer time.

"I could have told yuh that," Tug said. "Run it the other way."

This time most of the exerted pressure on the flippers was extracted from the program as if the chopper had torn open the elevator with soft-leaded bullets. Again the clock began at zero. Water was pumped in. By seven minutes and nine seconds, with seventeen tons of liquid surging about in the forward belly, the nose of the 270 lowered to a three-degree down angle. The frames slowly started to buckle once more. They watched closely for the revealing split in the pink outer skin. Forty seconds—nine actual minutes—slipped by with a soft bending of the jet's after section. Then, according to the imaging, the collapse slowed down. The Trent computer people increased the time frame mode. Twenty minutes. Thirty minutes. Forty minutes. Never!

"Now see how much has to be jettisoned for a nose up," Henry said. His staff had even estimated the water outflow from the opened landing gear doors. Eleven tons flowed out in twenty-two seconds. The nose came up. In theory they had landed. Whiskey Charlie was on the runway and in one piece.

Henry reached for the phone.

"Lucky, there's no doubt about it. You have to hit

that tail. If you don't, we show a total airframe separation in less than five minutes. It happened very suddenly."

"What if I landed in four minutes . . . before the final breakup?"

"Here's the problem. Once you have the nose down, you're aiming for the runway. At the last minute you must raise the nose by dumping the water. You're going from nose down to nose up. You can't do that with the frame failing. The weight of the water suddenly disappearing will reverse the pressure. You'll break up before you reach the runway. The only chance is more bullets through the tail . . . And I agree, it's one hell of a risk. But we can't see any other way."

"I get it," Lucky said. "Well, if it has to be, that's it. Here I go."

2:14 P.M. CST (Over TULSA INTERNATIONAL AIRPORT)

•

LUCKY ORDERED THE SECOND tanker plane to position itself overhead. The temporary cockpit hatch was removed. André was on the ladder to the lower bunk area with a rope twisted about his thin midsection, ready to dive down into the ballast water to open the hatch to the wheel well.

Their altitude was 5,500 feet. Lucky ordered that the tanker below them nose up, and inch by inch the Air Force KC–10 fell back with the bridle flipping along the aircraft's skin, sending off more sparks as it reached the nose and snapped free. Jeff Goodwin stared through the windshield, seeing the cable bound up into the air, then loop into a figure eight, as he dipped his nose down and flew under it, thanking God that he was free from that bondage.

"Lucky, I'm reading nine minutes to fuel exhaustion, the nose is coming up now, have to feed in power. Our airspeed is off," Connie cried out, as she pushed up the two thrust levers. Lucky looked at the decaying airspeed.

"As soon as we shoot the water in here, the nose will drop. We'll go to idle thrust. That should give us more fuel time."

"Hope our calculations are right," she said.

Lucky ordered his work crew to drop below with the safety lines, open the hatch, and back off the shackle bolt to free the cable that was hanging below the 270.

Lucky made a slight turn so that the massive bridle would fall far to the side of the airport runway where hundreds were lined up: not spectators but fire fighters and medical teams. The newsmen were posted on prefabricated steel towers that had been erected hastily on each side of the runway for better camera coverage. With nineteen cameras, they wouldn't miss a detail.

"While you're dropping the cable, Lucky, I'd better start my runs," Charlie Hoover said.

"Go ahead."

"Everyone stationed back aft?" Connie asked into the phone. The dread of an explosion gripped the crew of Whiskey Charlie and millions of others around the world.

The chopper opened fire!

Whiskey Charlie's work crew dropped down the stairs. Only Alex and two others remained to take the tankers jet's drogue nozzle and force it into the six-inch hose line. Connie was in the left seat. Lucky stood next to her, ducking to get a sight of the chopper. Connie rubbed his arms, trying to feed the blood toward his hands.

"Those hands, Lucky. I'm terribly worried about them," she said.

"You worry about the wrong things, my love. Don't pray for my hands, just our asses. It wouldn't be fair after playing this game for hours to have an explosion back there."

They listened but all they heard was zinging wind

funneling around the glass cockpit. Above that, but faintly, they detected the muffled rat-tat-tats of the machine gun fire.

This was the deciding moment. Explosion or no explosion? They would not know until the chopper had finished its work of punching bullet holes in both elevators. Lucky decided he couldn't afford to spend the time just waiting. If it was going to happen, he couldn't do anything about it now.

"There's no sense standing here doing nothing. Connie, tell the tanker jet above us to extend their fuel transfer line. You'll see their rigid boom."

They had fastened the mouth of the fire suction hose Frank had sent down through the opened cockpit hatch. Alex and his crew, with short lengths of one-inch rope, stood ready to snag the boom, a stiffened hose that peeled out from the after end of the tanker like a long unbending twig with a bump on the end, the delivery nozzle. Those who were experienced in air-to-air fuel transfers knew how to feed out the stiff line with particular skill: By coordinating the boom's downward direction with pitches of added or retarded thrust from the turbines, they could almost thread the eye of a needle. It was just about an exact science. The tanker plane, by a series of finite movements, brought the head of the nozzle to the hatch easily. Alex, with a slipknot loop in his hand, reached outside. Even though the power of the slipstream bashed his wrist back against the hatch frame, he was able to flip his loop around the coupling of the delivery nozzle.

Four others in the work crew lashed the nozzle to the fire hose section.

Lucky checked his altitude on the glass panel. He saw his nose continuing to rise. At the controls, Connie was spooling up to prevent the stall.

"Shit, there's not enough bullet holes in the elevators yet," Lucky said. "Charlie, continue to blast it, my nose is still high. I'm going to order the ballast water right now. We're sucking our tanks dry!"

"Be careful, Doyle, don't rush that," Tug Stiles said. "There's still backward pressure on the tail. Yuh don't want to break yuh jet in half after all the hell yuh been through."

"I don't want to run out of fuel either. Each is a wipeout."

Lucky switched over to the emergency power to bypass the main system that would short out when drenched in water.

Ten seconds later the black suction hose started to dance and flip about as the ballast water surged through, splashing into the lower compartment. Lucky moved over by the stairs and ducked his head.

"You ready to take your dive, André?"

"Ready as I'll ever be," he yelled back.

The flooding of the bunk compartment happened much faster than Lucky had imagined it would. A lather of bubbling white water started to creep higher almost immediately.

Alex, who had the walkie-talkie pressed to his ear, picked up a call from the work crews aft.

"Lucky. There's smoke back there. We got a fire!"

"A fire!" he yelled. "Thank God!" He turned to Connie.

"Do you hear that, Connie? We have a fire back aft."

"I heard you, Lucky. We're burning our ass up. Isn't that great!" she cried mockingly.

"Darling, if you only knew. It's the best break we've had all day."

How ironic, Connie thought, to celebrate an in-flight fire. But *fire* meant no explosion, so one of the two greatest fears of rational airmen: a fire raging in the fuselage, not out on a wing, was for the moment, their salvation. (The other great threat was being caught in the vise of a thunderstorm packed with shearing winds, hail balls, and lightning).

"If there's a fire back there, it means oxygen." Lucky crowed. "If there's air instead of fumes in our rump end, there can't be a pop. No explosion. Alex, you were right. There had to be air getting in the tail cone. Go back there. Give me a report."

"Lucky, you're not thinking this out quite right," Connie said.

"We have a fire. That means no explosion. Why aren't you glowing? We've won, darling."

"Listen to me. The pressure bulkhead is airtight."

"Of course. Any fool knows that," Lucky yelled out.

"I always thought you were so air smart."

"No. You were the smart one."

"Well, 'Mr. Clever,' think this out. If the pressure bulkhead is airtight, how is the smoke escaping?"

Lucky was stumped. Then he suddenly solved another riddle. "*Now* I know what was happening! A while ago, I started to feel funny. Distances became very different to my eyes. Did you feel odd?"

"I did. Thought it was just fear."

"It was the beginning of hypoxia. That fucking bulkhead back aft *wasn't* airtight. It must have pulled away from the outer skin after the collision."

"Are you saying we were never totally pressurized?"

"That's what I'm saying. When we hit seventeen thousand, we began to feel the beginning of hypoxia. Not knowing what was happening, we could have all gone to sleep, forever."

"But the gauges up here don't show a loss of pressure."

"It was a subtle loss. Maybe they weren't reading it right."

Connie was not going to get into that discussion.

It had been worn thin by that time, and there were too many other things to consider.

"I can't fly the airplane, Connie." Lucky went on. "No feeling in my hands. You bank it around . . . then fly the outbound course . . . take off some thrust. See, the nose is coming down nicely. Gear up now." She flipped the landing gear handle and the wheels folded back into their wells, and the doors closed behind them. "Call up that fuel situation on the tube." Again her fingers raced over the buttons. The low quantity mode on the fuel gauge was blinking bright red.

"Five minutes and fifty seconds." Connie said.

"Now come on around very, very slowly. Hit your timer on the back course. Fly three minutes outbound, make an easy one-eighty and establish yourself on final."

"Lucky, this fire is smoking us out," Alex called from his position in the aft cabin.

"I'll be right back. Hand me the phone, Connie."

She put it in front of Lucky's face and depressed the button.

"Ladies and gentlemen. We are four minutes to touch down. Water is already being pumped into our forward section by the tanker plane overhead. I'm coming aft to vent that smoke out of a hatch. The fire is contained beyond the pressure bulkhead. There shouldn't be a danger of its spreading. Keep in your seats. Make sure your belts are fastened."

"We're getting a lot of smoke out here," Charlie Hoover said as the three other choppers flew alongside Whiskey Charlie.

"I'm going aft."

"Lucky, are you leaving me to take this bird in?" Connie cried.

"I'll be right back. I want to make sure we control that fire."

The chief pilot had stripped down to his shorts.

"Go to it, André," Lucky said. "I'm heading aft. We have a smoky one back there. Okay, Connie start your outbound leg."

"Just have someone yank on the line when you want me to crack the hatch," André said once more.

Lucky looked down and winked at André. The ballast water was already up to the bottom of the bunks and rising rapidly. Two young men held the ends of the tether that was wrapped around André's waist.

Lucky opened the door to first class, which was thick with smoke and acrid fumes. The farther he made his way aft, the thicker the smoke became. Coughs and high-pitched voices filled the cabins. He entered the crossover galley, where Linda Glen and three of her girls were belted in.

"Help me jump into this, quick. My hands are frozen."

They unbuckled themselves, and held Lucky as he climbed into the pants and then the boots. They pulled the fire resistant parka over his head and laid the helmet on. Finally the air pack was fixed over his outstretched arms. He called into the voice-activated mike attached to his visored helmet.

"You guys hear me?"

"Better hustle back here. Smoke's getting worse. Should we hit the foam?"

"Do you see flames?" Lucky asked.

"Not yet. But it's heating up like hell," Alex said.

"Hold on. I'm coming."

Lucky raced through the second coach section, where the passengers were coughing and wiping their eyes. One woman was screaming, but her companion calmed her down. Lucky was hidden by the suit and the dark visor; no one recognized him.

In the last cabin, he found the smoke much thicker than he expected.

There were two sides to venting a fire. If he introduced more air, he would let the smoke off, but give the fire more oxygen, causing it to spread faster. He reached up and opened an escape hatch to give the thick smoke a way to get out.

The view from the outside, which was picked up by the camera planes following Whiskey Charlie, made it appear that the fire involved much more than the tail cone. Smoke had entered the ducting system and the black, curling waves poured out of the forward section. The whole jet trailed a tumbling dark plume of curling smoke. Connie picked up her walkie-talkie as the fumes reached the cockpit.

"Nose is even, Lucky. Water's still pouring in. It's smoky up here."

"I'm preparing to shoot the foam," he answered.

"Two miles from touchdown. I'm damned high," Connie said.

"Get some air brakes in. Go to full flaps for the landing."

"My gear's up. Now my nose is coming down, way down now."

"Spool up, spool up, honey! Don't get behind the power curve!"

"I'm looking at the gauges on empty. Four hundred pounds more. We're running dry, Lucky."

"Forget the fuel gauge. Concentrate on your landing."

Lucky tried to peer through the black smoke as he sucked in the air from his backpack. Through the smoke, swirling as it was whipped up by the air careening in through the open escape hatch, he saw a flash of orange. The kerosene flowing from the ruptured APU fuel tank had formed a lake in the tail cone. In the jet's nose-up condition, the four hundred gallons of kerosene had slopped around the far end of the tail. But as soon as the pressure was removed from the elevators by Charlie Hoover's bullets, and with the water ballast bringing the nose down, the flood of burning kerosene cascaded forward. It slapped up against the pressure bulkhead. No one, not even the Bristol pessimists, had forecast that this massive bulkhead would be ripped free of the outer skin. Now there was an escape route for the kerosene.

As soon as the smoke became dense, the passengers in the aft section evacuated, finding seats in the two forward cabins. With an oil field worker holding the nozzle of the CO_2 mounted on a small dolly, Lucky proceeded into the empty last section. Suddenly he saw the faint orange glow erupt into a fireball. A gushing river of tumbling, fuel-fed flames came down the two aisles toward the center crossover galley. Alex with CO_2 and the others watched the river of fire gushing down the two aisles.

"We'll have to stop it here. Once it gets into the center cabin, we're all dead!" Lucky yelled.

The two rivers of flame slapped into the galley and the crew shot the CO_2 in one massive blast. The gray-white muck seemed to smoother the flames for a couple of seconds and they thought that they had the fire halted.

Just at that point Lucky felt an oppressive heat build up. The entire third cabin had reached the flash point. The carpet, seats, and liners were now blazing just as a second river of flame tumbled into the galley. Their only hope was cutting the fire off there. If the flames started to incorporate the center cabin and move forward, the passengers would have nowhere to go, no escape. For a minute Lucky thought of that final horror: hundreds of people charred to death on top of each other at the far forward end of the first cabin, a mound of black human flesh piled up against the bulkhead and the locked cockpit door. What a sickening irony, Lucky thought. Connie would grease the 270 on like a feather, and after all their struggles of the last hours, they'd end up dead in a fire.

"Lucky, what the hell do we do? Hold here, or go in there?" Alex yelled, lifting his face mask and pointing to the last cabin.

"We have to make a fire break. If we can smother the flames across the last four seats in the aft section, I think we'll have it."

Immediately the eleven-man crew charged into the edge of the flames with their six CO_2 bottles. The fire was about half the way up the last cabin and moving toward them as a flaming wall. They squeezed the handles of the bottles, covering three rows of seats with a layer of thick foam. The fire had picked up heat now. Just as they finished foaming the seats, hoping that the fire break would work, the air became as hot as a furnace. They retreated back into the center galley which was smoky but cooler.

"Think we got it?" Alex asked.

"We'll see in a second."

As the flames reached the foamed seats, the fire seemed to halt. Then it leaped up to the carry-on luggage bins. The overhead liners burst into flames. For a second they thought they were safe. The jet was now at a down angle on final approach. Then Lucky saw one of the most frightening sights of his life. While the flames were charring the top of the last cabin, two more tumbling rivers of fire came cascading down the aisles. Added fuel must have escaped through the pressure bulkhead, Lucky thought. The fire rushed toward them like flaming lava from an erupting volcano.

"God, look at that!" Alex yelled. "Do we hold?"

"We have to try to cut this fucking thing off here!"

Half the crew retreated into the second cabin, shooting CO_2 to stop the flaming rivers before they made the turn into the galley. For a second or so, the foam halted the current of fire on its way to the second cabin, where the passengers were. The sight of them was obscured by smoke, but their screams rose above the sound of crackling flames and the explosions of the plastic liners popping one after the other.

In the galley, Lucky was directing Alex and a volunteer with their hoses. They were standing in three inches of white muck from the first assault with the CO_2. Small rivulets of flame entered the galley, but with only a shot or two, the men put them out.

"I think we got her stopped," Alex said.

"I think . . ."

As Lucky spoke, a long tongue of fire burst into the galley from above. The blaze swirled around them. Once more they hit the hoses, but the heat built up so rapidly that it sent the three of them charging out of the galley. In the next second, the entire row of buffets burst into flame with a sound like a shell going off right next to them.

Lucky and his firefighting crew spun forward through the middle coach section. The seats, the liners, the carpet, the overheads started to peel and wrinkle from the advancing inferno.

What Lucky saw next almost drove him mad. He had prided himself for never giving up. But some of the passengers, the older ones, had not been able to escape the second cabin. They clawed away at the seats, some were crawling up the aisles screaming. The flames curled around Lucky and leapt toward those passengers angling their way up the aisle through the coffee-colored smoke. Then an old lady's dress burst into flames. Lucky and his partner turned away from shooting the CO_2 on the rivers of fire that were devouring rows of seats as if they were made of light paper. They shot the foam on a group of passengers who were in danger of burning up. The CO_2 doused the flames, and the passengers screamed and summoned enough strength to pick themselves up and crawl further forward.

Linda Glen yanked the last of the crippled people out of the second cabin as Lucky turned toward the wall of fire that was charging toward him. The cabin was so hot he felt it would explode into one massive ball of fire at any second. The foam spat out of the nozzles, but nothing seemed to retard the inferno! The holocaust rushed toward them.

"Is it all over? Is this the end? To be burned alive after all we fought through?" Lucky asked himself.

Linda said it better. "Oh, shit. We're too close to making it to die now!"

Suddenly there was a series of small explosions, as various accessories of the airliner were blowing apart from the heat.

"Connie, we've got a bad fucking fire back here. It's gaining on us! Where are you?" Lucky said into his boom mike.

"About a half a mile from the threshold. My nose is down much too far. I have the trim reeled back all the way. Nothing happens."

"It's been destroyed by the chopper fire. Have the guys yank the line on André. Get him to open that hatch and dump the ballast water quick!"

Connie ordered one of the young members of the work crew to send André off. The chief pilot plunged into slopping ballast water, making a clean direct dive for the recessed hatch handle. He swung it up and the water pressure started to surge down and out, almost tossing André out of the jet through the wheel wells. But the tether rope stopped his descent, and the two oil field workers pulled him back up into the lower bunk compartment.

To the thousands standing on each side of the runway, the nose-down jet appeared to be urinating; the expelled water tumbled out so fast that the nose went from a down angle through the horizontal into a four-degree up pitch.

Retreating, Lucky and Alex ran into a stampede of people climbing over the seats; the river of flames was still cutting paths down the two aisles. There was no way out but over the seats.

"Connie, the flames are gaining on us. Where are you?" Lucky shouted into his mike.

"Just over the boundary. Lucky, I'm high and fast."

"Hit the spoilers, get this baby on, quick!"

Connie pushed up the spoiler handle, and small flaps popped up on the top of the wing like a series of baffles, intercepting the air and destroying lift. The jet started to fall toward the runway. As it did, Lucky saw an old woman trapped between the seats. Through the smoke and just short of the flames, he reached over and dragged her forward.

The flames increased their speed now, sent on by the rear energy of the fire. The heat rose to unbearable levels. The passengers had drawn themselves into a knot in the large first compartment. They began to panic, squeezing into one another through the smoke wall that was advancing in front of the flames.

The escape routes were sealed off! Again the thought of death by fire overwhelmed Lucky. It was almost certain to happen. They would be on the deck in a matter of seconds. With piles of people jammed against the forward bulkhead, and far back in the section standing on seats, the flames would consume the passengers before the rescue crews could enter. The fire was that energized, that incessant. Those who didn't die by fire would be smothered to death as one body piled up on another. Alex and Lucky turned to see the walls of fire coming at them like a blazing steamroller, moving forward with such power that their final spurts of CO_2 were mere tokenism—like trying to put out a forest fire with a water pistol. Lucky had never thought it would end like this.

"I love you, Connie!"

As he said that, his last words, he thought, there was a shuddering, clanking sound as the jet hit the runway. It was no landing but more like a crash, a fall into the soupy runway that was coated with a mush of foam. This was followed by a second crackling. The screams of the trapped passengers mounted. Another crashing sound followed. All Lucky saw at first was a burst of bright light puncture the smoke and flames. He didn't realize what had happened until the smoke cleared: It was actually sucked away. The heat of the fire vanished as if an icy shower had suddenly been turned on.

That wasn't even the most awesome part of it. In two seconds the rifts of smoke were entirely gone, replaced by cool fresh air. When it cleared, Lucky and more than three hundred others saw a phantasmagoric sight!

They looked out at the after section of the rolling jet. Connie's twenty-foot drop onto the runway finally broke the deformed and melting bones of Whiskey Charlie. Now there were two airliners. It broke just behind the massive wing box structure. The after end spun in the foam on the runway, the flames shot high. Even the vertical tail section disappeared in a geyser of shooting flames. But the wings didn't explode. There was no fuel left.

"Oh God, they lost half of them!" Henry Gibbons cried as he watched the fire equipment race toward the flaming after section on TV.

Lou Walters seized Ian's arm. "After all this, they're burned to death on the runway."

The front of the jet was out of control. It spun around and came to a halt some eight hundred feet from the far boundary of runway one seven left. And even after that twenty-foot drop onto the runway, the landing gear still stood up. Ron Alcott was on the first emergency truck to reach the forward end of the sheared-off jet, along with Frank A'hearn.

"Is anyone in the aft section?" rescue workers yelled.

"They're all in here! Safe," Lucky answered, his blackened helmet was removed by Alex.

"Thank God," Ron said. "Lucky! Good going!"

"And Frank, you see, we made it home long before dinner. We have plenty of time." Lucky tried to smile but his nerves and the pain in his burned arms finally erupted.

The passengers hugged him as ladders from the emergency equipment were pushed against the ragged edges of the sheared-off airliner. Lucky was the first one down. He wanted to do nothing but climb back up into that cockpit to be with Connie, who had miraculously made a perfectly horrible landing, thank God.

The only way he could reach her now was to climb down and re-enter the jet, up through the nose gear well. He ran through a thick shrubbery of outstretched hands, his ears filled with yells of congratulations. Men in bulky white asbestos suits clamored just to touch Lucky Doyle.

"Have to get back up in there. Have to go back," he kept saying, almost crazed with urgency.

A group of fire fighters hoisted Lucky up into the wheel well, and took him higher, through the jungle of retraction struts and drag braces. Three of the work crew had hands dangling down to help pull Lucky up. When his body had edged through the nose well hatch, they helped him up the dripping metal stairs as the entire work crew tried to embrace him at once. André was sitting on a wet bunk shivering, his face as white as chalk, but he was smiling.

"You did it, Lucky. You crazy bastard!"

"And you, André, became much more than a chief pilot."

Then Lucky was assisted into the glass cockpit. They slammed the door.

Connie was draped over the sidestick crying. She didn't know what had happened yet. She realized only that she had made the worst landing of her life: hitting the ground from twenty feet in the air. The giant jet had fallen the rest of the way. Her conclusion was obvious. The rough landing, or the fall from the sky, had dumped all the passengers back into the flames. She heard screams from everyone; somehow she knew they were all scorched to death along with Lucky.

When she saw his blackened smiling face, Connie thought he had come back from the dead. No one could have survived that landing while the aircraft was a roaring furnace. He kissed her and said,

"We made it. The old bird finally broke in half just as the computer said it would. But all the people were in the front half. We lost no one."

"Even after that terrible landing?"

"You screwed up magnificently. It was such a crappy landing that it broke the plane in half. If you had made the best landing of your life, we would have been burned to death."

They continued to hold each other. The dread that they had tried to avoid all that day, since 9:33 that morning, finally took physical shape in a series of shakes. Lucky looked at the digital clock on the panel of the glass cockpit. It read 2:22. He punched up the fuel condition on the glass panel. It read zero.

2:14 P.M. CST (Over TULSA)

"Lucky, can I ask you something?"

"Anything at this point." He sighed, feeling the pain in his arms.

"Did you ever think we were getting home for dinner tonight?"

"Want the truth?"

"Of course."

"Just before one o'clock, I said to myself that this isn't going to work."

"The time factor?"

"Exactly."

"Then how did you come up with the lasso idea?"

"I wasn't going to sit there and die doing nothing!"

"Did you feel that it would pull us out?"

"I don't know."

"Is that the truth?"

"Absolutely."

"So you didn't quite know what you were doing?"

"That's the whole trick, my dear. Never know too much. It fucks up dreams!"

She kissed his blackened face and said,

"Tell you something, Lucky. I'm not flying again. I've had it."

"So have I. Aviating isn't everything. Here's something strange. You know how I hate machines and computers?"

"Don't tell me."

"It was the lack of a machine that caused all this. If the tower had had ground radar, that private plane that hit us would have been detected. We could have saved all this by a simple radar that wasn't there."

"Such a simple thing."

"Yup. The need for machines was proven today."

"But *you* weren't disproven, even though you're being canned."

"Tell you the truth. I don't care. We'll find something else to do."

She looked at his rumpled clothes and stiffened fingers and called out.

"Medics, get someone up here to take care of the greatest pilot who ever lived!"

AFTERMATH

LUCKY DOYLE WAS RUSHED to a Tulsa hospital. His burns, while painful, were not serious. The doctors would be able to repair the damage to his hands; he would not lose any fingers.

Late the same afternoon, Intra-Continental's banks in New York called to say that they would be glad to refinance the Tulsa airline. Within hours after Whiskey Charlie landed, even though in two pieces, the I.A. reservations department received so many requests for seats that they had to charter in equipment to handle the new load factor for the next month.

Ian told Ron Alcott that the Trent sales department confirmed 240 new orders for their 270. The jet had been brilliantly reborn.

Three months later, the board of Intra-Continental met to consider a number of changes. Ron Alcott, André Bouchard and Lou Walters had all decided to retire. The retirements were acknowledged, with regret.

New executives were needed at once for the burgeoning company. The choice was made quickly and unanimously. The new president of Intra-Continental would be Glen "Lucky" Doyle. His copilot in this ground operation, the executive vice president, would be the one who had been in the right-hand seat all along: the new Mrs. Doyle, still known as Connie Esposito.

The flyers had made a happy landing.